A Family
to
Call Ours

Front Porch Promises
Book 4

Merrillee Whren

Give, and it will be given to you. A good measure, pressed down, shaken together and running over, will be poured into your lap. For with the measure you use, it will be measured to you."

Luke 6:38 NIV

CHAPTER ONE

The sideways rain drenched Caleb Fitzpatrick as he slogged down Main Street. He dodged puddles and wielded his umbrella like a shield against the precipitation coming from the dark-gray clouds, but his attempt to stay dry proved unsuccessful. Why had he traded a sunny beach in Florida for the dreary early October weather in Hawthorne, Massachusetts?

Family. The family business. The family legacy. He was the only child who had chosen to walk in his parents' footsteps. He wanted to protect everything they had built and step into their shoes when they retired. A warm, sunny climate couldn't lure him away from this all-important obligation.

That was the most important reason. He'd gone to Florida to do a job for his family's accounting firm. That job was over, and despite the temptation to stay in the warm Florida sun, he had come home. His parents needed his help even if they didn't think they wanted or required it.

When he reached the tan brick building that housed the office of his family's accounting firm, he hurried under the awning that stretched across the front. But the green canvas flapping in the wind did little to protect him. Head down, he ducked inside and shook the water off his hair like a dog shaking its coat. Rubbing a hand down his face, he looked up and discovered an unfamiliar female sitting at his mother's dark-cherry desk—a desk he almost didn't recognize because it was so neat.

The young woman's unexpected presence made Caleb realize how silly he must have appeared, shaking the rain from his hair. He quickly finger combed it and hoped he didn't look like a clown with his hair sticking out every which way. What was she doing here? And what had she done with his mother and her piles of paperwork? A bad feeling hit him in the gut.

The blue-eyed blonde smiled. Her cheery countenance belied the gloomy weather outside. "Good morning. May I help you?"

Caleb eyed the woman, who looked very efficient in her gray tweed jacket, black turtleneck sweater, and perky short hairstyle. "I guess—"

"Caleb, you're home." Sheila Fitzpatrick waltzed into the room before he could finish his sentence. "This is a surprise. We weren't expecting you so soon. Did you have a good flight?"

"I didn't fly. I drove."

"Drove? All that way? Why?"

"Because I wrapped up that project, and I plan to stay. I thought it would be a good idea to have my car here."

Sheila clapped her hands together. "That's fabulous."

"I'm sure this is a surprise." He made a none-too-subtle nod in the direction of the stranger.

His mother sidled up to the young woman and put a hand on her shoulder. "Caleb, I want you to meet Tara Madsen. She's our new receptionist."

Receptionist? Since when did they have one of those? Caleb could hardly wait to get his mother alone and find out what was going on. His suspicions made it difficult to smile, but he manufactured one anyway and shook Tara's hand. "Nice to meet you. I'm Tom and Sheila's son."

"Hi." Tara shook her head. "I'm sorry I didn't know you were their son. I thought you were a customer. I should've recognized you from the pictures in your parents' house."

"I don't look much like my college graduation photo anymore, so no problem." That would remain to be seen, because he sensed trouble brewing. He turned to his mother. "Where's Dad?"

"With a client."

"How long before he'll be through?" Caleb planned to corner his parents and give them a lecture and a half.

"I'm not sure." Sheila shrugged and nervously pushed her dark-brown hair away from her face.

Caleb eyed his mother. "When he's finished, I want to talk with both of you in my office."

"Your office is a bit of a mess right now." A little frown knit Sheila's eyebrows, her caramel-colored eyes not quite meeting his.

Now he knew where his mother's clutter had gone. He wasn't sure he wanted to see what had become of his office. "So I guess you've been using my desk while I've been away."

"Yes, but I didn't touch any of your stuff." His mother's expression resembled that of a school-aged child who'd been called into the principal's office.

"Will I be able to have my office back?" He gave her a wry smile.

"Yes, once I get my stuff out of the way." His mother gestured around the room. "I would've had it cleaned out when you got here, but you came home without warning."

"I didn't know I had to warn anyone that I was coming

home." He gave his mother a cheesy grin, then glanced in Tara's direction. "And just where are you going to put your stuff since we now have a receptionist?"

Tara looked back at him, wide eyed. "I can help you move everything right now."

"Yes." Sheila motioned toward the hallway. "Tara is such a good organizer and worker. She helped us clean out the storage area, and that's going to be my new office."

Caleb stopped, and for the first time since he'd arrived, he took a good look around. The place didn't look the same. The area was immaculate—much like the desk. A new piece of artwork featuring an autumn landscape hung on the wall behind Tara's chair. A cherry coffee table, adorned with an orderly stack of magazines and a silk flower arrangement, sat in one corner, along with two new chairs. He glanced in Tara's direction again. Was she responsible for the changes? While he contemplated the answer to his own question, he really looked at her for the first time. Her eyes were as blue as the cloudless skies he'd left behind in Florida, and her rosy cheeks made her pretty face glow. How had he missed her attractive features? Maybe because he'd been worried about the reason for her presence in this office, not her good looks.

Over the years, Caleb had been used to the people his parents had helped in numerous ways. Everyone from the down-on-their-luck vagabonds, to the troubled teens who continued their wayward ways while living in his parents' house. This didn't please Caleb, but he could understand his parents wanting to help them. And he had to admit that many people had benefited from the much-needed support and were eternally grateful for his parents' assistance.

Now he definitely had to be on guard. He couldn't let an

eye-catching blonde make him forget the reason he'd decided to move back to Hawthorne. He wanted to keep his parents from trusting the wrong people. Had they done it again—succumbed to another sob story? One way or another he was going to find out why Tara Madsen, pretty and efficient or not, was now the receptionist in an office that had never had one.

On the other hand, first impressions were important, and having a pretty receptionist with a clean desk was a plus. A spotless outer office, rather than his mother's chaotic paper piles, would inspire more confidence in a potential client. Besides, as long as he was here to serve as watchdog, Ms. Madsen wouldn't be able to harm his parents or their business.

He'd fallen down on the job before. He was supposed to have been their protector, but he'd become as much a victim as they were. Making up for that mistake was his top priority.

Caleb smiled, and this time it was genuine. "Let's start moving Mom into her new quarters so I can have mine back."

"Great. Let's start by putting all the furniture in place in your mom's new office." Tara popped up from her chair.

While she walked toward the old storeroom, he tried not to notice her tall, slender figure with curves in all the right places. He didn't need to be thinking about the young woman at all. He needed to think about getting his workspace back.

He let out a harsh breath as he followed her. He stopped short in the doorway, then turned to his mother. "Did you get new furniture?"

"No." Sheila waved a hand at Tara, who trailed behind.

"This young lady is a miracle worker. Some of this and the table and chairs in the front were in here covered in boxes and old files. Some of it was at home in the basement and in the old storage shed. Tara suggested we refinish several pieces, and others only needed a good dusting."

Caleb didn't want to turn around and acknowledge the younger woman's accomplishments, but he supposed he should. He didn't understand where she had come from, why she was here, or how she'd managed to turn his mother's penchant for stashing stuff here and there into something impressive. He glanced in Tara's direction. "Very nice."

"Thanks. It was nothing." She shrugged as a pink tinge colored her smooth, creamy complexion.

She reminded him of one of those models in the soap commercials. He stuffed his hands in his pockets to keep from reaching out and rubbing a finger across her flawless skin. He gave himself a mental shake. What had gotten hold of his brain that he was thinking about touching a woman he didn't know? He had to put his mind in another gear. "Who moved all of this? I hope Dad didn't try to help with his bad back."

"No, no." Sheila waved a hand at him. "Some of the men from church helped."

Tara's expectant gaze darted around the old storeroom. "Mrs. Fitzpatrick, where would you like your desk?"

Sheila sighed. "Tara, how many times do I have to tell you to call me Sheila?"

Shrugging, Tara grimaced. "I'll remember one of these days. It's just so hard because my grandmother always insisted that I not call my elders by their first names." Tara placed a hand over her heart and shook her head. "Oh, but you're not old or anything like that. It's just that you're older than me."

Sheila chuckled and put an arm around Tara's shoulders. "You know I'm old enough to be your mother, but try to call me Sheila. It will make me feel younger."

Caleb took in the exchange and hoped the apparent friendship between his mother and Tara wouldn't end in disaster. His mother had a fondness for taking in strays who eventually turned and bit her. While he watched the two interact, he wondered why the young woman mentioned her grandmother rather than her mother. He had a lot to learn about Tara Madsen, and the sooner the better.

As Caleb started the process of reclaiming his office, he hoped he could discover how Tara had wound up with this job in his small hometown. He helped his mother and Tara move furniture, files, and paperwork along with the odds and ends from his mother's desk. Tara focused her attention on the little details that made the new office not only a good place to work but an appealing room. She knew exactly which picture to hang on each wall. She even placed the photos of the grandchildren just so on his mother's desk.

Tara found a place for everything and made his mother's office the picture of organization. Caleb speculated about Tara's talent. "Have you studied interior design?"

Wide-eyed, she shook her head, a hint of sadness in her blue eyes. "My grandmother always said I had a knack for rearranging things. Drove her nuts that I moved my bedroom furniture every other week."

There was the grandmother again, and he gathered from her statement that Tara must have lived with her grandmother. And what about the melancholy look? Somehow he was going to find out what he wanted to know about this new employee. "Tara, are you from Massachusetts?"

"Well—"

"She's originally from Montana but has spent the last year here in Hawthorne." Sheila supplied the answer and left Tara standing there speechless. "You remember Molly and Kurt Jansen who run the bed-and-breakfast?"

Frowning, Caleb shrugged. "Not really. I believe you met them after I went to Florida, but you did mention them to me from time to time. What do they have to do with Tara?"

"Tara's been living at the women's shelter and working at the B and B, which are on the same property. Molly contacted me to see whether we needed some help." Smiling, Sheila turned to Tara and patted her arm. "I'm so glad we were able to hire her. She's done wonders for this office."

"It appears so." More questions about Tara filling Caleb's mind, he glanced around and nodded. "And I do remember you talking about the women's shelter."

At that moment, Tom Fitzpatrick emerged from his office, along with Howard Reed, who owned the local hardware store. Caleb's dad had been doing Howard's taxes ever since Caleb could remember. The two men shook hands, then Howard left. Seemingly preoccupied, Tom started to go back into his office.

"Hey, Dad."

Tom turned toward Caleb, his shaggy gray eyebrows, which matched the color of his hair, raised in surprise. "You're home. We—"

"Weren't expecting me so soon."

"Well, yes." Tom nodded. "I bet this weather makes you wish you'd stayed in Florida for a few more days." Tom gestured toward the window. "How were the golf and the beach?"

"I didn't spend my whole time golfing and sitting at the beach. We were working." Caleb wondered whether his dad was trying to make small talk rather than mention that they had hired a new receptionist. Caleb wasn't going to let his parents slide by on this one. "Mom, Dad, I'd like to see you in my office."

Tom narrowed his gaze. "Right now?"

"Yes, now." Caleb motioned toward the open door, then waited for his parents to precede him into the room. As he closed the door, he caught a glimpse of Tara settling behind her desk.

As Caleb stood behind his desk, his mother started waving a finger in his face. "I saw the way you were scrutinizing Tara. Don't you dare say anything unkind to her."

Holding up both hands, Caleb backed away. "Hey, I just want to know why we suddenly have a receptionist."

"Your mother's been doing that job in addition to her other work for too long, and it's about time she didn't have to pull double duty." Tom motioned toward the door. "Tara came along at just the right time."

Caleb narrowed his gaze and stood eye to eye with his father, both of them towering over his mother, who was nearly a foot shorter. "Yeah, while I was gone and didn't have a say. How long have you known about this? Is that why you were so eager for me to take on that business in Florida? So you could hire another needy soul?"

Sheila stepped in between the two men. "Now, Caleb, we only decided to hire Tara a couple of weeks ago. This is not like the other times."

Looking toward the ceiling, Caleb raised his hands. "Have I heard this before? I don't want a repeat of the Baxter debacle. That's why you're pulling double duty."

"We don't need to talk about that. It's history. Besides, you saw what Tara did with the reception area and my office." Sheila waved a hand toward the door. "Doesn't that speak for itself?"

Caleb shrugged. "I can't deny that she's done some good work, but that doesn't mean she'll continue to be reliable. Did you even interview her or get references before you hired her? Or did you just rely on Molly's recommendation?"

"Molly is a perfectly good reference." Sheila placed a hand on Caleb's arm. "Calm down and listen to your father."

Caleb let out a harsh breath as he glared at his dad. "Okay. I'm listening. What do you have to say for yourselves?"

Tom stared back. "We're doing charitable work. We're trying to help people who need it."

Sheila nodded. "And if anyone needs our help, it's definitely Tara. She's been caring for her very sick little girl."

"I'm all for helping people, but that doesn't mean you should let them take advantage of you. And that's what you've done—over and over and over again. When will you learn that helping every stranger who comes along isn't always wise?" Caleb figured it was useless to point out that Amy Baxter had been caring for a supposedly ill father.

"Jesus said, 'For I was hungry and you gave me something to eat, I was thirsty and you gave me something to drink, I was a stranger and you invited me in, I needed clothes and you clothed me, I was sick and you looked after me, I was in prison and you came to visit me.'" Tom frowned. "And besides, Tara isn't a stranger."

Nodding, Caleb bit back a harsh reply. He knew the Scripture from Matthew backward and forward. His parents had quoted it to him since he'd been a little boy. He was never going to convince his parents that they should be more selective in the people they helped. They weren't going to listen to him, so he might as well save his breath and get back to work. But he was here now to watch out for them. He'd make sure that no one misappropriated their money or their kindness ever again. He would be there to protect them this time.

CHAPTER TWO

Her fingers resting on the keyboard, Tara stared at the computer screen and tried to concentrate on the letter she was typing, but the muted conversation coming from Caleb's office tied her stomach in knots. She had no doubt he didn't like having her here. She'd seen it immediately in his gray eyes—a hue that matched today's stormy skies. His eye color painted a perfect picture of his blustery attitude. He'd attempted to cover his feelings, but he wasn't a very good actor.

Although Tara couldn't hear the words, the pitch of the muffled tones told her that Caleb and his parents were having a disagreement. Sheila had bragged about Caleb and had only good things to say about him. So what were they arguing about? Her?

Closing her eyes, Tara pressed her lips together and fought back the tears that stung her eyelids. Why had life thrown so much heartache at her and her daughter, Hailey? Tara pushed the troubling question away. She had to be strong for Hailey's sake. Her daughter was the most important thing in her life.

Tara hated having to depend on the Fitzpatricks, but she didn't have a choice. She'd spent her whole life depending on someone for help. First her grandparents, then Parker Watson, then the Jansens, and now the Fitzpatricks. One day she intended to stand on her own. She would be independent—needing no one. Right now that goal had to take a backseat to Hailey's health and giving Hailey a special Christmas.

Last year she'd been too sick to enjoy the holiday and all the fun things that went with it. This year Tara wanted to make the celebration perfect. Part of making it perfect was spending Christmas with her grandparents in Montana. She was saving every extra penny in order to buy plane tickets to Billings. She wanted nothing more for herself other than to give her grandparents a big hug and tell them in person how much she loved them.

She desperately needed to keep this job and the living arrangements. It kept her close to Hailey's doctors. Paying off her debts depended on it—debts that her deceased husband had accumulated without her knowledge. Every time she thought about how he'd saddled her with unpaid bills, she reminded herself that she didn't have good sense when it came to men. She always picked the wrong ones.

That knowledge should be enough to keep her from looking even sideways at another man. But when Caleb had walked through the door, his broad shoulders and a mop of wet, curly dark hair had drawn her attention immediately. She hadn't been able to look away. She didn't want to admit that his presence made her heart pitter-patter in rhythm with the rain. Not a good thing. She needed to focus her attention elsewhere. He was her employer's son, and besides, he seemed annoyed she was here.

The entry door opened, and a gust of cold, damp air accompanied a plump elderly woman into the room. She struggled to close an umbrella as she waddled toward the desk.

Tara's pity-party thoughts ground to a halt as she straightened her shoulders and smiled. "May I help you?"

While the older woman waved a finger in the air, her coffee-colored eyes stared at Tara through big round bifocals. "You're that new girl Sheila hired. Are they keeping you busy?"

"Yes." The word came out in a squeak. Why was she letting this elderly woman with the gravelly voice intimidate her?

"Good to hear it. It's a good place to work." The woman extended her hand. "I'm May Duncan. I own the Main Street Café—the restaurant down a few doors on the other side of the street."

"I'm Tara Madsen." Tara brought up the appointment schedule on the computer screen but didn't see May's name. "Do you have an appointment?"

"Well, no, not a formal one, but Sheila doesn't mind seeing me when I drop in." The older woman brushed the raindrops from her snow-white hair.

"Um…Mrs. Fitzpatrick is busy right now. Do you mind waiting?"

"Not at all. I'll just make myself comfortable over here." May toddled across the room and planted herself on one of the chairs surrounding the table.

As Tara turned back to the computer, the door to Caleb's office opened. Sheila and Tom emerged, not a hint of what had transpired—good or bad—in their expressions. Caleb lurked in the doorway, his stone face in place as well.

Tara hopped up from her chair and motioned toward the newly created waiting area. "Mrs. Fitzpatrick…I mean…Sheila, May Duncan is here to see you."

"Thanks, Tara." Sheila scurried strode strolled across the room. "May, what brings you by?"

The older woman pushed up from the chair, a grin brightening her wrinkled features. "Just wanted to chat about a business idea I have in mind."

"Well, come into my new office." Sheila motioned toward the far end of the reception area.

May glanced around as she followed Sheila. "You really have fixed up this place. Looks grand."

Sheila paused in front of Tara's desk. "And we have Tara to thank for that. She has made our office into a showcase."

May continued to survey the area, then fixed her gaze on Tara and nodded. "You do nice work, young lady."

"Thank you. It was nothing." Tara shrugged as heat crept up her neck and cheeks again. She hated not being able to control a blush.

"Looks like something to me, don't you think, Caleb?" Sheila looked at her son.

"She's made some excellent changes to the place."

At the sound of Caleb's voice, Tara jerked her head around. He still stood in his office doorway. He nodded, but the set of his broad shoulders and the way he had his arms crossed over his chest told her that he wasn't pleased with the conversation. For some reason, he had a problem with her presence in this office. She wished she knew why.

Sheila smiled and held her clasped hands in front of her. "I can't thank Molly Jansen enough for sending Tara our way. This office has never run so smoothly."

Caleb's stance didn't change, as if he was waiting for someone to convince him that his mother's statement was true. Sheila's smile did nothing to relieve Tara's unease about Caleb.

May stepped toward Caleb and tapped his arm with her umbrella. "I'll expect you to bring this young lady to lunch over at the café today."

Caleb nodded again as a strange look passed between him and his mother. "That sounds like an excellent idea. That way I can get to know Tara better."

Something in Caleb's voice told Tara that despite his positive response, he wasn't really excited about having lunch with her. And now she was cornered into going with him. He probably felt the same way. Trapped—the unintended consequences of well-meaning people.

***

Tara slipped into her jacket as she traipsed across the reception area to join Caleb.

"The rain's still coming down hard." Not even venturing a glance in her direction, Caleb stared out the nearby window. "Do you have an umbrella?"

"No, it wasn't raining when your parents and I came to work, so none of us brought one."

His expression didn't give her much comfort. Even though an inhospitable glint radiated from his eyes, she was determined to get through this lunch with a smile. She was thankful for his parents' help, no matter what he thought.

She couldn't figure out why, with his unwelcoming attitude, he was still insisting she go to lunch with him. He said it was a chance to get to know her, but she didn't believe he wanted to know her at all. Since she had no umbrella, she would have to share one with him or get wet.

She didn't know which prospect was more troublesome.

"No problem. We can both fit under mine." Still without a hint of enthusiasm, he held open the door for her.

While they stood under the awning, he opened the umbrella. "Duck under here with me, and we'll dash across the street and hopefully not get too wet."

Tara managed a smile and joined him under the umbrella. Although she'd never considered herself short, Caleb seemed to tower over her. All too aware of his nearness, she tried to keep up with his long strides as they hurried to the crosswalk and sailed across the street. After the way Caleb had marched his parents into his office this morning, she figured he was not pleased they had hired her. The rain splatting against the umbrella gave her a sense of foreboding even as she tried to generate a more positive outlook.

The smell of freshly baked bread greeted Tara as Caleb held open the café door. Heads turned, and several people spoke to him. He acknowledged their greetings but didn't stop to talk. She didn't recognize any of them.

What did she expect? She hadn't met that many people since arriving in Hawthorne, because she'd spent all her time working or taking care of Hailey. Although Tara had lived here for a year, she had never set foot in the Main Street Café. Eating out was a luxury she couldn't justify. Besides, Molly served delicious meals at the Hawthorne Inn.

While they made their way to the back of the restaurant, near the kitchen, speculative glances followed them. Were these people wondering why a strange woman was accompanying Caleb?

When they reached the counter where the waitstaff

handed in their orders, May appeared from around the corner. A flour-covered apron hugged her plump figure. "Well, I see you two made it. I'm glad this inclement weather didn't keep you away."

Putting an arm around May's shoulders, Caleb looked down at her. "You know nasty weather isn't going to keep me away from your great cooking. I missed it while I was away. Nobody in Florida makes biscuits or bread as good as you."

May gazed up at him, admiration in her eyes and a blush on her round cheeks. "Now you're trying to butter me up."

Caleb grinned. "You've got me there. I was hoping for the best seat in the house."

"I have the perfect table." May looped an arm through Caleb's. "One by the window. Although it would be better if we had a sunny day."

"Your food can brighten even a gloomy day."

May giggled like a schoolgirl. "You really are laying the charm on thick today, aren't you?"

Winking, Caleb gave her a crooked smile. "I'm only telling the truth."

Chuckling, May waddled up the aisle with Caleb in tow. Tara followed close behind and took in the neatly arranged tables covered with off-white linen tablecloths and surrounded by oak ladder-back chairs. Tiny vases sporting real flowers sat in the middle of each table. The place reminded her more of a fancy tea room found in a big city rather than a small-town café.

May directed Caleb toward a table for two in a little alcove near the front window that looked out on Main Street. He pulled out a chair and motioned for Tara to sit.

She did so while Caleb continued to stand as he talked with May about his time in Florida.

Caleb laughed and joked with the older woman. He seemed like a different person with May, more relaxed and not all uptight like he'd been at the office. She hoped the troubling undercurrent between him and his parents didn't have anything to do with her, even though she suspected it did.

Despite the delicious aromas and May's friendly countenance, Tara's stomach churned, and she feared she wouldn't be able to eat. While Caleb and May chatted, Tara closed her eyes and took a slow, deep breath in an attempt to summon courage to get through this lunch.

When Tara opened her eyes, May was staring at her. "Are you all right, my dear?"

Tara blinked and bit her lower lip. How should she respond? She really wasn't all right, but she didn't want Caleb to know he was making her nervous. "I'm just taking in the marvelous smell of that bread."

"Well, let's get you some of that bread right away." May glanced over at Caleb. "And how about some of my vegetable soup to go with it?"

"Nothing like a hot bowl of soup on a rainy day." Looking at Tara, Caleb pulled out the chair on the opposite side of the table but didn't sit immediately. "Soup okay for you?"

"Sounds perfect." Tara plucked her napkin from the table and placed it on her lap. Her head down, she wiped her perspiring hands on the cloth. She promised herself she wouldn't let him intimidate her, but when she looked up again and his storm-cloud gray eyes met hers, that promise faltered.

"Good. Alicia will be here in a minute to wait on you." May nodded.

"Thanks, May." Caleb managed to fold his tall frame onto the chair across from Tara. "My parents told me that you've been caring for a sick child."

Tara nodded, wondering whether Caleb really cared or whether he was just making conversation. "My daughter, Hailey. She's been battling cancer. Rhabdomyosarcoma."

Just then, the waitress, a tall, attractive brunette, appeared and placed a small cutting board containing a miniature loaf of multigrain bread on the table. "Hi, Caleb. It's a surprise to see you back in town."

"I wrapped up the Florida business, and it's good to be home." Caleb glanced across the table, then back at the waitress. "Alicia, have you met Tara Madsen?"

Smiling, Alicia shook her head. "A friend of yours?"

"Our new receptionist."

"Oh, nice to meet you, Tara." Alicia immediately turned her attention back to Caleb, not even giving Tara a chance to respond. "May says you want the vegetable soup, right?"

"Yes, and I'll take some water." He glanced at Tara. "Water okay for you, too?"

Tara nodded, feeling as though she was a second thought for both Caleb and Alicia. Tara had the distinct feeling that Alicia's interest in Caleb went beyond taking his lunch order.

"Anything else? A salad?"

"Not for me." Again Caleb glanced across the table. "You?"

Tara shook her head, wishing this whole lunch thing had never come up. But she would make it through this meal even it meant enduring Caleb's scrutiny.

CHAPTER THREE

C aleb watched Tara, who was staring at her lap. What did he say now? Alicia's arrival had interrupted the previous conversation, and he didn't know how to start it again. Cancer. Her little girl had cancer. Sympathy for her situation welled up inside him, but he cautioned himself not to be sucked in by another sad story.

He'd been fooled before, along with his parents, when he'd first returned to Hawthorne two years ago. His brother, Joshua, had been suspicious of one of their parents' charity cases, but Caleb had dismissed the notion that Amy and Frank Baxter were misappropriating their parents' kindness. Caleb hated thinking about how wrong he'd been, but his mind rehashed the disaster anyway.

Caleb couldn't understand people who deliberately used his parents' kindness for their own gain. He hated that these con artists took advantage of Tom and Sheila Fitzpatrick's help. When fake claims on their time, sympathy, and money had come to light, Caleb began to question all comers, no matter how legitimate their situation appeared. He had lent his trust and his heart too easily before and had both of them broken. Never again.

Although the circumstances with Tara's daughter sounded completely legitimate, Caleb determined not to let his guard down. He would make sure she didn't exploit his parents' charity. She seemed very closed mouthed. If she was hiding something, he was going to find out what it was.

"I'm sorry to hear about your daughter. How old is she?"

"Thank you. She's eight. The last year's been tough for her."

Caleb didn't miss the sadness in Tara's blue eyes, but he also noticed the way she ran her fingers up and down her water glass in a nervous gesture. She obviously wasn't going to give him more information unless he asked. Did she not like talking about her daughter's illness, or did her reluctance to talk spell trouble?

"My mother said you came from Montana. Where in Montana?"

"A place you've never heard of."

"Try me."

"Stockton."

Caleb smiled wryly. "You're right. I've never heard of it. Is it close to anything I might know?"

"Billings."

"Okay." Caleb nodded. "Any family there?"

"Yeah, my grandparents."

The grandparents again. "Parents?"

She shook her head. "My parents left me with my grandparents when I was four. Probably the best thing they ever did. They weren't the kind of people who should've had kids. Thankfully, I'm their only child, and I haven't seen them in years. I don't even know where they are or whether they're still alive."

Before Caleb could say anything, Alicia reappeared with their soup. After she set the bowls on the table, she lingered. "Caleb, are you going on the outing with the church group to pick apples?"

"I don't think so." Caleb wished that Alicia would find someone else to capture her attention. She was twenty, and at twenty-nine, he felt too old for her. She was an attractive young woman, but her all-too-obvious interest in him made him want to run the other way.

"You'll miss a good time if you don't go."

Caleb cut a slice of bread from the tiny loaf and slathered it with butter. He hoped Alicia would get the hint and move on to other diners. "I don't have any free time. I've got to catch up on things now that I'm back."

Alicia shrugged. "Guess I'll see you on Sunday. Maybe in two weeks you'll get caught up on your work and change your mind."

"Not likely." Caleb breathed a sigh of relief as Alicia moved on to another table. If Tara weren't with him, he'd have rolled his eyes heavenward. Women. They were more trouble than he cared to think about.

"Seems to me you've got an admirer." Tara's whispery-soft voice brought his attention back to her.

Should he agree, or would that make him appear too full of himself? What difference did it make? What she thought about him didn't matter. "Maybe so."

"No doubt about it." A little smile tugged at the corners of Tara's mouth—a very kissable mouth.

Whoa! Why had that thought popped into his brain? Must be the whole admirer thing, but then he'd had that thought about touching her flawless skin earlier. Whatever the cause, he had to shut it down. Now. "We'd better eat before our soup gets cold. I'll say a blessing."

"Okay."

Caleb bowed his head. Yes, prayer was what he needed.

He gave thanks for their food and then began eating his slice of bread, the whole time wondering how to get more information out of Tara without barraging her with questions. She didn't wear a wedding ring. Was she a widow, divorced, or a single woman with a child? He shouldn't ask. Maybe he would find out eventually.

"Do you have a problem with my position in the office?"

Caleb jerked his head up. Tara didn't blink as she skewered him with her ice-blue stare. So, despite his efforts to display an affable disposition, his true thoughts were completely transparent—no point in denying his feelings. "Maybe not a problem—just questions. We've never had a receptionist before. I didn't know we needed one."

"I hope I can prove my worth to your firm and that we can work together without difficulty."

"That's fair enough." Caleb admired the way she tackled his reluctant acceptance head on. "The whole thing took me by surprise."

"Is there some reason why your parents didn't tell you about hiring me?"

Caleb stared at his bowl of soup. How was he going to explain that without implying Tara was out to take unfair advantage of his parents? How deep would she dig if he gave her a generic answer? He really didn't want to offend her. He just wanted to be sure that she didn't hurt his parents. Maybe he should have quizzed his mom and dad more about Tara rather than end their conversation because he'd been frustrated with their never-ending Pollyanna attitude.

When he looked up, Tara was still eyeing him. She

hadn't touched her food. "How about discussing that after we eat, so our soup doesn't get cold?"

Not breaking eye contact for even a second, she picked up her spoon. "It must be a long explanation if you're worried about our soup getting cold. You don't have to sugarcoat anything for me. I've spent most days during the past year hoping for the best for Hailey but expecting the worst, even though I'd been praying. Sometimes God seemed pretty far away when the news was bad, but I lived through it all. It's made me stronger, so I can take whatever you have to say."

Begrudging respect for Tara pricked Caleb's mind. Her pluck made him see her in a different light. He was beginning to like her, but he had to keep his reservations in place as a defense against the unknown. He didn't know enough about Tara Madsen to set them aside. She would have to win his trust. He wasn't sure what it would take to do that.

Caleb sighed. "Let's just say that my parents don't have a stellar record when it comes to hiring people."

"So you think I'll be a bad employee?"

"I didn't say that." He smiled wryly as he shook his head. "I just wish they would've consulted me first."

"Would you have told them not to hire me?"

Caleb stifled a chuckle. And he'd been worried about asking her too many questions. She wouldn't let up—like a dog that latched on to a pant leg and wouldn't let go. "I'd have treated you like anyone else I hire. I would've insisted on an interview and references."

"So you want references? I can give you those." She grabbed her purse from her lap and fumbled through it until she came up with a pen and a scrap of paper. She started to write on it.

Without thinking, Caleb reached across the table and covered her hand with his in an attempt to stop her from making a list. A big mistake. She looked up at him with those big blue eyes, and his pulse pounded in his head.

"Sorry." He immediately withdrew his hand. "You don't need to give me references. It's a moot point. You are the receptionist, and I accept that. I just wanted to be totally honest about the whole situation."

A slow smile lit her face. "I like honesty. Let's me know exactly where I stand."

He tried not to dwell on her pretty face made lovelier by that smile. "Good. Let's eat."

She picked up her spoon and dipped it into her soup. "I bet our soup isn't exactly hot anymore."

He took a spoonful, then looked back at her. "It's warm enough."

"And this bread is delicious. May certainly is a good cook."

Caleb nodded, feeling a little less like an ogre. "May's café has been here since before I was born. The menu has changed over the years, but May's great cooking has sustained the place in good times and bad."

For several minutes, Caleb and Tara ate in silence. Now he was in the same position that he started in—wanting to know more about the woman sitting across from him. She had turned the tables on him and asked all the questions. She said she liked honesty.

"I'm surprised your admirer hasn't been back to the table to check on us."

Tara's comment pulled Caleb from his woolgathering. He pinched his eyebrows into a little frown. "Why?"

"Any good waitress always comes back to see whether the customers are satisfied with their food."

"And you know this because?"

"Because I used to work as a waitress when I lived in Montana, then at the Hawthorne Inn before I started working for your parents."

"Your experience as a waitress gives you the qualifications to be a receptionist?" Caleb puzzled over Tara suddenly giving him unsolicited information.

"Yes, I worked with the public."

Conceding the point, Caleb nodded. "That's true, and my parents seem satisfied with your work."

"I hope you will be also." Tara broke eye contact and started eating again.

Before Caleb could respond, Alicia reappeared. "How's everything?"

"Delicious as usual." Caleb hoped she wouldn't linger, even though the moment was lost to reassure Tara he would give a fair assessment of her employment.

"Good. Is there anything else I can get you?"

"No. We're good." He glanced at Tara. "Right?"

Tara nodded, a little smile curving those kissable lips.

There was that crazy thought popping into his mind again. Maybe he should start thinking about Alicia, but he really didn't want to think about women. Period. Or at least, that was what he kept telling himself.

Every time he was with his brother or his buddies who were all married, he couldn't help being just a little envious that they had found women to share their lives with, while he was still alone. He wanted to think not about just any woman but about the best woman for him. Only God knew who that was. Caleb definitely didn't have much wisdom when it came to finding the right one, and he wasn't about to open himself up for more heartache and betrayal.

When Alicia moved on, Caleb breathed a sigh of relief.

"Your friend did come back, but she didn't stay long."

"That's okay. So does she get a good grade?"

"I shouldn't be judging." Tara grimaced. "After working as a waitress for so many years, I just couldn't help noticing that she hadn't returned to check on us. It's hard work, but it could be fun, too. I enjoyed getting to know the regulars who came into the Steakhouse in Stockton."

Caleb decided to take advantage of Tara's sudden openness. "How did you decide to come all the way from Montana to Massachusetts to find a doctor for your little girl?"

Tara glanced out the window and then back at him, almost as if she didn't want to talk about it. "When Hailey became sick, one of my former high school teachers, who had lots of contacts because he's a medical writer now, helped me find the best doctor. That led us here."

"Is your little girl's doctor in Boston?"

"Yes, but thankfully, we don't have to live in the city now." Tara shook her head. "I'm a country girl. The city's big and noisy, and I never slept very well there—too many sirens and honking horns in the middle of the night."

"We sometimes have sirens in the country, too." Caleb raised his eyebrows and waited for her comment, hoping she would continue to talk.

"Not very often. I've been sleeping very well. Hawthorne is incredibly quiet compared to where we lived in Boston. The Hawthorne Inn and your parents' home are very peaceful places."

As Caleb took in this piece of information, he hoped the consternation didn't show on his face. Why hadn't he guessed that his parents had not only given her a job but taken her in as well? He should've known as soon as she mentioned seeing his photo in his parents' house. "Yeah, it is quiet out there."

She gave him a curious look. "Do you live near there?"

"I'm your closest neighbor." He smiled wryly. "I live in that little white clapboard house with the front porch just as you turn off the main road onto our lane. My paternal grandparents used to live there."

"Oh, I wondered who lived in that house. I never saw anyone around there, so I thought maybe the place was empty. Now I know why. You were in Florida." A pleased expression brightened her face. "I'm glad that house isn't empty. It looks so inviting with that front porch. It reminds me of the one at my grandparents' house in Montana."

He opened his mouth to respond but snapped it shut when he realized he had almost invited her to come over and sit on his front porch. Close call. He would see her often enough at work without having her hanging around his house. "I don't use it much."

"That's too bad." Tara tore off a piece of bread and popped it into her mouth.

"If I want to relax, I take a walk around the lake."

"The lake does look peaceful. I can see it through the trees when I look out my bedroom window, but I haven't walked down there yet."

"It's definitely better in the summer, not this time of year."

"But it's pretty now with the colorful foliage reflecting in the lake."

"Yeah, I suppose so, but I prefer summer when the weather's warm. Then I take the rowboat out and do a little fishing. My grandpa taught me how to fish when I was a kid. Those are good memories." After Caleb finished talking, he wondered why he was telling her all this. But for some reason, once they started conversing, he found he wanted to talk to her, not just pump her for information. Was he letting a blue-eyed blonde suck him in again?

"My grandpa used to take me fishing, too. And Hailey before she got sick."

"So you and your little girl are living in the in-law suite?"

"I guess—if that's what you call the little apartment in your parents' house."

"That's what we call it. After my grandpa died, my grandma's health wasn't good, so she lived there until she passed away."

"I'm sorry you've lost your grandparents." Tara grimaced. "My maternal grandparents are still living, and I really miss them. I want to go back to Montana. Then we can be near them again. I never knew my father's parents."

"My paternal grandparents live in New Hampshire, so I get to see them several times a year."

"That's nice."

So Tara didn't plan to stay here. Was that a good sign? Amy had made him believe she wanted to stay, but she'd only been stringing him along. "Do you plan to go back to your old job?"

"Someone else has taken my place, so maybe I'll look for a receptionist position." Shrugging, Tara grinned. "I'll have some experience to put on my résumé."

"You've gotten off to a good start." Whether that would

continue remained to be seen, but he wasn't going to say
so.

"Thanks. I can do anything I set my mind to." Tara
looked away, a shy smile showing her pleasure.

After hearing only a portion of her story, Caleb didn't
doubt that she could do anything she wanted. Maybe his
parents had been right to hire her, but he'd let a blue-eyed
blonde muddle his mind before. That relationship had
ended in disaster for his whole family. He wouldn't let it
happen again. He wouldn't let Tara Madsen worm her way
into the family fabric and tear it apart.

CHAPTER FOUR

··

While Tara finished her soup, she tried to put their lunch conversation into perspective. Caleb had said she was doing a good job. That was welcome news, but she had to admit he was right. His parents hadn't followed any standard business practices when they'd hired her. They'd taken Molly Jansen's recommendation without question. Tara was grateful for that, but she couldn't blame Caleb for wanting better assurances when hiring someone new.

At least she'd managed to stand up for herself. She'd learned to do a lot of that in the past year.

"Are you finished?" Caleb signed the check, then placed his napkin on the table.

Nodding, Tara pushed back her chair and stood. "That was delicious. Thank you for inviting me to lunch. I don't usually go out for lunch, so it was a treat."

Caleb motioned for her to precede him as he picked up his umbrella. "Then I'm glad I could treat you."

Tara couldn't help wondering whether that was actually true. She was pretty sure he had asked her to lunch so he could find out what kind of person his parents had hired. "Looks like the rain has stopped."

Caleb waved his umbrella. "Then we won't need this."

Tara fell into step beside Caleb as they walked to the street corner. "We had our first snow about this time last year."

"I'll have to get used the cold winters again after spending last winter in Florida."

"Why did you move back here?"

Caleb smiled wryly and shook his head. "You mean why did I move back to this awful weather?"

"Yeah."

"My parents needed me to work with a client who had moved to Florida, so I went there for almost a year until everything was settled with their accounts." Caleb acted as though he was going to say something else, but he stopped talking when he opened the office door and stood aside so Tara could go ahead of him.

When Tara stepped into the reception area, Sheila was talking on the phone and waved Tara over to the desk. Concern dominated Sheila's expression.

"Yes, yes. I'll let her know immediately." Sheila hung up and hurried from behind the desk. "Tara, that was the school nurse. She called because Hailey isn't feeling well."

"Did she say what was wrong?" Tara's heart sank.

Sheila shook her head. "She wasn't sure. She said Hailey wasn't running a fever, but she complained of an upset stomach. Do you want to go get her?"

"I think I should." Tara nodded and started for the back entrance. She didn't wait to see Caleb's reaction but raced out the door as if the building were on fire. She prayed that everything would be okay with Hailey. She'd thought the worst was behind them. Was she wrong?

She turned the key in the ignition, but the car didn't start. She tried again. The motor only groaned. Now what? She raced back into the office and nearly plowed into Caleb as she entered the reception area.

He grabbed her shoulders. "Whoa. Is something wrong?"

"My car won't start."

Sheila turned to Caleb. "Since you have no appointments for today, you can drive Tara over to the school to get Hailey."

Tara wanted to protest. Why should Caleb have to drive her? Couldn't she borrow a car, or would that be too presumptuous? In this case, the old adage Beggars can't be choosers probably applied.

"Sure. I'll be glad to help."

Caleb's response surprised Tara even more. "Thanks. We'll have to get her booster seat out of my car first."

"No problem."

Tara wondered whether that was really the truth as they hurried to her car. She shook the negative thought away. She shouldn't be worrying about Caleb's reaction, but she couldn't help herself.

While Caleb drove to the school on the edge of town, Tara realized she couldn't have driven his car anyway. She didn't know how to drive a car with a stick shift. Her mind buzzed with all kinds of thoughts. Lunch had gone much better than she'd expected, but she worried that he might think she was unreliable because she had to leave work to take care of her daughter.

Tara kept waiting, but he didn't say a word about this errand, just stared straight ahead. She should be glad, but somehow his silence made everything worse.

When he stopped in front of the elementary school, he finally looked her way. "I'll wait right here while you go in."

Nodding, Tara got out and sprinted to the entrance.

Please, Lord, let Hailey be okay. The prayer flitted through Tara's mind while she took a deep breath and entered the school office.

The woman sitting at a desk behind the counter looked up. "May I help you?"

"Yes, I received word that my little girl, Hailey Madsen, is in the nurse's office."

The woman stood. "I'll check."

A minute later, the woman returned with Hailey, who raced into Tara's arms. Tara held her daughter tight for a few moments and stroked the barely there, short blond curls that covered Hailey's once-bald head.

The little girl clung to Tara until she held the child at arm's length. "Mommy, I want to go home."

"We'll have to go back to my office first. Is that okay?"

Hailey nodded, and relief surged through Tara. She didn't know how she was going to handle a sick child and her job, too. Having to leave work wouldn't help her win Caleb's vote of confidence. After signing all the appropriate forms, she led a subdued Hailey out of the building.

As they drew closer to the car, Hailey tugged on Tara's arm. "Where's your car, Mom, and who's that man?"

"That's Mr. and Mrs. Fitzpatrick's son, Caleb. I'll introduce you." Tara opened the back door.

Before Tara could say anything, Hailey hopped into her booster seat and started introducing herself. "Hi, my name's Hailey. My mom said your name is Caleb. Are you a spy like the guy named Caleb in the Bible?"

"Hailey, please call him Mr. Fitzpatrick." Hailey suddenly didn't sound very sick. Tara couldn't imagine what Caleb was thinking about the whole situation.

Caleb chuckled and winked at Hailey. "That's okay. She can call me Caleb. It's not every day that someone calls me a spy. You know your Bible stories very well."

Hailey giggled. "That's cuz my great-grandma told me Bible stories all the time when we lived with her in Montana."

Heat rose in Tara's cheeks while she buckled Hailey into her booster seat. This child didn't resemble the little girl who had come running to her in the school office. What kind of game was her daughter playing? "Do you still have a stomachache?"

Hailey shook her head. "I never said I had a stomachache. I said I hurt here." She pressed her hands to her chest. "My heart hurts."

Tara frowned. What could Hailey possibly be talking about? Was the cancer returning in a different place? "Do you mean your chest? Are you coming down with a cold?"

"No, Mommy. My heart. Some kids teased me, and it made my heart hurt right here." Hailey patted her chest a couple of times.

Tears stung Tara's eyes at the thought of other kids teasing her child, but she blinked them away as she closed the door and slid into the front seat. Even though Tara's heart hurt, too, she couldn't let Hailey or Caleb see any tears. Why were children so cruel to each other? Was Hailey already experiencing the bullying that Tara had seen reported on the nightly news? Surely eight-year-olds weren't involved in that. Didn't that just apply to teenagers?

Caleb remained silent as he drove back to the office. Tara didn't know what to make of his silence or his intense countenance. Had Hailey's plight touched him? The way he'd joked with her and made her laugh surprised Tara. Although she'd glimpsed this lighter side of him when he'd talked with May, Tara couldn't shake the feeling that he was assessing her every move.

***

Back in the office, Caleb watched his mother fuss over Hailey. His mom was not only taken with Tara, but also with her child. He prayed that his tenderhearted mother wouldn't find disappointment in this relationship. He had vowed to keep his parents from further harm, but a helpless feeling inundated him. How was he going to do that when the little girl with the tight, fuzzy blond curls and big blue eyes like her mother's tugged at his emotions, too?

"Caleb, what do you think?"

Caleb looked up at his mother. He didn't have a clue what she was talking about. "I—"

"Oh, I couldn't expect him to do that." Tara joined the conversation, leaving Caleb more confused.

Sheila waved a hand at Tara. "It's no trouble. I think he can handle one little girl for a few hours."

A sinking sensation hit Caleb right in the gut when he finally got the drift of the discussion. They were volunteering him to babysit. He didn't have much experience with kids. He only spent time with kids a couple of weeks a year when he and his brother got together. And then he was never solely responsible for his niece and nephew, who were three and five years old.

Shrugging, Tara stared at him. "Are you okay with this?"

How could he say yes? But how could he say no? He

would appear unsympathetic if he didn't agree to this adventure. Yeah. That was how he had to look at this situation that was completely out of his comfort zone. He tacked on a smile, then winked at Hailey. "Does that work for you, Miss Hailey?"

She smiled shyly at him and nodded.

"Okay, I'll get my umbrella, and we'll go to my car." Caleb headed for the door.

"Caleb, please wait. I'd like to talk to you for a minute before you go."

Tara's request made him turn around. "Sure."

"Alone?" Tara bit her bottom lip.

"Okay. Let's go into my office." Caleb motioned toward the other side of the reception area.

After Caleb shut the door, he turned to look at Tara. Uncertainty painted her face. "It's very kind of you to agree to watch Hailey, but I would understand perfectly if you didn't want to do this. Besides, I'm pretty sure she isn't sick at all. She's just upset."

Caleb smiled, truly feeling at ease for the first time today. "Thanks, but it isn't a problem, and I think you're right in the assessment of your daughter's behavior."

"I'm not sure how to handle this." Her shoulders slumping, Tara turned away from him and walked toward the one window in the room and stared outside as if she could find the answer there. "She's never done anything like this before."

"I understand why she did it. It's not fun to be teased." Caleb came to stand beside her. "When I was about her age, I was overweight and got teased a lot. My brother, Josh, joined in the teasing."

She turned to face him. "I'm sorry. That must've been

tough. What did you do?"

"I pretended to be sick and spent a lot of time trying to find ways to torture my brother." Caleb laughed halfheartedly. "So don't be too hard on her."

"It's not a matter of being hard on her. It's a matter of how to handle this. Do I talk to the teacher? If she calls these kids out, will it make it that much harder on Hailey?" She looked up at him, tears welling in her blue eyes. "What did your mother do?"

"She gave Josh a warning and then let the whole thing run its course."

"Did the kids quit teasing you?"

"Yeah, after I grew into my weight and quit eating jelly doughnuts." He gave her a wry smile.

"Do you think they'll quit teasing Hailey?"

Caleb shook his head, surprised at how much Tara's discomfort made him want to reassure her that everything would be okay. "I can't answer that. Times are different. Who is Hailey's teacher?"

"A Mrs. Lesniak. Do you know her?"

"Yeah. Her husband and I played high school football together. She was a year behind us in school. Would you like me to talk to her?"

Tara shrugged. "I don't know. I appreciate your offer, but maybe I should see how things go before we involve her teacher."

"I'll do whatever suits you."

"Let's just wait then." Her tentative smile told him she still wasn't sure she was doing the right thing. Being a parent was a tough job—one he didn't envy. Maybe he should remember this episode when he started wishing he had a family like his brother and friends.

"Do you want her to lie down when I take her home?"

Tara shrugged. "Since I don't think she's really sick, maybe keeping her quiet is the best thing. She likes to read, and we have lots of books."

"Okay, guess I'll be on my way unless you have more instructions for me."

"No, and thanks again."

"Think nothing of it."

Caleb followed Tara to the reception area and watched while she talked to Hailey. Then the duo accompanied him to his car. When Caleb had come into the office, he'd never imagined what this day would bring. He prayed he could handle one little girl and not get too caught up in the life of her mother.

***

High-pitched giggles and the rumble of male laughter greeted Tara as she opened the door to the one-bedroom apartment that had been added onto the Fitzpatricks' cedar-sided ranch house. She quietly closed the kitchen door and leaned against it, taking in the delightful chorus. Hearing Hailey's happiness drained away most of Tara's tension, but she still had to deal with Hailey's problems at school and an unexpected attraction to the handsome man who was watching her child.

Tara peeked around the corner just as Hailey raised her arms above her head in victory. "I won again. You'll have to practice more, Mr. Fitz."

Tara stepped into the living room, where Hailey and Caleb sat on the blue plaid couch. "You seem to be feeling much better."

"Mommy, you're home." Hailey jumped up and raced across the blue braided rug. She flung her arms around Tara, then stepped back. "I beat Mr. Fitz in every game."

Tara turned to Caleb, who was still holding the secondhand game console. "What are you playing?"

Caleb grinned. "Something called Smash Brothers."

"Now I understand why you're losing." Tara couldn't help smiling. "I never win either. Hailey is unbeatable at that game. She spent hours playing it this past year."

"Your daughter is doing well." Caleb stood and patted Hailey on the back. "So I'll be heading home."

"Thanks for your help, and your mom said to tell you that she's expecting you for dinner." Tara looked over at Hailey, then back at Caleb. "We're invited, too."

"That sounds good." Caleb gave Hailey a fist bump before heading to the door. "See you soon."

Hailey cheered, but Tara wasn't sure she was prepared to spend another meal with Caleb, but there was no way she could have turned down his mother's invitation. Tara knew she would've seemed ungrateful. But she still wasn't comfortable around Caleb, despite his kind gestures.

She didn't want to have to impress him, but she sensed her employment rested on his good favor. And then there was that attraction for him that she wanted to put completely out of her mind. How could she do that when they would be working in the same office every day?

After Caleb left, Hailey tugged on one of Tara's arms. "Mommy, I like Mr. Fitz. He's fun."

Tara lifted her eyebrows. "Why do you call him Mr. Fitz?"

"So he knows I'm talking to him instead of his dad, Mr. Fitzpatrick."

"But I thought he said you could call him Caleb."

Hailey nodded. "But I know you like me to call adults Mr. and Mrs., so I call him Mr. Fitz, and he calls me Miss Hailey."

"What did you and Mr. Fitz do besides play Smash Brothers?"

"I read a book to him, and he read a book to me." Hailey took a big breath, her little chest puffing out. "Then he talked to me and told me not to worry about kids teasing me."

"And how did you feel about that?"

"Not so good at first, but then he told me about how he got picked on at school, too." Hailey giggled. "He said to ignore the people who tease me about my hair."

The way Caleb connected with Hailey was one more reasons to like him, but Tara didn't want to find things to like about him. There wasn't any wisdom in letting herself have an interest in any man—kind or not.

A little while later Tara and Hailey traipsed across the soggy lawn to the Fitzpatricks' front porch, which ran the length of the gray house. Before Tara could ring the bell, Caleb opened the door.

"Hi, Mr. Fitz." Hailey bounded into the front hall.

"Hi, Miss Hailey."

Hailey held out a folded piece of paper to Caleb. "I drew you a picture."

"Thanks." Caleb unfolded the paper and exclaimed over the drawing.

"Hailey, are you doing better?" Sheila entered the hall.

"I am." Hailey waved another paper at Sheila. "I drew a picture for you and Mr. Fitzpatrick."

"Well, thank you. This is a lovely surprise." Sheila took

Hailey's hand. "Let's show Mr. Fitzpatrick, and then we can put it on the refrigerator."

Tara watched as Hailey skipped away with Sheila.

"Your daughter's quite an artist. Did she get her talent from you?"

Tara turned at the sound of Caleb voice, her heart racing as she nearly stumbled into the brown tweed sofa. Unable to speak for a moment, she shrugged. Taking a calming breath, she wished he didn't have this effect on her. "I don't know where she gets her talent, but she loves to draw."

"Maybe from you, since you like to decorate."

"Could be." Tara shrugged again. "I want to thank you for talking to Hailey about how you were teased. I think it will help her cope, knowing that you went through something similar."

"No need to thank me."

Before Tara could reply, Hailey reappeared. "Mom, Mr. Fitz, you're supposed to come into the kitchen."

Tara and Hailey joined Caleb at the round oak table in the kitchen nook. Hailey made sure to get a seat next to Caleb. With her chin barely above the edge of the table, she looked so small in the big oak chair. Her little girl had been through so much in the last two years, and Tara didn't want her to have to deal with more problems.

Caleb put a napkin on his lap, then helped Hailey with hers. "Miss Hailey, you are in for a treat. My mom makes the best chicken parmesan."

"And I make the best garlic bread and salad." Tom put a bowl of each on the table.

"Everything looks really good." Tara looked over at Sheila, who carried a platter. "Is there anything I can do to help?"

Sheila shook her head as she placed the platter on the table, then sat next to her husband. "Tom, please say the blessing."

Tara bowed her head and prayed her own silent prayer. *Lord, please help me to trust in You and not worry about what the future holds.*

As everyone passed the food and started to eat, Tara tried to keep her prayer in mind. Learning to trust God had been hard this past year. Every bit of good news heightened her trust, but with every piece of bad news, the doubts took over. Trusting God through the bad times wasn't easy. For too many years, she had resisted letting God have a place in her life. Now she understood her grandparents' faith so much more.

When the meal was almost over, Sheila turned to Tara. "Tom and I invited you and Hailey, as well as Caleb, to dinner because we've been discussing an idea. I've been talking with Heather Watson, whose fiancé is coming up on the one-year anniversary of his bone marrow transplant. She's planning a celebration, and Molly Jansen and I thought it would be a good time to have a big fundraiser for her House for Families project. We thought we could get folks from both Hawthorne and Oakton to join this venture."

Tara wasn't sure how to respond. The Fitzpatricks were always doing some kind of charity work, like giving her a job and a place to live. "That sounds like a fabulous idea. What did you have in mind? I know the House for Families project can always use more funding."

A wary expression crossed Caleb's face. "And what exactly is the House for Families? And how do you know this Heather?"

"My friend Heather is an oncology nurse. She started a campaign to buy a house where families of cancer patients can stay while their loved one is being treated at the clinic where she works."

"So why aren't you staying there?"

"Because Hailey had finished her treatment before the house was a reality, and besides, her doctor was in Boston."

"So what brought you to the women's shelter?"

Tara tried not to be annoyed. "When Hailey finished with her treatments, I needed a job and a place to live. Molly Jansen offered me both."

"Then why did you quit your job there and start working for my parents?"

Did he think she was some kind of charlatan? "Because I was taking up space that they needed for women who were fleeing abuse. Your parents' request came at just the right time. Hailey was finished with her treatments, but we still needed to be close to her doctor for regular checkups. It seemed like an answer to prayer."

"It certainly does." Despite Caleb's agreement, skepticism clouded his expression.

Tara forced a smile, but she wondered how the man who had played with Hailey and had her laughing appeared so negative now.

Sheila looked at Caleb with a tentative smile, almost as if his badgering had embarrassed her. "I'm so glad you're on board with this idea. Heather gave a presentation about this project to our ladies' Bible study a few weeks ago. I thought it was a perfect project for our fundraising community."

Caleb stared at his mother. "So you're raising funds for this place?"

Sheila nodded. "Caleb, there's so much that's happened while you were in Florida. I guess we'll have to catch you up on all the events."

Caleb nodded. "You will."

"Maybe Tara would be the best person to give you all the information." Sheila laid a hand on Tara's arm. "Could you do that?"

Tara didn't know what to do other than agree to the Fitzpatricks' plan, but she didn't understand why Sheila couldn't do this herself. "I'll be glad to fill Caleb in on what I know."

"Caleb, your father and I think you would be the perfect person to spearhead this project."

Tara was afraid to see Caleb's reaction, so she refused to look in his direction. Instead, she studied the squiggles of marinara sauce left on her plate. If he took on this project, would it require them to work together? The thought created a swirling sensation in her midsection.

"What exactly do you have in mind?" Caleb's question didn't indicate any irritation.

Sheila glanced around the table. "That's up to you, but there are dozens of ways to get the community involved."

"Are we going beyond Hawthorne and Oakton with the fundraising?" Caleb raised his eyebrows.

Sheila shrugged. "We'll concentrate on those two communities, but we can always include other groups if they are interested. You can go as far and wide as you want."

"Absolutely." Nodding, Tom brought his hand down on the table. "You've got the organizational skills for an undertaking like this."

"I'm glad you have confidence in me, but are you expecting me to organize this by myself when I've been gone for nearly a year?" Caleb looked from one parent to the other.

"Oh, no, I thought Tara could help you." Sheila patted Tara on the back. "Isn't that right, dear?"

Trying not to show her insecurity, Tara finally looked at Caleb. What could she make of his expression—guarded, uncertain, or annoyed? Maybe all three. "I'll do whatever I can."

Caleb stared at his mother. "Aren't you railroading Tara into this?"

Sheila grinned. "Actually, we're railroading both of you."

Caleb chuckled. "And you're good at it. You always have been."

As Sheila joined the laughter, Tara tried to figure out what to say. Caleb didn't appear surprised or too upset by his parents' admission. She shouldn't be either. Too many times today she'd gone along with something because she didn't want to appear ungrateful. She had to quit being pushed along as if she didn't have a mind of her own. She could make her own decision. "Caleb, your parents have a worthy idea. We should talk to Heather and see what she thinks."

Caleb nodded. "Okay. Will you set up a time when you can introduce us?"

Tara nodded, not sure how all of this would work out, but she wouldn't let any of this intimidate her. She'd survived the ups and downs of Hailey's illness—she could survive this, too.

"Wonderful." Sheila stood and started to clear the table. "Dad and I will clear the table, then play a game with Hailey so you two can talk about this endeavor."

Standing, Caleb finally smiled. "Let's go into the living room and kick around some ideas."

"Okay." Tara thanked Sheila for the meal and instructed Hailey to be on her best behavior, then followed Caleb. She hoped working with a man who made her pulse race wasn't going to be a mistake.

CHAPTER FIVE

His parents' living room felt more like a prison than a place to chat. Why were his parents pushing him and Tara together? Were they trying to be matchmakers when they barely knew the woman? Was he being overly cautious?

He had to quit speculating and deal with the situation. Caleb waved a hand toward the seating area containing a couch and two arm chairs. "Have a seat wherever you'd like."

Tara gave him a forced smile as she sat at one end of the couch. "I know you just got back into town, and I'm sorry your parents have roped you into this. I'd understand if you'd rather not be involved."

Caleb wondered about her contradictory statement. Was she on board with this idea, or did she want him to back out? "So how do you actually feel about this project?"

Tara frowned. "What do you mean?"

"I'm wondering if you're putting on a good show for my parents, then giving me an excuse to back out."

"Am I doing that?"

"I don't know. Are you?"

Tara stared at him as she fingered the cross pendant hanging on the chain around her neck. "I…I thought maybe you were the one who didn't want to get roped into doing this. So I was giving you an out."

Nodding, Caleb let out a feeble laugh. "I see. You do want to do this, but you're afraid I don't. Is that it?"

Tara pressed her lips together, then let out a heavy sigh. "Yes. I'm sorry if I misjudged you."

Had she misjudged him? He wasn't exactly thrilled, but maybe this was the perfect opportunity to keep an eye on Tara Madsen and learn what she was all about. He'd let his parents down once before because of a woman. He wouldn't do it again. "It's not a matter of misjudgment. It's a matter of being honest with each other. I appreciate your honesty. Now let's see what we can accomplish."

Tara gazed at him, her smile more genuine. "Okay. Do you have any ideas?"

"I thought you were the idea woman—the creative, artistic one." Caleb gave her a lazy grin.

Tara's smile turned shy as she fluttered her eyelashes and lowered her head. He had embarrassed her. Not his intention.

After a few moments of silence, she finally looked up at him. "I'm thinking a little ahead of where we are in the calendar right now, but what do you think about having the kids in the church youth group bake cookies and make ornaments to sell to the people who come out for the holiday parade?"

"The ornaments are a good idea, but I'm not sure about the cookies."

Tara frowned. "Why no cookies?"

"I'm not sure, but we might have to jump through some government hoops if we do something with food. All kinds of regulations have come about in the last few years regarding food preparation." Caleb waved a hand in the air. "I don't think we want to deal with it. Too much trouble."

Tara let out a heavy sigh. "So you're saying a cookie sale is out?"

Caleb nodded. "I think it will be easier that way."

"Do you think selling ornaments will be enough?"

Caleb wasn't sure what he could contribute to this endeavor. His artistic talent was nonexistent. "So tell me your plan."

Tara looked at him wide eyed. "I thought you were the organizer."

"I can't organize unless you tell me what I'm organizing."

"Maybe you should write something down." Tara glanced around the room. "Do you have paper and something to write with?"

Caleb opened the drawer in the nearby end table and produced a small pad of paper and a pen. Then he gave her a cheesy grin. "What would you like me to write?"

Tara let out a heavy sigh. "We need to find a place to make the ornaments and decorations."

"Got that down. What else?"

Tara drew her eyebrows into a little frown. "And we'll need the materials for the decorations."

Caleb scribbled Tara's instructions on the pad, trying to figure out his role in this project. "What do you need in the way of materials?"

Tara pressed her lips together, that little frown still in place. "I'll have to get back to you on that."

"Okay, but what other things can we do before this Christmas stuff?"

Tara stared at him as she bit her lower lip. "You have any ideas?"

Caleb let that question roll around in his mind, as he

hoped it might trigger something brilliant. Instead, a pair of beautiful blue eyes had his brain in a whirl. He was letting a woman scramble his thoughts again. He would not let that happen. "Does the town still have that fall festival with the pumpkin patch?"

"I think so." Tara shrugged. "Hailey was really sick last fall and couldn't participate in many activities, so I didn't pay much attention."

Caleb scribbled a note to himself. "That's something I'll find out. If they do, I'll talk to the coordinators about letting us sell the decorations and ornaments at that event, too."

"That's a wonderful idea." Tara gave him an expectant gaze. "I know we haven't discussed this, but I thought maybe we could make gingerbread houses. What do you think?"

"I suppose we could do that as long as we aren't selling them as food."

"I thought we could provide the materials, and then folks could pay a fee to assemble and decorate them."

"Do you think folks will pay to make gingerbread houses?"

Tara shrugged. "People buy kits to make them. You see them on sale all over. I think it's worth a try."

Caleb took in her request, his heart filling with reservations. Her request brought visions of Amy to mind. He could still see her begging him for money to pay for her father's doctors and medicine. Without hesitation, he had given it to her, never dreaming she was duping him and his parents. But Tara's plea wasn't for something she would use for herself. So why did it invoke memories of Amy's duplicity? Maybe the hurt ran so deep that he couldn't shake it.

"I don't know. You should talk to my mom to see what she thinks." Caleb's mind was so filled with doubt that he couldn't make a decision, and here he thought his parents needed help. He was the one who was still carrying the burden of betrayal, while his parents had moved on with their lives.

"Okay. If that's what you think I should do." Tara fished her phone from her purse and tapped on the screen. "I'll make myself a note to talk to her."

Caleb was almost sure his mother would agree with whatever Tara wanted. He reminded himself this was a good thing—nothing like Amy's false needs.

"I hope we can make the houses. My grandmother used to make one every year when I was a kid, and then again with Hailey."

"I'm sure Hailey would like to make one."

"You're right." Tara nodded. "I want to make this the best Christmas ever for her."

"I hope it is the best." Caleb couldn't fault Tara for wanting to give her daughter a Christmas to remember. He had to help and keep his negativity at bay. "I'll make the inquiries, and you get me a list of the things you need. We don't have much time. When will you get back to me?"

Worry clouding her eyes, Tara grimaced. "Is Monday soon enough"

Caleb had the urge to reach out to comfort her. Instead, he gripped the pen tighter. Her vulnerability tugged at his heart. He didn't want to fall into his parents' trap, but he couldn't be hardhearted either. Was there a spot somewhere in between the two? He would have to find it. "Please don't worry over it. You can get it to me as soon as you can."

"But you're right. We can't waste time." She jutted out her chin. "I'll get that information to you tomorrow."

"Great." Caleb took a deep breath. "We can talk over our plans again when you give me that information."

"Would you like me to introduce you to Heather Watson, since she's the person who spearheaded the original drive for the House for Families project? She's a dynamo when it comes to fundraising."

Caleb leaned back and laced his fingers behind his head. Did he want to get caught up in his parents' world of do-gooders? That was a cynical attitude—one that should be eradicated even though he'd had a bad experience with charitable efforts. "Yeah, that would be good."

"Then I'll talk to Heather, too. We have a Montana connection. Her uncle has been my benefactor. I can never repay him." Tara took a deep breath and let it out in a rush. "So many people have helped me along the way. That's why I want to be a part of this fundraising—so I can give back at least a little bit."

Caleb's cynicism reared its ugly head again. Was this young woman sponging off multiple people? He pushed the thought away. She said she wanted to give back. He couldn't continue to compare Tara Madsen with Amy Baxter. He had to let go of the past without falling into the same trap.

***

Monday morning brought little change to Tara's suspicion that her presence in this office made Caleb unhappy. He was polite but distant. He would probably shut her out completely if it weren't for his parents. She stared at the closed door to his office. It held no welcome. What would she find on the other side of that door this morning? She had the information he had requested Friday night, and she had an invitation to issue.

Tara held up her hand to knock, then dropped it to her side. She bowed her head and said a short prayer. Letting him intimidate her wouldn't help with anything. Despite his agreement to work with her, she had no doubt that he came as a reluctant participant. And she couldn't forget the unwanted attraction she had for the man, or maybe it was only the intimidation factor that had her heart beating in overtime.

Taking a deep breath, she pushed the questions without answers aside and rapped her knuckles on the door.

"Come in." Caleb's deep voice sounded through the door.

Tara turned the doorknob, its coolness reminding her of Caleb's somewhat frosty attitude, except when it came to Hailey. The man appeared to like her child even if he didn't like her. That was another problem. Hailey had a tendency to adopt whatever male figure came into her life, but that was something Tara would deal with later.

The door swung open. Caleb sat behind his desk, a mask of indifference hiding his thoughts. Tara tried to smile as she waved the papers in her hand. "I've got that information you wanted, and your mom thought that making the gingerbread houses is a marvelous idea."

"I thought she would." Caleb stood. "And you're very prompt with your information."

The compliment should make her feel better, but it didn't. "I know we need to get started, so I wanted to get this to you right away."

"Thanks." He nodded. "And I've made arrangements to use the church fellowship hall for the crafts."

"When do you plan to start?" Tara asked.

He stepped around the desk as he took the papers from her and studied them. "As soon as we get these supplies and contact the folks we want to get involved."

"How long do you think that'll take?"

Caleb shrugged. "All depends on how fast we can garner support for this project."

Holding tight to her cross pendant, Tara saw this as her opening to introduce Caleb to Heather. "We talked about having you meet Heather Watson. I talked to her yesterday, and she invited us to meet her for lunch tomorrow if you're free."

Caleb grabbed his cell phone from the desk and tapped the screen several times. "Let me see what's on my calendar."

Tara held her breath. He had no reaction to the invitation. It was merely business for him—another appointment he would have to fit into his schedule.

She wanted this man to accept her role as receptionist, but was it more than that?

Surely not. She didn't need a man to muddle her already too-complicated life, but she couldn't deny her attraction to him. Stupid. Stupid. Stupid. She couldn't repeat her previous bad decisions about men. Besides, she couldn't let herself hope for another relationship.

She'd fallen in love with Blake Madsen the moment he'd grinned at her while she'd waited on his table at the Steakhouse in Stockton. The handsome cowboy had breezed into town to work on a nearby ranch. In a matter of weeks, he'd won her heart, and against her grandparents' wishes, Tara had eloped with him. She'd been young, only eighteen, and so naïve and foolish.

"So what do you think?"

"I'm free." He glanced up from his phone. "Time and place?"

"Out at the Hawthorne Inn at noon."

"Great. I'll drive." He started to turn away, then stopped and looked at her. "By the way, how's your car?"

"It was a dead battery. Your dad put in a new one for me." Tara hated that she was always depending on someone for help.

"Dad's always been good with cars." Caleb's expression didn't give Tara a clue as to whether he was happy that his dad had fixed her car.

Tara forced a smile and turned to go.

As she returned to her desk, she couldn't help thinking about her life and how it seemed to be a never-ending stream of calls for help. Ever since Blake had suddenly died and she'd discovered the credit card debt he'd accumulated without her knowledge, she'd been depending on someone. First, she'd moved back in with her grandparents, who watched Hailey during work hours, while she ever so slowly tried to chip away at the debt. She earned pretty good tips as a waitress, but the inconsistency of her income made it hard to plan ahead.

Her new job gave her an income she could count on, but it still didn't pay a lot. Not enough to completely pay down the debt that hung over her. The debt had dwindled over the years, but the expenses of Hailey's cancer had ended her attempt to get rid of the balance on that credit card. The bill was a monthly reminder of Blake's irresponsibility.

Regret over the bad decisions she'd made weighed her down as well. She'd thrown away the opportunity to go to design school when she'd married Blake just weeks after graduating from high school. She was determined not to let another handsome man turn her head.

Somehow she always got separated from the people she loved. Her parents left when she was young. Blake died. She'd had to leave her grandparents in order to treat Hailey's cancer. Hailey was the only one Tara had managed to keep close, and every day she feared that cancer would separate them, too. Her main focus was Hailey, and nothing could change that. Nothing.

Shaking away bad thoughts, Tara tried to concentrate on the spreadsheet on her computer screen. She was learning how to use different computer programs on this job, and she was grateful for the opportunity to further her skills. She wanted to be the best she could be so she could prove she deserved to be here.

While she input information, Caleb came out of his office and strode to her desk. She looked up and swallowed the lump in her throat. He didn't look happy. "May I help you?"

"Yes." He looked at the list in his hand. "I showed this to my mother, and she insists that you go with me when I shop because she says when I shop, I often buy the wrong things. She thinks I need your assistance."

Now Tara understood his annoyed expression. Something told her that no matter what she said, it wouldn't be right. "Maybe I should just pick up the things we need, and you won't have to bother."

His expression morphed from annoyance to suspicion. "I'm supposed to use the business credit card for the shopping trip."

Tara tried not to frown. Was he insinuating that she couldn't be trusted with the business credit card? Of course, she might not be authorized to use the card anyway. What would it take to show this man he didn't have anything to fear from her? "I understand."

The frown Tara had suppressed appeared on Caleb's face instead. "I don't think you do."

"Sure I do. Your mother thinks you need help, and she expects me to give you that help because you're the one authorized to use the company credit card." Tara produced a less-than-genuine smile. "It's as simple as that."

"I'd like to go after work, if that's okay with you." Caleb raised his eyebrows as he stared at her.

Tara wasn't surprised that he never agreed with her assessment of the situation. "Who will watch Hailey while I'm out helping you?"

"My mother has that covered, too." Caleb smiled wryly. "She probably planned the whole thing so she can watch Hailey."

"You're sure she doesn't mind?"

"Hailey's a good substitute for the grandchildren who live too far away." A shrug accompanied Caleb's crooked smile. "You might as well get used to having my mom snatch time with Hailey at any possible moment."

Tara couldn't help the little chuckle that escaped her lips. "I think Hailey has adopted your mom, too. We lived with my grandparents before we came here, and I know Hailey misses them a lot."

"So are you still planning to go back to Montana?"

Tara let that question and all of its implications settle in her mind. Was he hoping she would? Why did that thought prick her heart? "I do want to go back, but I'm taking this all one day at a time. We need to stay here for the time being to be close to Hailey's doctors and the treatment center."

"Yeah, that's probably the best way to look at it." Caleb let his gaze drop as if he wished he hadn't asked the question. He looked up again as he took a step back. "I'd better let you get back to work."

Tara watched him disappear into his office. The man was a puzzle. Sometimes he seemed genuinely annoyed that she was here, and other times he seemed sympathetic to her circumstances. She thought this job situation had been an answer to prayer until Caleb showed up with his less-than-enthusiastic approval. Could she talk to anyone about this? Only one person came to mind. Molly. Maybe she would understand.

***

Tonight's shopping trip would test Caleb's ability to push away the past, at least for a few hours. He had finally realized that what had happened with Amy still sat like a stone in his heart, weighing him down with destructive emotions. A year ago, he'd welcomed the assignment in Florida. It had given him a change of scenery, but fleeing to another state hadn't taken away the hurt of Amy's betrayal. The thought of spending more of his day with another pretty blonde didn't improve his mood—only made it worse.

As Caleb held the door open for Tara, a grim, cloudy sky greeted him, painting a picture of his mood. He didn't want to feel this way, but he couldn't help thinking that his mother was pushing Tara at him with this bogus shopping trip. He was perfectly capable of buying the things on the list. How could he mess that up?

"It certainly looks like it's going to rain." Tara's statement snapped Caleb out of his troubling thoughts.

He shrugged as he unlocked his car. "Haven't you noticed that we have gray skies here more often than not from now until summer?"

Tara slid into the passenger seat and buckled her seat belt. "I guess I've been too busy worrying about Hailey to notice. Last year there was so much snow."

Tara's comment reminded Caleb that he had life easy. He shouldn't be feeling sorry for himself. He had no sick child to cause him concern. He had a loving family and a good job. And he shouldn't have unkind thoughts about Tara, but Amy's duplicity lurked at the back of his mind and told him that he was a poor judge of women, maybe people in general. He had no good response. So he spent the rest of the drive on I-495 in silence. The less he said, the better.

Minutes after parking the car, Caleb pushed a cart into the huge hobby and craft store and looked over at Tara. "We can start by finding the aisle with the paints we need.

"Do you know where that is?" Tara asked.

Caleb shrugged. "It's been a while since I've been here."

"Maybe we should ask someone."

"We'll find it."

"So you don't believe in asking for directions?"

Caleb stopped and stared at Tara, his hands gripping the cart until his knuckles turned white. It was a simple question. Why did it bother him? He forced a smile. "Only when I need them."

"Sounds like we need them."

Caleb loosened his hold on the cart. "You can find someone to ask."

"Sure." Tara turned her head, looking around the cavernous store. "There's someone."

As Tara trotted off to speak with the man who was stocking the shelves in a nearby aisle, Caleb took a deep breath and closed his eyes. *Lord, I'm doing a rotten job of showing kindness. Help me do better.* When he opened his eyes, Tara was back and staring up at him. He hoped she didn't think he was… He didn't know what he hoped. "Did you find out what we need to know?"

She cocked her head as she peered at him. "Are you okay?"

He let out a deep sigh. "I'm sorry my mother felt it was necessary to push us together."

"We'll survive."

"Yeah." Caleb cringed inwardly. He was making a mess of this. Why had he opened his mouth? Now Tara would think he didn't like her.

That was the whole problem. He liked her too much— too much for his own good. He didn't need a woman to complicate his life, but his mother was determined to place Tara there. Thinking of a new relationship couldn't happen until he buried the hurt from the old one, and success in that endeavor had failed.

"Let's get started so we can be done with our mission as soon as possible." Tara charged ahead.

Pushing the cart, Caleb followed and wished he could undo the last few minutes. Tara didn't deserve the brunt of his lingering unhappiness. In the long run, maybe the declaration he'd made concerning his mother would make Tara wary, despite their forced togetherness over the next few weeks.

When they reached the aisle with the paints, Tara rifled through the little plastic tubes. "I think we'll need lots of green and red. What do you think?"

"If we need lots of red and green, can we find bigger containers?"

"Well, we'll need different kinds for different surfaces—wood, metal, or plaster."

"Okay. Guess my mother was right. I do need a helper."

Tara let out a little laugh. "Thanks for making me feel useful."

"You're welcome." Caleb smiled, realizing she was useful all right—useful for showing him what a dunderhead he could be. Begrudgingly, he was learning how to appreciate her contribution to their office. "Show me what paints we need, and I'll put them in the cart."

"Besides the red and green, we'll need the other primary colors, gold, silver, and some with glitter."

"Okay." Shaking his head, Caleb grabbed some bottles of paint and tossed them into the cart. "You are making me see that I know very little about craft projects."

"I didn't expect that you would." Tara moved down the aisle and picked out more types of paint. "We'll need brushes, too."

"Pick up whatever you need." Caleb pushed the cart and stopped next to her as she looked through the paint brushes.

Finally she looked up at him. "I've got everything I need in this aisle."

"Where to next?"

Tara looked down at her list. "Wherever they have plaster of Paris and molds."

"Let's try the next aisle." Caleb maneuvered into the main aisle, then stopped and motioned to his left. "Looks like I guessed right."

Nodding, Tara headed for the large bags of plaster. "A couple of these will be perfect."

Caleb rounded the cart. "That's got to be heavy. Let me help."

"It's okay. I've got it." As Tara lifted the bag, she lost her grip.

Caleb grabbed the bag before it fell. Their hands touched. Their eyes met. He swallowed hard. This was worse than he thought. He was letting a pretty blonde turn his head again.

She smiled as they carefully put the bag into the cart. "Thanks. That was a lot heavier than I thought. I can't imagine the mess if I'd dropped it."

"Glad to assist." Caleb took a deep breath and let it out slowly. The plaster was safely in the cart, and Tara obviously didn't have any romantic notions about him. He was the only one feeling the sparks. Why did the latter thought disappoint him? The propensity to fall for pretty blondes afflicted him like a virus—one with no cure.

"I'll let you do the lifting from now on." Tara looked at her list as she moved down the aisle. "You can get a second bag."

Caleb put another bag into the cart and proceeded to follow Tara, doing her bidding as he went.

When they finally had everything on the list, she turned to him with a smile. "This is going to be so much fun."

"If you say so." He grinned.

Despite his wariness, Tara's enthusiasm lightened Caleb's heart. He had to admit that her fortitude made him examine his own life. She'd dealt with a lot, and yet she forged ahead without complaint. He should take a lesson from her instead of comparing her to Amy. Would he be opening himself up for heartache if he put aside his reservations? He shook away the question as they gathered the other items and headed for the checkout. He'd think about that another day. After all, he was going to spend plenty of time with Tara in the coming days.

CHAPTER SIX

An earthy smell permeated the air as the sun warmed the moisture-soaked earth. The early morning rains had given way to clear skies and balmier weather. The sun warmed Tara's cheeks as she accompanied Caleb to his car. She was looking forward to their lunch with Heather, but he strode ahead in brooding silence.

Tara guessed that he didn't share her enthusiasm for the day's adventure. What could she expect? He didn't like to be around her, and she couldn't exactly figure out why. He'd been surprised that his parents had hired her, but that couldn't be the entire reason.

Tara slipped into the passenger seat and buckled her seat belt, the question sticking in her mind like the crimson leaf plastered to the windshield. The rain and blustery wind had denuded a lot of trees, and colorful leaves lay everywhere. Leaf-peeping season was just about over. The Hawthorne Inn would grow quieter in the weeks to come until the Christmas season started. She had always enjoyed the little respite between this time of year and Thanksgiving when she'd worked at the inn.

"You're quiet." Caleb's deep voice interrupted Tara's thoughts.

She glanced his way. "You're one to talk. You haven't said much since we left."

"I was waiting for you to start the conversation."

"Really? Why?"

"Safer that way. I can't say anything that would get me into trouble."

Tara gave him a little frown. Had she given him any reason to think she would disapprove of what he said? She hated this pins-and-needles feeling she had whenever they were together. "What have I done to make you dislike me?"

He looked at her as he stopped before turning onto the main road. "Did I ever say I disliked you?"

"Not exactly."

"Then why do you think that?" He raised his eyebrows as he continued to stare at her.

Tara wished she could take back the question. If he hadn't disliked her before, he surely did now. "Just a feeling."

"We're good." He shifted gears as he maneuvered the car down the road that wandered through the forested area. "I'm still getting used to having a receptionist who also lives in my parents' home. That's all."

"Okay." Her response came out in a squeak. She wasn't at all sure she believed him, but she wasn't going to argue. Would she ever feel completely comfortable around him? Maybe it was good that she couldn't relax. Then she wouldn't succumb to her attraction to the man.

Caleb was everything Blake hadn't been. Caleb was grounded, responsible, and serious. Was that what attracted her? She gave herself a mental shake. She'd been wrong about Blake, so maybe she was wrong about Caleb, too. Wishing she could steer her thoughts in another direction, she could hardly wait to get to the inn.

They rode in silence for a few minutes. Tara didn't

usually mind a quiet ride, but today it lent itself to thinking time she didn't want or need. "I'm glad you're going to get to meet Heather. She's such a good-hearted person. And Molly, too. They are some of the most giving women I know."

"Do you know a lot of those kinds of women?"

Thinking his question was odd, Tara stifled a frown. He made it sound like they weren't the kind of people she should be around. "I know a lot of people who share an interest in helping others, especially those who have cancer, and I'm grateful to have met them."

"I'm sure you are."

"They've been my lifeline." Tara wondered why Caleb's inquiries seemed to put her on the defensive. Was he implying something about her activities?

"I'm happy to meet some of your friends."

"You'll like them." She wasn't convinced Caleb was actually glad he'd be meeting Heather and Molly. "Our turn is coming up just around this curve in the road."

Minutes later, Caleb drove down the lane toward the ornate pale-blue Victorian house with the white trim. As he parked the car, he glanced in her direction. "I'm surprised my mother never mentioned this place. How long did you say it's been in operation?"

"They've been open a little over two years."

"How long did you work here?"

"A little over a year." Tara opened her door. "Molly and Kurt are fabulous people to work for. Kurt did all the renovations on the property."

"He did a great job. It looks like the perfect bed-and-breakfast that I see in brochures."

"You'll have to tell him."

Caleb walked around the car and joined Tara. "I'll get to meet Kurt, too?"

"Maybe. He may be off working on a restoration somewhere." Tara took in the piles of leaves in the yard on the right side of the inn. "Looks like Kurt left the leaves for the kids to play in."

"Kids?"

"Yeah. Kurt's twins, Emily and Eric. And some of the women who come to the shelter have kids, too." Tara fell into step with Caleb as they moseyed up the front walk. "When Hailey's health permitted, she used to love playing with the kids. That's the one thing I miss about living here. Playmates for Hailey."

"Are you sorry that you've moved?"

Tara shook her head. "Oh, no. It has been better for everyone that I moved out and opened up a space for someone else. Hailey will make new friends."

"You sound confident of that, despite the problems from the other day."

Tara sighed. "She's good at handling challenges. She's battled cancer."

"I'm glad you have confidence in her."

"I try to keep my worry to myself." Tara straightened her shoulders. "Hailey doesn't need to see that from me."

"You're a good mother."

Tara drank in the compliment. "Thank you. I appreciate your saying so."

"You're welcome."

"There's Heather." Tara motioned toward the wraparound front porch. A moment later, Tara embraced her friend, then introduced her to Caleb.

"It's nice to meet you, Caleb. I've met your mother.

She's a dear person." Heather pushed a strand of her shoulder-length dark-brown hair behind her ear. "I hope you don't mind, but Max, my fiancé, is joining us, too."

"Wonderful." Tara turned to Caleb. "I'm so glad you'll get to meet Max. He's been a role model to Hailey."

"I think Max would say Hailey's been a role model to him." Heather patted Tara on the shoulder. "He isn't here yet, but I'm expecting him any minute. In the meantime, we can go to our table."

"Sure." Tara glanced over at Caleb, who had been politely quiet. Was he wishing he wasn't here? She had to quit trying to figure out what he was thinking. Pushing aside her concerns, she walked alongside him as Heather led the way into the inn.

Heather stepped through the door and waved a hand around the foyer, where a staircase turned at a right angle as it led to the second floor. "Isn't this a fabulous restoration?"

"Wow! This is magnificent." Caleb surveyed the area. "The dark woodwork is gorgeous. I can tell a real craftsman did the work."

"You see the tall woman with the strawberry-blond hair talking with the couple over there?" Tara nodded her head toward the dining room on the right.

"Yeah. Is she the owner?"

Tara nodded. "That's Molly Jansen. You can tell her."

"I hope I get the chance," Caleb said.

"I'm sure you will. Molly makes a point to stop at each table to chat with her guests for a few moments." Heather gave her name to the hostess.

The threesome settled at a table beside a window that looked out on the side porch. While they studied their menus, Max arrived, and Heather introduced him to Caleb.

Standing, Caleb shook hands with the man. "I'm glad you could join us. Now I won't be the odd man out."

Max chuckled as he took a seat. "Yeah, these two women can steamroll a guy before he knows what's happened."

Heather gave Max an annoyed look but couldn't hide the smile lurking behind the frown. "Just because you think I like to run things doesn't mean you should lump Tara in with me."

"I've seen you two together." Max turned to Caleb. "You'll soon learn that Heather is the planner, but Tara eagerly takes up the cause. Then everything is settled before a guy can say a thing."

Caleb nodded. "That pretty much sums up why I'm sitting here."

Tara couldn't tell if there was even a hint of levity in his statement. She wondered what Caleb thought of Heather and Max's playful teasing. Caleb was always so serious, even when he was sharing time with Hailey. Tara tried to relax and not stew over his participation, while the waitress took their orders.

Caleb gazed across the table at Heather. "So Tara tells me that you have a house for the families of cancer patients?"

"Yes, we opened it earlier in the year." Heather smiled. "It's been a big help to the families who have to stay here for an extended period while a family member receives treatment."

"It wasn't available when I was getting my treatments, but it would've been a big help for my folks when they came to visit." Max reached for Heather's hand. "Even though I kid her about being a steamroller, she's a mighty fundraiser."

Heather smiled at Max. "Thanks, honey. Let's find out what Tara and Caleb have in mind for their fundraising project."

Glancing at Caleb, Tara wasn't sure whether to take the lead. "Actually, Caleb's mom was the one who came up with the idea, but she put us in charge."

"Caleb, can you tell us about it?" Heather laid down her menu.

"She hopes to involve the children in our church and other area churches so the kids can learn about giving in a personal way." Caleb glanced at Tara, seeking confirmation.

Tara nodded. "We want to involve all ages from kindergarten through high school. We're planning to have the kids make Christmas ornaments and decorations and sell them at a number of events this fall. We bought a lot of supplies today, and we'll have age-appropriate projects for everyone. We'll be working in the fellowship hall of the church we attend in Hawthorne."

"Your project sounds like quite an undertaking," Heather said. "Do you have everything in place for your tax-exempt status?"

Caleb rubbed a hand over his chin. "That's a good question. We didn't discuss that, but I'm pretty sure my mom has it covered, or she wouldn't have made these plans. You can talk to her about that."

Tara hoped they didn't think she was rushing into something without the proper planning. "I know this is kind of last minute, but I saw it as a way to get the kids involved in an activity that benefits others. We plan to start next week on Wednesday night, which is the night our youth group meets."

"That would be a perfect time for our youth." Heather smiled. "And if anyone can pull this off, it's you."

"Thanks." Tara wondered if Caleb had the same confidence in her. Why did she care what he thought? This wasn't about him. It was about helping people affected by cancer. It would be her lifelong cause.

While Tara tried to stifle her worry about Caleb, the waitress came and took everyone's order.

As the waitress left, Max looked around the table. "Hey, I've got an idea. The one-year anniversary of my transplant is coming up at the end of October. My grandparents who live here are planning a big event to celebrate. They've rented a hall, and I'm sure they'd let you set up a table to sell items there."

"Do you really think so?" Tara didn't want to get her hopes up. "I got my invitation to your party, so Hailey and I are already planning to attend."

"That's great." Max turned to Caleb. "I'll send you an invitation and talk to my grandfather about your project, especially since the funds will go toward the House for Families."

Caleb nodded. "I appreciate that."

"My grandfather has made a point of helping with any project that involves raising money for cancer. Last summer he surprised both Heather and me with a Fantasy Day at Fenway Park." Max glanced at Heather. "We both love the Red Sox, especially this lady. When she broke her leg last year, she got a red cast."

"I take it you both like baseball." Caleb chuckled. "Sorry about your broken leg. Looks like you're fully recovered."

"Thanks. I am." Heather smiled. "But the most important recovery is Max's. That's what we're going to celebrate."

"And our little project would like to be part of your celebration," Tara said.

"And it will be." Max nodded. "Looks like our food's here."

After the servers placed all the dishes on the table, Max offered a prayer of thanks. Tara said a silent prayer of thanks for friends who shared a common cause, and she prayed that she would find the right balance in her relationship with Caleb. In minutes the group helped themselves to the family-style dishes that accompanied the entrees, while the conversation centered on upcoming events.

Tara drank in the camaraderie, even with Caleb. He seemed to be enjoying the company, too. She hoped that was a good sign for their upcoming project. She had to quit fretting about the future, but worry had been her constant companion throughout the last few years. Trusting God to see her through each crisis didn't come easy. Why couldn't she remember that God had brought someone into her life to help her with each and every predicament? One day she would lean on Him and learn not to worry. That was a promise.

***

The food churned in Caleb's stomach while he watched Tara laugh and talk with Heather and Max as if everything was right with the world. He shouldn't be bothered that she always seemed uptight when she talked with him. Could he blame her? He hadn't exactly welcomed her with open arms.

If he was honest with himself, he would admit that he was afraid to let her get too close. Could he be her friend without letting his attraction to her grow into something more than he wanted? He couldn't continue to torture himself this way. He would be her friend, starting now. He could do this.

"Molly's coming our way." Tara's statement interrupted Caleb's thoughts.

"Hi, everyone." The tall strawberry blonde stopped beside their table. "I hope you enjoyed your meal."

A chorus of yeses emanated from the group. Then Heather jumped in and made introductions.

Molly looked at Caleb. "I've met your mother. We've done some fundraising projects together."

"Yes, my mother seems to know everyone. I guess that's a good thing." Caleb realize that his parents were possibly trying to orchestrate his life. With all the people they were putting in his life, he couldn't help thinking that.

"And we love your mother, and your dad, too. They are going to start doing our books and giving Tara a chance to learn accounting firsthand." Molly patted Tara's shoulder. "We really miss her around here, but working for your parents is a real plus."

Caleb forced a smile, his misgivings going into full gear. He couldn't get over the way this was all playing out like the situation with Amy. She had come to work for his parents, who had offered to teach her how to keep books. Had his parents learned nothing from that bad situation? Were they blindly walking into a similar set of circumstances? They had never mentioned anything about Tara learning the accounting side of the business. She was supposed to be the receptionist. He would have a talk with his parents first thing in the morning.

"Did I hear correctly that you're going to involve the kids in a fundraising project?" Molly asked.

Tara nodded, then went on to explain their tentative plans.

"Emily and Eric will be so excited to participate," Molly said.

Tara smiled. "And Hailey's looking forward to it, too."

"And I'll check with the children's program director at our church to see if they want to participate." Heather glanced over at Tara. "I'll report back to you after I find out."

"Sounds like your plans are moving right along." Molly glanced around the table. "I just had a thought. We have a booth at the fall festival here in Hawthorne, and we could easily let the kids sell their stuff in our booth. That way you won't have to go to the expense of renting a booth for your project."

"That would be perfect." Tara clapped her hands. "We were talking earlier about whether there is a fall festival. Now we know."

"When you get everything set, let me know the final plans. Now I need to get back to work." Molly nodded. "Thanks again for coming in."

"Thanks for your help." Tara stood and gave Molly a hug. "I'll be in touch."

As Molly hurried away to talk to other guests, Caleb let his earlier thoughts sift through his mind. Had God brought all these charity-minded people into his life to show him that he'd been wrong to worry about his parents' giving nature? Despite that question, he wasn't ready to let his guard down yet. He'd ask Tara about his parents' plan, but this wasn't the time or place.

Heather finished the last of her meal and looked over at Tara. "Tell me about your plans to learn bookkeeping."

"I'm so excited about it. Sheila asked me the other day if I would like to learn about accounting and suggested that I take some online classes." Tara's face lit up with excitement. "So I'm registered and everything. I can hardly wait to get started. I always did like math in school."

Taking in Tara's enthusiasm, Caleb almost felt guilty for his doubts about her. Almost. He wasn't ready to let go of his skepticism, but he was glad for Heather's inquiry. At least he knew where the idea had come from, and he had the sneaking suspicion his parents were paying for Tara's classes.

"That's fantastic. I know you'll do a great job," Heather said, then glanced his way. "Caleb, can we recruit you for our PMC team?"

"You mean the Pan-Massachusetts Challenge?" Caleb wasn't sure he was up for the hundred-mile trek on a bike, even if it was for cancer research.

Heather nodded. "Yeah, that's the one. Hailey's been our Pedal Partner for the past two years."

"She's going to do one of the kids' rides this year. She is so excited about that." Tara grimaced. "I just have to make sure I get her a bike for Christmas."

A bike for Christmas. Caleb could see his parents chipping in on that deal. They had practically made Hailey an honorary grandchild. He gave himself a mental shake. What could be bad about giving a child a bike? He was letting old hurts make him a Scrooge. Hailey deserved whatever she wished for Christmas.

"She'll love that." Max grinned.

"The ride's not until next August," Caleb said.

"True, but we like to start getting our team together and training early, so we have plenty of time to do our fundraising." Heather looked over at Tara, then back at Caleb. "Tara's going to ride this year, too."

Caleb wondered if that was supposed to be an incentive for him to join the team. Was Heather thinking of Tara and him as a couple? He hoped not. He didn't need more matchmakers in his life. His mother was more than enough. "I don't know. I'll have to think about it. It all depends on how busy we are and if I have time to train."

"You'll have time if you get started now. I'm going to ride this year, too." Max reached over and took Heather's hand. "She didn't get to ride last year because of her broken leg, and I was getting chemo. But this year we're going to be there in full force."

As Caleb watched the other couple interact, their love for each other clearly visible, he wondered whether he could ever trust a woman enough to surrender his heart again. He didn't see a clear path to that happening anytime soon.

"So what do you say?" Max ran a hand through his dark-brown hair. "A year ago I was as bald as bald could be, but it all grew back. I'm feeling great and looking forward to new adventures."

Caleb looked over at Max. He appeared healthy, not a sign that he'd been through months of chemo and a bone marrow transplant. If Max could ride, Caleb knew that he should, too. He had no excuse. "Okay. You've convinced me."

When the group had finished eating, Tara glanced around the table, her gaze finally landing on him. "Do you all have time to take a quick tour of the grounds here at the inn?"

Heather nodded. "I'm off today, and Max is his own boss these days. So we're good."

Tara looked Caleb's way. "Okay with you?"

He didn't want to seem disagreeable, but he wondered about the time away from the office for her. Was this part of the plan his mother had in mind? He was probably reading all kinds of things into this meeting because his mind and heart were twisted into knots of guilt, distrust, and hurt. "Okay, but we can't linger."

"We won't." Tara stood and pushed in her chair. "Let's get started."

Caleb frowned. "Don't we have to pay the bill?"

"No. Molly said it was on the house." Heather popped up from her chair. "The Jansens are very generous people."

"Yes, they are." Tara smiled at Heather.

Wishing that smile had been for him, Caleb placed his napkin on the table, then stood. He didn't understand why one minute he was doing everything in his power to keep her at a distance and the next minute making a foolish wish like that. "Okay, Tara, you lead the way."

After the group gathered their belongings, Tara led them toward the other side of the dining room and stopped in front of a swinging door. "The kitchen's through this door, but we won't go in and disturb the work. Molly gives culinary instructions to some of the women who come here."

"She takes in a lot of women who are just getting out of

prison, right?" Heather asked.

Tara nodded. "She helps all kinds of women in need. She helps them learn a skill if they need it to get back on their feet and be productive in society."

Caleb wondered if the Jansens ever had problems with any of the women they helped, but he wasn't going to ask. Amy's betrayal colored all his thoughts about charitable work. He wished it wasn't so, but it rifled through his thoughts like a gunshot every time people stepped out to give help to the less fortunate. Silently, he followed the group into the foyer.

Tara stepped toward the stairway. "Most of the rooms are occupied, but Molly told me there's one we can look at."

As everyone climbed the stairs, Caleb took in the stained-glass window that looked out on the landing where the stairs turned at a right angle to the upper floor. As they walked down the hallway, a young woman pushed a cart out of a room.

When she saw Tara, she rushed forward. "Tara, it's so good to see you. Did you bring some visitors?"

"Yes, Jenna." Tara gave the other woman a hug, then introduced everyone.

Caleb contemplated the reunion between the two women. Tara seemed to have friends wherever she went. So had Amy. As the group took a few minutes to inspect one of the rooms, he tried to wipe the comparisons from his mind by concentrating on the attention to detail in the furnishings that represented a bygone era in elegant style.

"The rooms are all gorgeous." Tara motioned toward the front door. "Now I'll show you the rest of the facilities here."

Max held open the door. "Caleb, Tara told me that you've recently come back from Florida."

"Yeah. On some of these cold days, I miss the warmer weather."

"What brought you back?"

Caleb couldn't share his worries with this group, no matter how friendly they were. Part of his mission was protecting his parents' business, not sharing their problems. Any discussion about Amy and what she'd done to him and his parents was off limits. "My assignment there was finished."

"You weren't tempted to stay?" Max asked.

Caleb fell into step beside Max as they walked across the parking lot toward a blacktop drive that wound its way into a forested hillside. "Hawthorne is my home. It's a good place to be."

"Yeah, I miss my grandparents back in Montana." A sad little smile curved Tara's lips as she turned to look at Caleb.

His heart sank. He didn't understand the feeling. Why should he care if she wanted to go back? She wasn't like Amy, who had declared her undying love and promised to stay in Hawthorne, only to leave in the middle of the night, not only with his parents' money but with his heart as well.

Max eyed Caleb. "Do you mind if I ask about your business in Florida?"

"Not at all." Squinting against the sun, Caleb strode ahead, determined not to think about Tara or her leaving. "We had a client from Hawthorne, who owned a business. We did his books and taxes for years, even after he retired and spent most of his time in Florida. When he became incapacitated, his wife asked if someone could manage their affairs. My dad gave me the assignment. Their estate was quite extensive, so it took me nearly a year to get everything in order."

"So it wasn't all fun and games?" Max asked.

"Not really." Caleb shrugged. "It was hard to see a once robust man unable to handle his affairs, and it was a little daunting to have these folks depend on me to get things settled for them. Handling other people's money carries a big responsibility."

"You must feel good about the trust they put in you," Heather said.

Caleb nodded, unable to push away thoughts about how Amy had broken his trust. "My parents have built their business on trust. I definitely want to carry on that legacy."

"Did you have time to golf while you were down there?" Max asked.

"I did." Caleb wondered where this line of questioning was headed. "I have to admit that the beach and golf were easy to handle in my free time.

"Good." Max reached into the pocket of his jacket. He held out a brochure. "I hope you'll sign up for the charity golf tournament my grandfather is sponsoring this coming weekend at his club."

"Are you participating?" Caleb asked.

Max chuckled. "Even though I'm not much of a golfer, I am. I just hope for good weather."

"Yeah, I'm not much for golfing in the rain or the cold, especially after golfing in sunny Florida." Caleb could wish for a day like today for the golf outing, but in a week's time the weather could be rainy and cold again. But this event wasn't really about the golf. It was about the money that the sponsors would collect to help a worthy cause. "You can count me in. I'll see about teaming up with my dad."

"Perfect. I look forward to seeing you there." Max looped arms with Heather as they came to a stop at the end of the blacktop drive.

A parklike area with benches and children's playground equipment stretched out in front of Caleb. If he closed his eyes, he could hear the delightful laughter and squeals of children as they played here.

Kids. The only thing that made him want to get back in the dating game. He loved kids and wanted to have some one day. If he wanted to do things right, that required a wife. Every time he thought about dating again, the fear of rejection grabbed hold of his heart and wrung it out until it was dripping with pain. He glanced at Tara, and for a moment wished things could be different. He pushed that wish away and bolstered his resolve to stay away from a pretty blonde whose ambition would lead her back to Montana.

Tara motioned toward the two buildings on either side of the open space. "These two buildings house the women and children who come here for help. The main building is named after Bonnie Jansen, Kurt's first wife, who was tragically murdered. His former mother-in-law, Virginia Spencer, has funded much of this project."

Caleb wasn't quite sure what to say. He remembered the incident that had happened when he'd been in college. Kurt Jansen had been sent to prison, accused of manslaughter in his wife's death. Years later, he was exonerated and the real killer put behind bars. He hadn't realized that Molly's husband was that Kurt Jansen until now.

These folks sharing this day with Caleb had suffered the death of a spouse or had someone they loved suffer with cancer. They had put their lives together and moved ahead. Why couldn't he? His problems were small in comparison to theirs. In addition, despite the tragedies in their lives, they had all stepped out to help others in need. His attitude had a long way to grow.

As they made their way back to the inn, Tara came up beside Caleb. "I hope you got a better idea about the wonderful work they do here at this place."

Caleb gave her a wry smile. "I did. You're a one-man, I mean one-woman cheering squad for charitable works. No wonder my parents hired you."

"And you aren't in favor of their charity?" Tara eyed him with disapproval.

Her look created a sick feeling in the pit of his stomach, or maybe it was something he'd eaten. No, it wasn't the food. Her disrespect churned his insides. "Did I say that?"

"No, but sometimes I get that feeling."

Did he try to explain or just admit his failings? He feared explanations would only make things worse. "I think charitable work is commendable."

"Why do I sense an unsaid *but* in that statement?" She gave him another one of those looks that sent his insides on a roller-coaster ride.

"I don't know." Raising his eyebrows, he grinned.

"Okay. I'm jumping to conclusions."

"You said it. I didn't."

"Hey, you two. Are you going to let us in on your tête-à-tête?" Heather asked.

Without missing a stride, Caleb turned to look at her.

"We're just discussing charitable events. Seems to be a lot going on in that arena these days."

Heather nodded. "There's a lot of stuff happening in the next few weeks, whether it's charity related on not."

Max made a thumbs-up sign as they reached the parking lot. "Charity golf, kids' ornament making, apple picking, fall festival, my celebration. Do we think that will keep us busy and out of trouble?"

"Apple picking?" Narrowing his gaze, Caleb looked at Max. "A group from our church is going in a couple of weeks. When are you going?"

"Probably the same time." Max glanced at Heather for confirmation.

"I believe it is the same weekend. It's church Saturday or something like that at the orchard on the other side of Oakton. They donate ten percent of their revenue for the day to local charities. So even the apple picking is a charity event." Smiling, Heather surveyed the group as they approached the cars. "Hey, I've got a great idea. Let's go together."

The invitation swarmed through Caleb's thoughts like a thunderstorm with lightning and plenty of black clouds—clouds of foreboding. He could hardly reject the invitation without appearing antisocial, but accepting would mean one more outing with Tara. Maybe she would turn it down. He could only hope.

"That sounds like a great idea. Hailey will love it." Tara looked over at him. "Of course, Caleb may be too busy."

He looked into her bright-blue eyes and read the challenge there. She was giving him an out, but at the same time daring him to accept. He'd decided to try to be her friend. This was certainly the first test. "I can probably find time to do some apple picking."

"Fabulous." Heather opened the door to her vehicle. "I'll discuss it with Tara and let you know the final details."

Max grinned and extended his hand toward Caleb. "You see what I mean? Heather plans, and Tara takes the reins."

"I do see." Shaking Max's hand, Caleb grinned in return. "Good meeting you. And thanks for the golf invitation. See you on Saturday."

During the good-byes, Caleb pushed aside any worries about the impending activities. Determined to make the best of it, he got into the car. When Tara joined him and smiled, his heart skipped a beat. Confidence about the wisdom of his decision fled. As he started the car, he gave himself a mental pep talk. He wouldn't let Tara's presence determine his attitude. He'd promised himself that they could be friends, and that was going to happen. Friends. Nothing more.

CHAPTER SEVEN

The following Monday evening, Tara's cell phone rang as she helped Hailey with her homework. Tara picked it up from where it lay on the pock-marked wood of the oak kitchen table. Heather's name popped up, and Tara punched at the screen with her index finger. "Hi, Heather."

"Hey, Tara. I'm calling because I talked to our youth sponsors at church yesterday, and they're all excited about being part of your project to make Christmas decorations." Genuine excitement came across in Heather's voice. "We'll be there in full force on Wednesday. What time?"

"We'll meet at five thirty and have pizza before we start working."

"Great. We'll see you Wednesday. And I have something else I want to mention."

"What's that?" Worried tension crowded Tara's thoughts.

"Max, Caleb, and Kurt are all participating in the golf tournament next weekend, and even though it's Molly's busy season at the inn, I convinced her that she should put one of her residents in charge and take the night off so she can attend the dinner afterwards."

"And she agreed?" Tara couldn't keep the incredulity out of her voice.

"She did." Heather chuckled. "She had no answer to my persuasive argument."

"I believe I've run into your buzz saw of persuasiveness before, so I know she had no chance to say no." Tara laughed.

"I'm glad to hear that, because you're coming to dinner, too."

"But I don't have anyone to watch Hailey."

"Oh yes, you do. I've already talked to Sheila. She has volunteered."

"But I probably don't have anything to wear to a country club."

"That is no excuse." Heather's sigh sounded loud over the phone. "It isn't some formal occasion. Anything you wear to work will do."

Tara knew she was doomed to accept the invitation. She guessed that the two other women had conspired to make sure she and Caleb attended this dinner together. Tara closed her eyes and took a deep breath, trying to ward off the displeasure that welled up. Was there any getting away from the man when everyone around her was making them a couple? If she read Caleb correctly, he wasn't any happier with the situation than she was. So they could grin and bear it together. Did she dare mention the matchmaking to him? No, absolutely not. Better left unsaid.

"Okay, I guess I have no excuse."

"That's right. I'll pick you up and give you a ride to the dinner. Caleb will bring you home. I'll tell you what time on Wednesday. Sound good?"

Not really. "I'll see you Wednesday."

"Okay."

As Tara ended the call, a knock sounded on the door. Hailey jumped up from the table and scrambled to open it.

Tara raced after her child and grabbed hold of her arm just before she reached the door. Hunkering down, Tara looked into her daughter's questioning eyes. "You do not open the door. Ever. You can't tell who's on the other side."

"But, Mommy. It's probably Mr. Fitz to help me with my math homework."

"And why would he be doing that?"

Another knock sounded before Hailey could answer. "Mommy, answer the door."

Tara straightened, hoping her warning would soak in.

Even though they no longer lived in the city, she still tried to teach Hailey caution. The child acted like they still lived in the tiny Montana town where everyone in town knew each other and hardly anyone locked their doors, her great-grandparents included.

Tara looked through the small rectangular window at the top of the six-panel door.

Sure enough. Caleb stood on the other side. Hailey had never said why Caleb was coming over to help her with math homework. Tara was perfectly capable of doing that. Was her child matchmaking too?

Tara let the door swing open. "Hello. To what do we owe this visit?"

Stepping into the room, Caleb gave her a curious look. "Didn't Hailey tell you?"

"She mentioned something about her math homework, but I've been helping her with that." Tara closed the door as she looked from Caleb to Hailey and back.

Caleb shrugged. "Sunday morning she said you didn't like to help her with math, or some such thing."

"I think we should have a conversation with her." Tara turned to see her daughter scamper back into the kitchen.

With a sigh, Tara looked back at Caleb. That matchmaking conversation was going to happen whether she wanted it to or not. "This is a little embarrassing, but I believe my daughter is trying to do a little matchmaking."

Caleb burst out laughing. "Does this mean you're going to uninvite me?"

"No. It wasn't my invitation." Tara pressed her lips together as she tried to gain control of mixed emotions. She wasn't sure what to make of his laughter or her own feelings. Did he think the idea of them as a couple was humorous or the whole situation humorous? She pushed the question aside.

"You don't have to be embarrassed. Maybe this is something we need to talk about." He raised his eyebrows as he gazed at her. "What do you think?"

Think? How could she think when he was standing there gazing down at her with those mesmerizing gray eyes? "Okay, if you say so."

"You don't sound too sure."

"I'm not."

"Then I'll give you a few minutes to think about it while I help Hailey with her math, and you can do whatever else you have to do." He raised his eyebrows again. "Okay?"

"Sure." Tara started to go, then turned back. "I have laundry to fold."

"Good. We can talk after you finish and put Hailey to bed." Removing his jacket, Caleb didn't wait for her agreement but headed for the kitchen without a backward glance.

Tara picked up the basket of clothes sitting on the floor in front of the bedroom door. While she folded the clothes, she tried to figure out what she was going to say to Caleb. She practiced half a dozen scenarios in her mind. None of them seemed right. Maybe she'd let him take the lead.

As she put the last piece of clothing into the drawer, Hailey skipped into the room. "Mommy, I've finished all my homework."

Tara turned. Caleb stood leaning against the doorjamb. "I'll just wait in the living room while you two do your thing."

"Sure." Tara looked down at Hailey. "Say good night to Mr. Fitz."

"Ah, do I have to?" Hailey stuck out her lower lip.

"Yes."

"Can he read me a story first?"

"You ask him." Tara glanced up to gauge Caleb's reaction to the request.

"If your mom says okay, I will." Caleb pushed away from the doorjamb.

Tara hesitated. If she went along with Hailey's request, would it foster the child's tendency to attach herself to another father figure? Not that it would be all bad. Max had been a positive influence, and Hailey hadn't tried any matchmaking there. So why did she seem to be doing that with Caleb? "All right. One short book."

"Yippee!" Hailey pranced over to the bookcase and plucked a book from the shelf. All smiles, she hurried across the room and handed it to Caleb.

Smiling, Caleb took the book and went into the living room with Hailey. They sat on the couch while Tara remained in the bedroom doorway. She gritted her teeth at her daughter's defiance. The child had chosen a book that wasn't short at all, but she wasn't going to confront her daughter in front of Caleb, at least not at this moment. Hailey looked over her shoulder, as if waiting for a reprimand. Tara ignored her.

Fifteen minutes into the book, Tara approached the couch. "Storytime's over."

"But we're not finished—"

"Too bad." Looking down at Hailey, Tara held her hand out for the book. "If you'd chosen something shorter, you would've had time to finish."

Hailey didn't say another word as she got up and gave Tara the book.

As Hailey shuffled toward the bedroom, Tara tapped the top of Hailey's head. "Don't you have something to say to Caleb?"

Her eyes downcast, Hailey stopped in her tracks. "Thank you."

Caleb stood. "You're welcome. Maybe we can finish the book another time."

"Okay. Good night." Hailey's voice barely sounded above a whisper.

Tara looked over at Caleb. "I'm going to put her to bed, and you can leave if you want."

"I said we had some things to talk about, so I'm not going anywhere until we do."

"Okay. I'll be back in a few minutes." Tara scurried away, not looking forward to the conversation.

Ten minutes later Tara traipsed into the living room, where Caleb sat on the couch, reading the devotion book she had left on the end table, his ski jacket lying beside him. His dark curly hair shone in the lamp light, and for a second, she had the strange urge to run her fingers through it. She took a deep breath and shoved that completely inappropriate thought far away.

Sitting on the very edge of the royal-blue chair that sat at an angle to the sofa, she looked over at Caleb. "Sorry about Hailey's behavior. She's testing me. I hate to think what she'll be like when she's a teenager."

"You don't have to apologize. She's just a little girl."

"I know, but I have to stop letting her take advantage of me and others. While she was really sick, I catered to her every whim. That most likely was a big mistake. Now she thinks she can get away with whatever she wants."

"I don't blame you. It's hard to see kids suffer."

"Thanks for your vote of confidence." Tara wondered why he was being so agreeable. "So what do you want to talk about?"

He laid the book aside, then leaned forward. "The matchmaking thing."

"Yeah. What about it?"

Caleb just gazed at her and didn't say a thing, seemingly weighing his words. Then he shook his head and lowered his gaze. "I thought I knew what I was going to say, but now it all sounds so...so wrong."

Tara didn't know what to make of his uncertainty. He came across so confident, so sure of himself. He had always intimidated her. "What's wrong?"

One side of his mouth curved in a wry smile as he looked up at her. "Let me start over. We both see what's happening around us. My mother, your daughter, and a host of well-meaning friends and acquaintances seem to think we would make a good couple. So they're trying their best to push us together."

"I'll agree with that. There's no subtlety in their methods."

"Yeah, excellent observation." Caleb chuckled, then lowered his gaze again. He didn't say anything for a moment, going back into his uncertainty mode.

Tara stared at his lowered head, that curly hair beckoning her again. She closed her eyes and took a deep breath. She had to get this conversation over in a hurry before she did something outrageously stupid. "So what do you plan to do about it?"

Caleb jerked his head up. "Nothing."

"And what do you mean by that?"

"Nothing. Just nothing."

"You mean ignore them? Pretend that it's not happening?" Tara held her breath. Could they really do that?

His gray eyes studied her, and her heart raced. "Probably not possible."

"Then please explain what you intend to do."

Caleb rubbed the back of his neck as he stared at her. "I just want you to know that my objection to these matchmakers is nothing personal. You're a talented and attractive woman, but I'm coming off a relationship that ended badly, and I'm not interested in a new one."

"I understand." Inexplicable disappointment inundated Tara. She didn't want a relationship any more than he did, so why did she have this letdown feeling? "So we just go along with it, knowing that neither of us is interested in a relationship? That's what you want to do?"

Standing, Caleb nodded as he picked up his jacket and shrugged into it. "Yeah, I think that's the best way to approach it."

"Sure. That works for me." Tara joined him as he walked toward the door. "Thanks for helping Hailey with her homework, even though I could've done it."

Caleb gave her a lopsided grin. "She's a cutie, and I don't mind at all."

"Well, I don't want that cutie to make a nuisance of herself."

"She won't." Caleb put a hand on the doorknob. "I suppose you know about the golf dinner."

Tara nodded. "Heather called right before you came over. So I guess that'll be the first big test of our plan."

"Unless you count Wednesday night with the decoration project."

"That won't be quite the same." Tara smiled. "We'll be surrounded by dozens of kids."

"True." Caleb returned her smile. "I'd better get out of here."

"Thanks again."

Nodding, Caleb opened the door and stepped onto the porch. "We'll make the best of this. Good night."

"Good night." Tara closed the door and leaned against it. How could she have a good night when her thoughts and probably her dreams would be filled with Caleb? She wasn't any more eager to have a relationship than Caleb was, but she couldn't deny the attraction that had her second-guessing that thought. She couldn't waver. When Hailey's doctor gave the okay, they would head back to Montana. There was no point in even considering a relationship.

***

The sun hovered just above the tree line as Caleb drove down a side street to the church. He eagerly anticipated the plans for the Wednesday night youth group project. He didn't want to believe his eagerness involved spending more time with Tara, but he couldn't get rid of the thought. He saw her at work every day, but he was in his office, and she was out front answering the phone and doing clerical work. They didn't interact much.

When he reached the parking lot, he glanced at his mother, who occupied the passenger seat in his SUV. "Looks like we're the first ones here."

His mother grinned. "That's the way I planned it. We'll unload the supplies and get everything set up so we can go right to work after the kids have pizza. Delivery time is all set."

"You've got everything planned down to the last detail." Caleb brought his vehicle to a stop near the entrance to the fellowship hall of the white clapboard church with the steeple that rose to the blue October sky. The color reminded him of Tara's eyes. Wow! He was in trouble when even the sky reminded him of her.

"Well, Tara did a lot of the work." Sheila eyed Caleb as she reached for the door handle. "Speaking of Tara—"

"Let's not." Caleb got out of the SUV and went around to the back. He was having enough trouble not thinking about her without his mother adding to the problem.

"Why not?" Sheila joined him as the hatchback rose into the air, revealing the cargo area full of their supplies. "She's a lovely young woman, and I think you two would make a wonderful pair."

Caleb tamped down his exasperation. "Yeah, I figured that out, and so has she. Neither of us is interested in a relationship."

Sheila frowned as she lifted a box from the cargo area.

"And you've discussed this?"

"As a matter of fact, we have." Caleb grabbed a box and hurried ahead to open the door for her.

"When did you do this?" Sheila hurried through the door and put her box on a long table that sat against the wall just inside the door.

"The night I helped Hailey with her homework." Caleb set his box down and eyed his mother. "I believe you and that little girl conspired to make that happen."

"So what if we did?" Sheila found the light switches and flipped them.

The fluorescent lights came to life and brightened the room filled with long tables surrounded by chairs. Caleb wished the lights could brighten his outlook. After his talk with Tara, he'd had second thoughts about their plan, not because he wanted to date her. He'd thought about cute little Hailey and what she might think about the whole thing. If she was conspiring to bring her mother and him together, she was probably thinking about having a father. He didn't want to disappoint her. How could he talk to Tara, or even his mother, about that?

"It's not a good idea."

"I think it is." Sheila headed back to the SUV.

Caleb hurried after her. "You're wrong."

As Sheila picked up another box, she gave him a no-nonsense look. "Caleb, it's been over a year since the incident with Amy. You should be over her by now. Nothing heals a broken heart like a new love."

Caleb took a deep breath and blew it out in a rush as he carried another box inside. Why did his mother have to interfere in his life? "So what makes you think Tara's any better than Amy? You don't know much about Tara."

"I know enough. She's nothing like Amy." Sheila strode back to the SUV.

"But you bought Amy's story hook, line, and sinker, just like me. So how can you be so sure?" Caleb grabbed another box and marched back inside, not waiting for his mother's response.

Sheila hurried to catch up to him. "Not really."

Caleb raised his eyebrows as he stared at his mother. "You mean you suspected she wasn't what she said she was?"

Sheila nodded. "Your father and I both suspected she wasn't being completely honest with us."

"Then why didn't you say something to me?"

Sheila sighed as they worked together to bring in the last of the supplies. "Sometimes I wish we had, but we didn't because we thought you wouldn't believe us, and that would only drive you closer to her."

"So you let me fall for her without a word of caution?" Caleb didn't know whether to be angrier with Amy or with his parents.

"Would you have listened? Would it have made any difference?" Sheila started to arrange the items so they could be used in an assembly-line fashion.

Working alongside his mother, Caleb shrugged and let the question stew in his mind. He couldn't say for sure. All his feelings were in hindsight now. He could see things so much more clearly. He should have seen the warning signs, but he'd been so blinded by love that he hadn't seen the truth about Amy until it was too late. "I don't know, but I'm not jumping into another relationship. So please leave it alone."

"I'm not asking you to jump into anything. Just open up

your heart again, and see what happens."

"So I can have my heart stomped on again? No thanks." Caleb glared at his mother. "Why didn't you find her and press charges?"

"We didn't want the bad publicity." Not meeting Caleb's gaze, Sheila put together the workstations. "It would've done no good to pursue her."

"I still don't understand why you let things go on with Amy when you suspected her duplicity. Did you ever think that letting her go free will allow her to do the same thing to someone else?"

Looking up, Sheila shook her head. "We hoped and we prayed that the love of God would change her heart. We still do. We wanted to give her a chance to come clean and ask for forgiveness, but instead she ran."

"Yeah, and now she's probably out there doing bad things to who knows who." Caleb narrowed his gaze. "I hope you don't eventually regret your decision."

"I'm going to leave that in God's hands." Sheila stepped back and looked over the tables. "Looks like we're ready."

"Seems so." Did his mother's statement signal the end of this conversation? He should leave it at that and take a lesson from her to leave it all in God's hands. He had a hard time doing that. "I'm going to move my car."

As Caleb turned, he caught sight of a banner hanging on the nearby wall. The Scripture from the third chapter of Proverbs inscribed there jumped out at him. "Trust in the Lord with all your heart, and do not rely on your own insight. In all your ways acknowledge him, and he will make straight your paths," he read aloud. Had he forgotten to rely on God instead of himself? The answer was obvious. Could he do things differently now?

He hurried out with those thoughts churning in his mind like the fallen leaves that swirled in the breeze. Right now he didn't want to think about the things he'd done wrong or the things he might do in the future. He was going to concentrate on tonight and the project at hand. As he parked in one of the marked spots, he welcomed the sight of Heather and Max. They arrived with several children, who scrambled out of the car and raced to the building. The group would serve as a buffer between him and his mother and Tara.

Caleb greeted Max and Heather as they walked inside together. "Are you ready for an interesting evening?"

"I hope I'm going to supervise, because I have no artistic talent." Max chuckled.

Heather patted him on the back. "You surely can use a pair of scissors."

Max put an arm around Heather's shoulders. "If that's all you ask me to do, then we'll be fine."

Caleb took in the way Max and Heather kidded with each other. They weren't just in love. They obviously enjoyed each other's company. Caleb didn't want to think about love, but it stared him in the face. Even without his mother's prompting, he was thinking about Tara.

While Caleb and Max set up additional tables, more children and youth sponsors arrived. In minutes, joyful chaos ensued. When Tara arrived with Hailey, his heart did a little jig. Nothing had prepared him for that reaction, and he wished it away. It had to be his mother's influence. She'd put romantic thoughts about Tara front and center in his mind. He wouldn't succumb to his mother's suggestions. Nothing good could come from letting down his guard where Tara was concerned.

"Hey, there's Tara." Heather motioned toward the doorway.

Caleb pretended he hadn't noticed. "Looks like Ms. Hailey is excited about this activity."

Heather nodded. "It's been my observation that she gets excited about almost everything now that she's finished with the grueling chemotherapy regimen."

"I can relate to that." Max ushered Heather toward Tara and Hailey and gave the little girl a fist bump. "Hi there, Ms. Hailey. How are things going?"

"Good." Hailey's gaze drifted toward Caleb. "Hi, Mr. Fitz. Are you going to help, too?"

"I am." Caleb couldn't explain why Hailey's question brightened his day. He couldn't deny that a tender spot for Hailey had sprouted in his heart. She made him smile even when he didn't want to. She appeared to affect all the adults around her in the same way. Max, Heather, and his mother were all under the child's charm.

"Yay! I want you to help me make my decorations."

"I think we can arrange that." Caleb didn't dare look at Tara for fear that all kinds of feelings would engulf him, especially after their talk the other night. He didn't know how to say no to this sweet little girl. She had him wound around her little finger.

Just at that moment the pizza arrived, and Caleb went to pay for it while Hailey tagged along. Several of the teenagers grabbed the pizza boxes and put them on the counter between the kitchen and the fellowship hall.

As Caleb stuffed his wallet back into his pocket, Hailey grabbed his hand and pulled him over to one of the tables. "I want you to sit here beside me while we eat."

A powerful protective feeling overwhelmed him as he held her tiny hand. Was this what it was like to be a father? To know that a child depended on you to take care of her? He'd never felt this close to a child, not even his niece and nephew. "Okay. You sit down, and I'll get our pizza."

"Yippee!" Hailey scrambled onto a nearby chair.

As Caleb got in line for the pizza, Tara came up behind him. "Don't let Hailey become a pest."

Caleb turned to look at Tara. "She's not a pest."

Heather chuckled as she stood next to Tara. "You know Max is going to be jealous that you've replaced him in Hailey's world."

Heather was kidding around, but he wondered whether they suspected, as he did, that the little girl was looking for a father figure, and he happened to be the flavor of the month. Grinning, he looked over at Max, who had joined the group. "Sorry, man, but you know how flighty females can be."

Max laughed. "Don't go breaking her heart."

"She's more likely to break mine." Although Caleb went along with the joking, he feared that it was all a little too close to the truth, not just because of Hailey, but Tara, too. Being drawn into Hailey's life meant having a part in Tara's also.

He didn't want to risk falling for her, but he couldn't get his mother's advice out of his mind. Would a new love take away the hurt or cause more? He had to decide if he was willing to find out.

CHAPTER EIGHT

Hailey tugged on Tara's arm. "Mommy, hurry. We'll miss the hayride."

"We won't miss it." Tara smiled. This was going to be a great day with sunshine and laughter and good friends, even if Caleb was nearby. He might not like her, but he liked Hailey.

"Miss Hailey, I'll make sure you don't miss the hayride. They have more than one wagon to take people out to the orchards to pick the apples." Caleb patted Hailey's head. "You'll get your turn."

The exchange between Hailey and Caleb made Tara's heart lighter. She couldn't deny his positive influence on her little girl. Tara promised herself that she would only think of the good things today, like the cloudless blue sky overhead and the fresh air swirling around them, warm enough that a light jacket would suffice. Caleb's friendship was one of the good things, too. She just had to remember to not let it drift into something more.

A flurry of activities had pushed Tara and Caleb together the last two weeks. The two meetings to make decorations resulted in hundreds of items ready to sell at the fall festival and Max's celebration. Thankfully, Hailey's presence during their work project had served as a buffer, making their time together somewhat less stressful.

The golf tournament dinner, on the other hand, entailed

wrestling with her emotions as well as the speculation of her well-meaning friends. At least she and Caleb were on the same wavelength when it came to the matchmaking that surrounded them. Yet Tara couldn't help wondering about the relationship that had caused him so much hurt, but she didn't dare ask for details.

Somehow, Tara had managed to survive his constant scrutiny. She wished she knew what made him view her with a jaundiced eye. She kept telling herself to ignore him, but her discomfort never dissipated. He'd never mentioned their discussion again, even though Hailey constantly bugged him to do things with her.

Caleb's kindness toward Hailey made it that much harder not to have feelings for the man. Dangerous feelings that could lead to heartache. But it was nice to have a responsible man around, one who took a real interest in Hailey instead of using her to get to her mother. After Blake had died, she'd run into several men like that. Not Caleb. Having him in Hailey's life was a good thing. Tara had to remember that while she kept her own feelings in check.

While they waited for the next wagon, Molly, Kurt, Emily, and Eric arrived. The kids greeted each other with excitement while Kurt shook hands with Caleb, and Tara and Molly welcomed each other with a hug.

Tara leaned over to Hailey. "Aren't you glad you had to wait? Now you get to go with Emily and Eric."

Nodding, Hailey dug the toe of her right sneaker into the loose dirt. Tara wondered about her daughter's sudden change in demeanor. Hailey's earlier enthusiasm had disappeared. While Tara speculated about Hailey, Max and Heather arrived along with several families from their church. As everyone made a new round of greetings, Hailey withdrew further.

Tara put an arm around Hailey's shoulders and drew her close. Was she not feeling well? As an empty flatbed filled with bales of hay pulled to a stop near them, Tara hunkered down to eye level with Hailey. "Are you not feeling well?"

Hailey shrugged, a tight-lipped expression on her face. "I'm okay."

"You don't seem okay. Is something wrong?"

Sidling up to Tara, Hailey laid her head on Tara's shoulder. "I feel bad because I don't have a daddy."

Tara pulled Hailey close and hugged her. Pain tore at Tara's heart. Of all the times for Hailey to have such thoughts, why now? Tara held her daughter at arm's length and looked into her sad eyes. "Tell me why you're worrying about that?"

"'Cause Emily and Eric have a daddy and mommy, and I don't." Hailey's little brow wrinkled. "Can you get married so I can have a daddy, too?"

Tara took a deep breath. This was not the time for a discussion like this. Did she dare put it off until later? She glanced up. Folks were getting on the flatbed, and Caleb, Kurt, and Max were talking nearby. Tara looked back at Hailey. "Sweetie, let's talk about this when we get back home, okay?"

Hailey stuck out her lower lip, but she nodded her agreement.

Tara stood, grabbing Hailey's hand. "Good. Let's find a seat. Do you want to sit with Emily and Eric?"

"Okay." Hailey stepped forward.

At that moment, Caleb appeared and lifted Hailey onto the flatbed, and she giggled. "Ready for your ride to the orchard?"

Hailey giggled again, and Tara knew without a doubt that her child had a daddy all picked out. Tara wondered whether she should clue Caleb in. They had come to an agreement on the matchmaking business, but this was a whole different kind of problem. At one point, Tara had worried about the way Hailey had adopted Max, but their friendship centered on their shared cancer experience. Tara had quit thinking about Hailey's yearning for a father figure until she had practically adopted Caleb.

As Tara climbed the steps, Hailey bounced on the bale of hay where she sat. "Mommy, come sit here, and Mr. Fitz can sit next to you."

"I thought you were going to sit with Emily and Eric." Tara gave Hailey a speculative glance.

"I changed my mind." Hailey grinned up at her as if she was hiding a big secret.

Caleb grinned at Tara as he joined her on the hay bale. He leaned closer and lowered his voice. "Our little matchmaker is working overtime today."

Silently, Tara nodded. He had no idea how much. Hailey's wish was something Tara would keep to herself. She hoped that it didn't wind up on the child's Christmas list. A bicycle would have to do, and a long-shot chance that they could go to Montana for Christmas.

Hailey's matchmaking held no subtleties. Mission accomplished, she changed her mind again and moved to the hay bale where Emily and Eric sat. Hailey smiled back at her mom. Tara didn't want to look in Caleb's direction, even though he was the one who had brought up the child's efforts to push the two adults together. Tara wanted to think about something else. Anything else. Even the lack of funds for a trip to Montana to visit her grandparents.

The ticket fund was slowly accumulating, but it wasn't growing very fast. She feared that the little she saved each week would never amount to enough. Every time she checked airfares, the prices were out of reach, and she was tempted to charge the tickets. But she could never do what Blake did—live beyond her means. Seeing her grandparents would probably have to wait until they could return to Montana to live.

"You seem lost in thought."

Caleb's statement made Tara jump. She'd certainly been lost in her own worry. "I was thinking about Montana and missing my grandparents. It's been nearly three years since I've seen them."

"Do you ever video chat with them?"

Tara shook her head. "They don't know how to do that."

"You should get a friend back in Montana to show them how. Then you could at least see them while you talk."

Tara turned to Caleb with a smile. "That's a good idea. I don't know why I haven't thought of it before. Hailey would love that, and so would my grandparents."

"Glad to help." Crossing his arms over his midsection, Caleb leaned back against the side of the hay wagon.

With the smell of hay and the great outdoors permeating the air, Tara relaxed and wondered whether he was warming up to her. If so, that could have its pluses and minuses. Plus—she would have someone to rely on. Minus—she might start liking him too much for her own good. And what about Hailey?

As the tractor started, the sputtering sound shook Tara from her thoughts. The wagon jerked forward, and the passengers clapped and cheered. Hailey's laugh mingled with the sounds, and peace settled over Tara's heart. Today she would enjoy this time with her daughter, who was happy and on the road to recovery. Savoring the good topped the list of important things. Other decisions could wait.

***

The wagon bumped and swayed along the dirt road that led to the orchard. Caleb resisted the urge to put his arm around Tara's shoulders as they rode together on the bale of hay. Her blond hair blew in the breeze generated by the movement of the tractor. She pushed it back from her face and gazed over at him. His heart thudded in rhythm with the noise coming from the tractor's engine.

Thankful for the sound that covered the beating of his heart, he glanced over at Hailey. The little girl's laughter touched him deep inside. Did he dare let down his guard and let this child and her mother get close? He couldn't help remembering how he'd been drawn into Amy's life and come to care greatly for her father. They had spent hours playing chess in the evenings or watching some sporting event together on TV. Then everything had come crashing down around Caleb when Amy and her father left town without a word.

"Now it's my turn. You seem lost in thought."

Caleb chuckled. "Yeah, but I'm not going to share my thoughts."

Tara frowned. "Is that fair?"

"Nobody ever said life was fair. At least that's what my parents told me time and time again while I was growing up."

"That's for sure." Tara sighed. "I've learned that all too well."

Caleb could only nod because he didn't have an adequate response. He had no good reason to feel sorry for himself. His life was easy peasy, as Hailey would say. If he didn't count the episode with Amy, he had a life a lot of people dreamed of. A great family, a good job, and a comfortable place to live. He hadn't been counting his blessings. Tara's entrance into his life had made that quite clear.

"So what do you plan to do with the apples you pick today?" Tara asked as the orchard came into view.

"Probably give them to my mom. I'm not much of a cook." Caleb raised his eyebrows as he looked at Tara. "And what are you going to do with yours?"

"I'm going to bake an apple pie for sure." Tara motioned to where Kurt and Molly sat. "I plan to make some things from the recipes Molly gave me while I worked at the inn."

"And there will be apples for lunches, crisps, caramel apples, apple dumplings, applesauce—"

"Whoa! You said you're not a cook. Who's going to make all that stuff?"

"You mean you're not going to make it and share it with your lonely neighbor?"

Tara laughed. "I would hardly call you lonely, and no, I'm not going to make all those things. Apples for lunches maybe."

"And here I thought you were the neighborly sort."

A smile hid behind the frown Tara tried to produce. "Now you know that I'm really hardhearted."

Caleb couldn't remember the last time he'd had so much fun flirting. Was he falling into Hailey's trap? If he was, today he didn't mind. He hoped he wouldn't be sorry tomorrow.

Could've fooled me. The words almost came out of his mouth, but he gritted his teeth. Would she fool him like Amy? He wished he could wipe the bad memories away, but they were wedged in his mind like the hay sticking to his jeans.

The tractor halted, saving Caleb from having to make a response. While folks scrambled off the wagon, he stopped to help Hailey. "Are you ready to pick those apples?"

The little girl frowned. "I'm too short."

"That's not a problem. I've got the muscles to lift you up." Grinning, Caleb flexed his right arm.

"See my muscle." Hailey held up an arm.

Caleb hunkered down and gently squeezed the little girl's bicep. "Yeah, you've got a pretty good muscle going there. You should be able to grab a lot of apples."

"Okay, you two muscle-bound people. Let's go pickin'." Tara looked over at Caleb as she held out her bag. "You have yours?"

"Right here." Caleb shook the bag out in front of him. "Ready to go. You want to lead the way?"

"Okay." Tara grabbed Hailey's hand as she skipped beside her mother.

Caleb quickened his stride to catch up. Apple trees, their leaves rustling in the breeze, stretched out ahead in neat rows like soldiers in review. As he walked up beside Hailey, she grabbed his hand and looked up at him with her bright-blue eyes, the color of the October sky. The trust in those eyes made a lump rise in his throat. How had he let this little girl steal his heart? And worse yet, he was beginning to think her matchmaking tactics were starting to work on him, despite all his fears about loving again.

For the next hour, Caleb helped Tara and Hailey fill their bag with a variety of apples for eating and cooking as he took delight in lifting Hailey high to reach the fruit. Her laughter went deep into his soul and made everything about today scary and exciting. He felt alive, like he hadn't felt in a long time.

With their bags filled to the top, Caleb trudged alongside Tara, while Hailey skipped ahead. "She's certainly full of energy today."

Sadness lingered inside Tara's smile as she nodded. "I just hope she hasn't worn herself out. Thanks for being so kind to her today. She really looks up to you."

"Guess that means I have to be on my best behavior." Caleb gave Tara a wry smile. "I wouldn't want to be a bad influence."

"I don't think you could be that."

"It's a good thing you didn't know me in my younger days. I was not the best example around."

"You can say that about a lot of people." Tara let her gaze drop. "A lot of people make mistakes when they're young."

Caleb couldn't help wondering if Tara was talking about herself. No. He didn't suspect that even a young Tara had done anything she regretted. He couldn't imagine what the neat, organized, and efficient Tara Madsen had ever done wrong.

As they continued their walk toward the red barn that served as a country store and restaurant, Alicia strode toward them.

"Caleb, I thought you said you wouldn't be able to participate in the apple picking."

Caleb shrugged, holding his bag of apples in one hand. "Things worked out after all."

"Great." Completely ignoring Tara and Hailey, Alicia slipped an arm through Caleb's. "Have you been in the store? They have some amazing stuff in there."

Alicia's brazenness completely shocked Caleb, so much so that he didn't say a thing as she steered him toward the barn. How could he extract himself from this female leech? Maybe Alicia's presence would cool his romantic thoughts about Tara, but he didn't want Alicia to think he had any interest in her either. Could he discourage her without hurting her feelings? What a mess!

"Mr. Fitz, wait for us." Hailey's high-pitched voice sound from behind Caleb.

He stopped and turned, using Hailey as an excuse to move away from Alicia. "Sure. We can all go to the barn together."

"Yippee." Hailey raced to Caleb's side and grabbed one of his hands, then turned to look at Tara. "Mommy, hurry."

Tara trudged along with a knowing expression on her face. "I can't hurry. I'm lugging this big bag of apples."

Caleb stepped toward her. "Would you like me to carry your bag, too?"

"No, I'll be fine. I just can't run with it."

Wondering what Alicia was thinking, Caleb turned back to her. "You remember Tara?"

Alicia nodded, her mouth pinched in a tight smile.

"And this is Hailey, Tara's daughter." Caleb tapped the little girl's head as she gazed up at him. Those big soulful eyes always brought out the protector in him.

"So where's your daddy?" Alicia stared down at Hailey.

"In heaven." Hailey's answer put Alicia's question on ice.

"Oh, I'm so sorry." Stepping back, Alicia looked from Tara to Caleb and back at Hailey. "I didn't know."

Caleb wanted to tell Alicia that she should think before she asked stuff like that. He didn't want to dislike the young woman, but she was making it hard not to. Women. Thoughts of them made his head want to explode.

"That's okay. It was a natural question." Tara smiled at Alicia as she put her free arm around Hailey's shoulders. "We've been managing on our own for a while, and we're getting used to it. But it's nice to have friends like Caleb and his parents in our corner."

Alicia gave Tara a tentative smile. "I'm sure it is."

"Well, let's go see what the country store has to offer." Tara forged ahead as if she wanted to leave the prior conversation behind.

Hailey slipped her hand into his and looked up at him with a smile. Had this little matchmaker pulled a fast one on them all? At least she had saved him from Alicia. Things were truly sad when he was letting an eight-year-old manage his love life. But somehow, for today, he didn't mind as they wandered through the store.

Within seconds Hailey dropped Caleb's hand and ran toward a display with rag dolls on it. She picked one up and turned to Tara. "Mommy, can I have this?"

Tara sighed. "Sweetie, I'd love to buy that for you, but I just don't have the money. We had to spend my extra money on new clothes for you."

Hailey stuck out her lower lip and dropped her gaze. She didn't argue.

Tara put an arm around Hailey's shoulders. "I'm sorry. I wish I could."

"That's okay." Nodding, Hailey looked up at her mother. "I understand."

Caleb watched the exchange, knowing that this sweet child deserved to have that doll. Sometime before they left, he intended to buy it for her. He hoped that wouldn't get him in trouble with Tara, but he was willing to take the chance.

After they finished wandering through the store, Caleb glanced over at Tara. "Would you like to take your apples to the car? Then we can wander over to the pumpkin patch to snag a few pumpkins. My mother requested that I get her some for the front porch. She likes to paint them, and I'm pretty sure she'd like some help. What do you think, Hailey?"

"Mommy, can we get some?" Hailey tugged on Tara's arm. "I want to help paint them."

Tara held up her index finger. "One for you. That's all."

Hailey nodded as she skipped along beside Caleb. "Will you help me pick one out?"

"I think I can manage that. We can help each other find the best ones in the patch."

As they headed for the parking lot, Alicia bid them good-bye as she rejoined the group she had come with. Caleb breathed a sigh of relief. Hailey had not only saved him, but she had given Alicia an easy escape from the potentially embarrassing situation she had put herself in. Would today's encounter discourage her interest in him? He could hope so.

"Mr. Fitz, do you like that lady more than my mom?" Hailey looked up at him, a serious expression on her face.

"Hailey! That is not an appropriate question. Alicia is his friend, and we are his friends. He likes all of his friends. We don't compare." Tara's cheeks held a hint of red as she stared at her daughter.

Hailey hung her head. "Sorry."

"Let's just think about getting those pumpkins." Tara tried to smile as she set her bag of apples in the back of Caleb's car.

"That sounds like a good idea." Caleb closed the car door. "Which way to the pumpkin patch?"

Hailey pointed toward the big orange pumpkin sign with an arrow in the middle. "That way."

While Hailey skipped ahead, Tara hung back to walk beside him. "I'm so sorry that Hailey is so obviously trying to push us together. I don't know what I should do about it."

Caleb chuckled. "Don't worry. I think it's kind of cute."

"But I'm afraid it will get out of hand."

"As long as we both understand what she's up to, there's probably no harm." Caleb shrugged, knowing he was beginning not to mind at all. He wondered where that thought would lead him.

"I don't know about that." Tara hesitated as she took a deep breath and let it out in a long sigh. "She wants a dad like the other kids have."

Caleb didn't know what to say. Hailey would surely be disappointed if her wishes didn't come true. Why had that thought never occurred to him? He'd only been thinking about his own heartbreak instead of thinking about what was really behind the matchmaking plans of a little girl. "Yeah. That could be a problem. How would you like to handle this?"

"That's a question I don't know how to answer. What do you think?"

What did he think? His thinking was about as unclear as the jar of apple butter he'd bought for his mom along with that rag doll the clerk had surreptitiously put in the bag. If he gave Hailey the doll, would that make things worse? Part of him wanted to let go of his fear and get to know Tara better, but he didn't want to break anyone's heart, especially that of a child. Stepping away was the better thing to do. "I don't know how we can discourage her hopes when we'll be in each other's company a lot in the next couple of months with the fundraising project, not to mention Max's anniversary party. And we not only have to deal with Hailey, but my mother, too. They make quite a team."

Tara let out a laugh filled with resignation. "I've thought about getting Hailey to understand that you and I are just friends and that she needs to put any other thoughts aside." Tara sighed again. "Do you think an eight-year-old will understand?"

"You're asking me?" Caleb let out a halfhearted laugh. "I'm the wrong person to give you advice on kids."

As Caleb and Tara continued to follow Hailey, they fell silent. Despite Caleb's reluctance to seek a relationship with Tara, her obvious indifference toward him was a hit to his ego. Alicia's fascination with him should take care of that, but he didn't share her interest. This whole day was making him crazy. He needed something to occupy his mind besides a cute little girl and her pretty mother.

Pumpkins would do for a start. He hoped.

With Hailey following right behind, Caleb roamed the pumpkin patch. Every step reminded him that he had to be a good example to this child. The responsibility weighed on him, but he could do this. He just had to make sure he didn't encourage her to think that her mother and he would become a couple. Was that an impossible task?

Shaking the question away, he stopped to check out some medium-size pumpkins. He picked one up and turned to Hailey. "What do you think?"

She tilted her head as she examined the orange orb. "Looks okay to me."

"But does it look fantastic?"

Hailey giggled. "It will after we paint it with a face."

Caleb raised his eyebrows. "Is this the one you want?"

Hailey nodded. "It's perfect."

"Good. Now you can help me pick out the ones for my mom." Caleb put the pumpkin in the little wagon that Tara pulled. "I'll tell her that you helped."

During the next twenty minutes, the threesome examined dozens of pumpkins and came away with just the right ones. Caleb took charge of the wagon as they headed back toward the car. On the way they met up with Kurt, Molly, Emily, and Eric. Hailey immediately joined the kids, who traded stories about their day's adventures. They stopped for a late lunch at the country store, then the Jansens said their good-byes.

When Caleb and Tara were settled in his car with Hailey in her booster seat in the back, he turned to look at her. "Did you have a fun day?"

Hailey nodded. "It was the best day ever."

On the drive back to Hawthorne, Hailey's words kept running through Caleb's mind. *The best day ever.* His thoughts exactly. Even though he worried about his growing feelings for the two females in his car, he had enjoyed this day more than he had ever expected. Could he let down his guard and love a little or maybe a whole lot?

CHAPTER NINE

O n the drive home, Tara glanced back at her daughter. "Looks like we wore someone out."

Concern filled Caleb's eyes as he turned to her for a second before returning his gaze to the road ahead. "Did we overdo?"

Letting out a little laugh, Tara shook her head. "No. She still gets tired, but the activity was really good for her. Thanks for being so kind and understanding about all the matchmaking stuff. You don't know how much I appreciate it."

"I enjoyed it, and I have apples and pumpkins besides. And no concerns about you-know-what." Caleb gave her a sideways glance. "I got something for Hailey, and I hope you don't mind."

"What?"

"That doll she wanted."

Tara let out a little sigh as she thought about how Caleb's kindness made it so hard not to consider the wishes of the people who wanted to see them together as a couple. "I guess this one time will be all right, but please don't spoil my daughter."

"Okay, I'll keep that in mind, but she's hard not to spoil."

Tara laughed again. "That's because she's not your kid."

"That's what my brother says to me when I spoil my niece and nephew."

"I know where he's coming from."

As Caleb pulled into the lane that ended at his parents' house, Tara couldn't help thinking how this place seemed like home. Montana was so far away. The thoughts of returning had begun to take a backseat to her life here. But she still missed her grandparents. She was torn about so many things. Caleb. Her finances. Her dreams for the future.

"Well, we're here." Caleb pulled his car to a stop in front of his parents' house.

"Where are we?" Hailey rubbed her eyes as she looked around.

"We're home." Tara turned to look at her daughter. Home. That was definitely what this place had become. "You fell asleep."

"Did I miss anything?"

"Nothing but the long drive back." Caleb opened his door. "Do you want to gather all your loot?"

Hailey unbuckled her seat belt and scrambled out of the car. She raced around to where Caleb was unloading the things from the backseat. "I want my pumpkin."

"Wait just a minute, and let us help you." Tara got out of the car.

Before Tara managed to go around to the other side, Hailey grabbed her pumpkin and started racing toward the house.

"Hailey! You can't run with that." Tara tried to grab at her daughter's arm before she got away, but she was too late. "Stop right there. You're going to be in trouble when I get you."

Tara's words went unheeded as Hailey sprinted ahead. Tara watched in horror as Hailey tripped over something in the yard. The pumpkin went flying and smashed into pieces. Her child hit the ground with a thud. Screams filled the air.

With Caleb close behind, Tara raced to where Hailey lay in a crumpled mess. "Honey, are you all right?"

"No." Hailey's wail echoed through the barren trees in the yard. "My pumpkin's smashed."

Tara knelt beside Hailey. "Let's not worry about the pumpkin. Let me see if you're injured."

Hailey sat up, tears streaming down her cheeks. Tara felt her arms and legs. The little girl's pants were torn and muddy. "Mommy, will I get a new pumpkin?"

Tara sighed as she glanced around. It appeared as though Hailey had tripped over some bricks. She glanced up at Caleb, who looked on with concern. "What are these bricks for?"

"My mom plants flowers in there in the spring and summer. Looks like they got covered up with leaves." Caleb kicked away a mass of leaves and exposed a circle of bricks. "Guess she'd better put out something to warn people they are there or clear away the leaves so people can see them."

"It's too late for that now, but it would be a good idea." Tara took Hailey's hand. "Can you stand?"

Hailey shook her head. "My leg hurts."

Caleb hunkered down beside Hailey. "Let me carry her to the house."

"Okay." Tara looked over at Caleb. "I just hope she hasn't broken something."

Once inside, Caleb laid Hailey carefully on her bed.

"I'll wait in the other room in case you need me."

"Thanks." As Caleb left the room, Tara nodded and turned back to Hailey. "Let's take off those muddy pants and see what your leg looks like."

"Okay, but be careful, Mommy." Hailey scrunched up her little face while Tara peeled off the blue leggings.

Tara inspected her daughter's leg. "Well, it doesn't look horrible, but I'm pretty sure you're going to have a really nasty bruise. Let's get it cleaned up."

After Tara bandaged the wound and got Hailey dressed in a new set of clothes, they returned to the living area, where Caleb sat on the couch. He stood and met them near the kitchenette. He patted Hailey's head. "How you doing?"

"Okay, but now I don't have a pumpkin." Hailey pressed her lips together in a frown.

"And why is that?" Tara gave her daughter a no-nonsense look.

"'Cause I didn't do what you said."

Tara nodded. "That's exactly right. Did you learn a lesson today?"

"Yeah."

Tara pressed her lips together in order not to let a smile escape. Hailey's begrudging response and expression made it hard to be stern, but Tara hoped that Hailey had learned a lesson. "Good. Then we hope for no more repeat performances."

"But do I still get a pumpkin to paint?"

Tara held out her hands and shook her head. "I don't see how that can happen now."

"But, Mom."

"No buts. You disobeyed, and now you have to pay the

consequences." Tara took in Hailey's pout and tried not to get annoyed. Tara turned her attention to Caleb. "Thanks for your help. You don't have to stick around and listen to this mother-daughter dispute."

"Is that my signal to leave?"

Tara didn't want to seem inhospitable, but the long day was wearing on her nerves. Too much time with Caleb was more like it. "I'm sorry. I didn't mean to be rude."

"I understand. It's time to call it a day, but I do have something I'd like to discuss with you in private before I leave."

Caleb smiled, and Tara's heart bumped against her rib cage as she looked at Hailey. "You need to go to the bedroom."

When Hailey skulked off to bed without an argument, Tara breathed a sigh of relief, even though she was surprised after all the previous protests on her daughter's part. As soon as Hailey closed the door behind her, Tara turned to Caleb. "Now what did you want to talk about?"

Caleb grinned. "That went well."

Tara raised her eyebrows. "You mean her going to the bedroom without a fuss?"

"Yeah. I don't think I've ever seen her quite so, so…"

"Disobedient?"

Caleb shrugged. "Maybe disappointed. She really wanted that pumpkin. She could have one of the pumpkins I got for my mom."

"Are you determined to spoil my child?"

"No. I wouldn't want to get on your bad side."

Tara wondered whether that was really true. Was she supposed to read anything more into his statement? That could spell trouble because she was beginning to like him too much, an interest he certainly didn't share, even if he was kind to her today.

"That's nice to know, so no pumpkin for Hailey. What did you want to talk about besides that?"

"Remember I bought that doll for Hailey, but with all the other excitement, I never gave it to her. I'm figuring after what transpired since we got back that you'd rather I didn't give it to her today."

"Good thinking." Tara smiled up at him, wondering why this discussion was so disheartening. Had she been hoping for something else? Despite everything she knew about Caleb's thoughts on the subject, had she been expecting him to suggest they eat dinner together, or to ask her out? She shoved that ridiculous thought away. He was kind to her daughter, but a date was a far stretch of his attention. After all, hadn't they agreed to ignore the matchmakers? "I'll let you know when it's a good time to give her the doll. Thanks again for everything today. I appreciate how you treat Hailey, even if she's trying to push us together."

"It's not all that bad." He gave her a wry smile.

"I'm glad you think I'm not too much of a nuisance."

"You're going to make me admit that you're a great addition to the office."

"You don't have to admit anything." Tara wouldn't put too much stock in his statement.

"But I should, just to set the record straight. You're doing a good job."

"Thanks. I always try to do my best in whatever I do."

"I can see that." Caleb walked to the door. "Time to get going. I enjoyed today."

"Me, too." Tara stepped out onto the porch with Caleb

as the sun sat just above the tree line. "See you tomorrow at church."

"Sure thing." Caleb loped off toward his car.

Tara stood on the porch and watched until his car turned into the drive at his house. She leaned against the door and took a deep breath. What was she going to do about her growing feelings for this man, especially when he didn't share them?

***

"So how was school today?" Tara took Hailey's backpack as she got into the backseat of the car.

Hailey shrugged. "Okay, but I don't like Mondays."

"A lot of people don't like them." Tara hoped her child wasn't still dealing with teasing, but she was afraid to ask. Would Hailey volunteer the information if that behavior was still going on? Tara didn't know how to handle this type of situation. Would Sheila be able to give some advice?

Hailey nodded as Tara started the car. "We just did regular school stuff. It's mostly boring."

"Yeah, sometimes it is." Tara chuckled, remembering her own school experiences. "I've got a surprise for you. Mrs. Fitzpatrick has invited us over to help her paint pumpkins we got over the weekend. We'll go after dinner and after you've done your homework."

"Yippee!" Hailey clapped her hands. "I can hardly wait. I don't have much homework."

At least the child was excited about something. Tara always wondered whether the two years of sporadic school attendance would keep Hailey from fitting in with other kids. Changing schools just weeks after the beginning of the school year didn't help either, but it was something that couldn't have been avoided.

After Tara and Hailey finished drying the dinner dishes, they put on their coats and raced next door through the cold night air. October had brought not only a colorful landscape but sunny afternoons and cold nights. The stars twinkled overhead, and Tara remembered wishing on a star when she'd been a kid. Wishing on stars was a childish activity, and she was no longer a child. She had adult responsibilities and an adult faith in the God who had made the stars. She would rely on Him. She clung to that thought as she rang the doorbell.

Sheila answered immediately. "Come in. Come in and get out of the cold. I can't believe how cold it is already tonight."

"It's nice and warm in here." Tara shrugged out of her coat as she looked at the fire crackling in the fireplace. "I thought I had smelled a fire burning as we walked over."

Sheila nodded. "We can sit by the fire and paint our pumpkins. I was going to have us work in the kitchen, but the fire was so inviting that I put paper down on the coffee table so we can work in here."

"Is Mr. Fitz going to paint pumpkins with us?" Hailey asked.

"Not tonight. He had other plans." Sheila set three pumpkins, several jars of paint, and paint brushes on the table. "I think I have everything we need."

As Tara sat on the couch next to the coffee table, she wondered what Caleb's plans were. Was it business or a date? She didn't know why she cared, but she couldn't deny that she did. Their time together on the day of the apple picking had her wishing for things that she shouldn't wish for—a romantic relationship with her employer's son. Knowing his presence would add tension to the evening, she was relieved he wouldn't be here.

She had to admit the tension wasn't all bad. It was the kind that made her heart race and dream impossible dreams. She tried to blot those thoughts from her mind, but they kept coming back over and over again. And well-meaning friends did nothing to discourage her runaway notions.

While Sheila helped Hailey decorate a pumpkin, Tara painted one of her own. When she finished, she leaned back to look at it, then looked over at the one Hailey was working on. "I've got mine all done. What about you?"

"Almost." Hailey dipped her brush into a nearby paint jar. "Yours looks really good, Mommy."

Tara smiled. "Thanks. It'll be perfect for our front porch."

"You have a very artistic eye. I noticed that while you were doing the makeover at the office." Sheila smiled.

"Thanks." Tara thought about mentioning her desire to go to design school but decided against it. The Fitzpatricks were kind enough to help her learn accounting. Being a designer was a long-lost dream that she could probably never recapture. She didn't need to resurrect it. "I've always liked art."

"You are very talented. I could see that when we were making the Christmas decorations for our fundraising effort." Sheila put a finishing touch on her pumpkin. "There. Mine's done."

"How's the pumpkin decorating?" Tom walked into the room.

Hailey jumped up and escorted him to the table. "Great! See my pumpkin. I just finished it, and my mom and Mrs. Fitzpatrick have theirs done, too."

"They look fabulous." Tom nodded. "We finished our church committee meeting earlier than I thought."

"You got everything accomplished?" Sheila put the lids back on the paint jars.

"We did." Tom took a step toward the kitchen. "I'm going to make some tea to warm me up. Anyone want some?"

"Certainly." Sheila glanced over at Tara. "Would you like some, too?"

Tara nodded. "That sounds wonderful."

"And how about some hot chocolate for you, Hailey?" Sheila stood.

Hailey nodded. "I'd like some, please."

"Would you like to help me make it?" Sheila held out her hand.

Hailey jumped up from the couch. "Yeah."

"Do you need my help?" Tara asked.

Sheila waved a hand at Tara. "You can put the rest of the lids on the paint jars and wash the brushes out in the laundry room."

"I'm on it." Tara put the lids on as she watched Tom, Sheila, and Hailey disappear into the kitchen.

After Tara cleaned the brushes, she headed toward the kitchen. Before she got there, Sheila walked into the living room with a tray containing a teapot, tea cups, and a plate of cookies.

Sheila set the tray on the coffee table. "We're all set. Tom's taking care of Hailey. He adores your little girl. She's a real charmer."

Tara recognized this conversation as her opening to talk to Sheila about Hailey and her possible problems at school. "Yeah, she can be, but I worry about the teasing that she received at school when we first moved here."

Sheila shook her head. "I'm sorry. I didn't know about that."

"I guess we never mentioned it to you, but Caleb knew about it." Tara joined Sheila on the couch. "Hailey's always been better with adults than other children because she's an only child and has mostly associated with adults, especially because she missed so much school in first and second grade."

"I just can't imagine that sweet little girl getting teased." Sheila poured Tara a cup of tea and handed it to her. "Why were they teasing her?"

"Her hair. When it grew back after the chemo, it was really, really curly and so short." Tara couldn't help remembering how she hurt for her child. The pain still weighed her down like a stone in the pit of her stomach. "It's a little better now."

"Has she said the kids are still teasing her?"

Tara shook her head. "She hasn't mentioned it, but I still worry. I shouldn't, but I do. She just doesn't seem to like school all that well."

"I would give it some time to see what happens." Sheila took a sip of her tea, then set the cup on the table. "I know you're concerned, but she seems okay to me."

"Yeah, I'm probably worrying for nothing." Tara picked up her teacup and wrapped her hands around it. The tea and Sheila's advice warmed Tara's heart and took away some of her concern. "Thanks for understanding."

"You can talk with me anytime about anything." Sheila

smiled.

"I'm thankful she has some good male role models like your husband and son. She hardly remembers her father. Mostly she knows him from the photos I've shown her."

"Do you mind telling me what happened to your husband?"

"We married young. It was a whirlwind romance." Tara thought back to the early days of her marriage when she and Blake were happy, before they had started to argue about money. Even at that time she'd had no idea how much he'd been spending.

"How old was Hailey?"

"Not even two."

"I can see why Hailey doesn't really remember him." Sheila broke off a piece of cookie and dunked it in her tea. "I'm glad she relates to Tom and Caleb."

"Me, too, since Hailey doesn't remember Blake. He was a rodeo cowboy and specialized in calf roping, but he did all the perilous things that rodeo cowboys do." Tara pressed her lips together as she remembered the tragedy that took his life. She took a deep breath and managed a little smile. "Ironically, when Hailey was a baby, he decided to quit living that risky life on the rodeo circuit and took a job with a local ranch so he could be home more. A few months after he started that job, he was involved in a freak accident. The horse he was riding spooked and threw him. His head struck a rock, and the trauma killed him."

Sheila put down her teacup and looked at Tara. "I'm so sorry that you lost your husband at such a young age and in such a tragic way."

"Thanks. It was hard, and then just when I was getting my life together, Hailey was diagnosed with cancer."

For a few minutes, the two women remained silent. Tara thought of how God, despite all of her troubles, continued to place the people she needed in her life. Sheila and Tom were some of those people. Was Caleb? And how did he fit—friend or something more?

As Sheila finished her cup of tea, she acted as if she wanted to say something, but she appeared hesitant. She took a deep breath as she gazed at Tara. "I hope you don't think I'm speaking out of turn, but I couldn't help noticing how you and Caleb had such a good time together while you've been working on the fundraising project."

Tara wasn't sure how to respond to Sheila's statement. "Caleb has been a big help."

Again Sheila hesitated. "I don't want to be presumptuous, but I was kind of hoping there might be something more than friendship developing between you and my son."

Wow! Now Tara really didn't know what to say. There was no way she could give Sheila false hope on that front. "I have to be honest. I enjoy Caleb's company, but I'm not sure he enjoys mine."

Sheila leaned forward as she poured herself a half a cup of tea, then took a sip, as if she was taking time to formulate her response. Sheila took a deep breath as she continued to hold her cup. "I want to tell you a little bit about Caleb. I know he would hate my interference, but I'm going to do it anyway."

"Okay." Tara wasn't sure about this whole conversation, but she sat back and waited to hear what Sheila had to say.

"A little over a year ago, Caleb suffered a devastating betrayal. In fact, the whole family did." Sheila shook her head. "But Caleb most of all. The woman he loved broke his heart. She wasn't who she pretended to be, and cheated our family out of some money, then left without a warning. He's never quite gotten over it. I was hoping a new relationship would help him in that regard."

Tara had so much respect for Sheila, but this conversation made Tara uncomfortable. "Caleb and I figured out that you were trying to push us together. He told me about this relationship that ended badly. No details except that he wasn't interested in a new one."

Sheila shook her head again. "I'm sorry if my meddling has put you on the spot, but I think so much of you. I was just hoping that you and Caleb would find an interest in each other."

Tara shrugged. "Like I said. He made it quite clear that he's not looking for another relationship."

"I have a feeling you could change his mind, so if he ever gets around to that point in his life, I hope you'll give him a chance." Sheila placed a hand over her heart and patted her chest. "It would do this mother's heart good. Forgive me if I've intruded on your life."

Tara steepled her hands in front of her mouth. She wouldn't let Sheila's hopes change things. "I know Hailey shares your wishes about Caleb, but I don't want her to rely on false hope."

Sheila gave Tara a halfhearted smile. "So you're telling me that I shouldn't hope that you and Caleb might get together?"

"Pretty much." Grimacing, Tara shrugged. She didn't want to say anything more about the subject.

"Okay. I understand. I won't mention it again, but I'm going to be praying about it."

Tara just smiled. She didn't want to pray about it or have someone else praying about it. She didn't want to latch on to Sheila's hopes and be disappointed, but in reality Tara's heart wasn't getting the message.

CHAPTER TEN

The following Friday night, the lights of a car flashed through the window as Caleb walked toward his kitchen. He stopped and peered through the blinds. It looked like a police car. Was there a problem at his parents' house? He grabbed his coat from the hook by the back door and shoved his arms into the sleeves as he rushed out.

Three pole lights along the drive illuminated Caleb's way, and a squad car and a late-model sedan were parked in front of the house. Two officers got out of one, and a lone woman got out of the other. Frowning, Caleb jogged toward them. They headed for the end of the house where Tara lived. His heart jumped into his throat at the thought of her having some kind of trouble. He quickened his pace and reached the spot where the cars were parked just as one officer knocked on the door

"Is there some kind of trouble here?" Caleb called out to them.

The threesome turned at the sound of his voice. One officer turned back to the door while the other came down the steps toward him. "What are you doing here?"

Caleb motioned toward his house. "I live right over there, and this is my parents' house."

"This doesn't concern you."

Taken aback by the officer's response, Caleb debated about arguing. "If there's a problem with my parents, it does concern me."

"We're here to see Tara Madsen."

"Is she in some kind of trouble?"

The officer frowned. "Like I said, this doesn't concern you. Go on your way."

While Caleb stood there debating about what he should do, the door opened. Hailey stood silhouetted in the doorway.

Tara's voice echoed from inside. "Hailey, I told you not to open the door unless I'm there."

Caleb caught Hailey's gaze, but Tara intercepted her daughter before she slipped outside. Tara stepped onto the porch and closed the door behind her, leaving Hailey inside.

With a sudden feeling of foreboding, Caleb retreated to the darkness on his parents' front porch. Maybe he could figure out, undetected, what was happening. He strained to listen to the conversation, but he couldn't hear what any of them were saying. Were the police planning to arrest her or only question her?

The old doubts crowded his thoughts. Had she done something nefarious, like Amy? After all, Tara had spent a good deal of time with the ex-cons who worked at the Hawthorne Inn, and she was still very close to some of those women. He tried to push the negative thoughts from his mind. He had no reason to believe Tara had done anything wrong. Coatless, Tara stood on the porch with her arms crossed over her midsection. From a distance he couldn't read her expression, even though the porch lights illuminated her features as she spoke to the officers. He didn't dare get any closer, and only muffled voices reached him. He tried harder to make out what they were saying, without any success. He debated with himself about stepping forward again but decided against it for everyone's good.

Then Tara's voice sounded loud through the night air. "You can't come into my house unless you have a warrant."

He swallowed hard. Did this mean what he had suspected? She was into some kind of criminal activity? But why would the police come to her door without a warrant? And what was that woman doing with them? A sick feeling hit Caleb in the gut.

While Caleb stood rooted to that spot on the porch, Tara's determined expression didn't change as she stared down the cops confronting her. The woman handed Tara a piece of paper, and she looked down at it and said something that Caleb couldn't make out. Then to Caleb's surprise, the police officers and the woman withdrew to their cars. His heart racing, Caleb backed farther into the shadows along the side of the house as the vehicles drove back down the lane to the main road.

As the red taillights disappeared, Tara reached for the knob behind her. The door swung open, and Hailey bounded into Tara's arms. The two clung to each other. Then Tara stood, and the two of them slipped back inside. The porch light went off. Caleb stared into the night. Was this any of his business? Surely it was since she was living in a portion of his parents' home. He would find out what was going on to protect them from any association with criminal activity.

He sprinted off the porch. Before he reached Tara's

door, the light came on again. He stopped as she stepped out the door and looked around. He waited silently as she grabbed Hailey's hand and raced toward the place where he stood.

When she got near, Caleb stepped out of the shadows. "Tara, what's going on?"

She let out a little yelp as she halted and placed a hand over her heart. "Caleb, you scared me. What are you doing out here?"

"I saw the police car and came to see what was going on."

"I need to talk to your folks." The catch in her voice told him she was close to tears, but she seemed to be putting on a brave face for Hailey.

She appeared to be upset and seemingly not interested in sharing this problem with him. "Their light's on, so they should be home."

Tara didn't say another thing. Without waiting for him, she hurried onto the porch and knocked on the door. When his mother opened the door, Caleb didn't miss the surprise on her face. "Tara, is something wrong?"

Tara nodded her head. "May I come in?"

"Certainly. Tell me what's troubling you." Sheila opened the door wider.

As Tara ushered Hailey inside, Caleb noticed the crumpled paper in her hand. Clinging to her mother, Hailey glanced back at him as if she was waiting for him to help in some way. He still didn't know what to say or do, but he was pretty sure his parents would.

Caleb followed Tara and Hailey into the house.

"Oh, Caleb." His mother stared at him. "You're here, too. Do you know what's going on?"

"I saw a police car drive toward your house and came to investigate. That's all I know." Caleb shrugged and waited to see what kind of explanation Tara had.

"Police car?" Sheila turned back to Tara. "Come into the kitchen and tell me what happened."

"Okay." Tara's voice cracked as she blinked back tears.

Before they reached the kitchen, Tara broke into sobs as she brought her hand up and covered her mouth. She closed her eyes, and more tears streamed down her cheeks. She wiped them away with the back of her hand.

"Mommy, did those people make you cry?"

Tara nodded. "They did, but you make me smile."

Hailey's question tore at Caleb's heart. Still not knowing what to do, he stood there.

"Tara, please tell us what's wrong." His mother hurried to Tara's side and patted her on the back.

Tara let out a heavy sigh and shoved the crumpled paper at Sheila. "The police and a social worker from the Department of Children and Families brought me this. They want to take Hailey away from me."

Sheila studied it, then looked up at Tara. "I don't understand this. Have you talked with Hailey about it?"

Tara shook her head. "As soon as the police and that social worker left, I brought Hailey over here."

"I'm glad you did." Sheila waved the paper in the air. "Why would they do this? It doesn't make sense. You're a fabulous mother."

Caleb looked at Tara as all his wrong-headed thoughts about her made him ashamed. How could he have had such unkind thoughts about the woman who, more often than not, captured his heart with her kind and loving nature? How could the authorities think she was a bad parent?

They needed answers.

Sheila turned her gaze to Caleb. "So you didn't know what was going on?"

"No. I'm as puzzled as you are." Caleb searched his mother's face, then glanced at Tara as he tried to bury his mistaken thoughts. "What exactly does that say?"

Tara took the paper back from Sheila and handed it to Caleb. "It's a summons for me to go to court about these allegations that I've abused Hailey."

He stared at the paper, the words blurring as he tried to focus on their meaning. How had he ever thought Tara was involved in something criminal? A sick feeling churned his stomach. Now she was being accused of something completely out of the realm of possibility. Who had made such a report? "We need to get you a lawyer."

"But I haven't done anything wrong." Tara stuck out her chin.

"That's reason enough to get one." Caleb handed the summons back to her.

Tara hung her head. "But I don't have the money to pay a lawyer."

Sheila put an arm around Tara's shoulders as they moved into the kitchen. "The court would appoint one for you, but we'll make sure you get a good lawyer, not one who's overburdened with cases and doesn't have time to make a good defense for you. Don't worry about that. Molly Jansen has a good friend who's a family-law lawyer. I'm sure we can work something out with him."

Tara's face brightened. "Yes, I remember Nick and his wife from when I worked at the inn."

"Good. Then I think we have a solution." Sheila smiled. "Now let's figure out how this report was made. Let's talk it over."

As they started to sit at the kitchen table, Tom entered the room. "I didn't know we had company, but I thought I'd heard voices."

Tara let out a harsh breath. "I'm not exactly company. I'm more of a burden than anything else."

Tom frowned. "Now why would you say a thing like that?"

"You'll soon find out." Tara pressed her lips together in a grim line as she showed him the summons.

Tom looked it over, then handed it back to her. "Wow! This is crazy."

Hailey tugged on Tara's arm. "Mommy, am I in trouble?"

Tara hunkered down next to her daughter as she sat in one of the chairs around the table. "Sweetheart, you are not in trouble. We just want to ask you a few questions. Can you help us figure something out?"

Hailey nodded, a solemn expression coloring her features. "I'll try."

"Thanks." Tara gave Hailey a hug, then stood.

Taking in the smell of freshly baked cookies for the first time, Caleb berated himself for his unkind thoughts. He had nothing to explain his judgmental attitude except his own problem getting over the past. Tara had done everything for her child, leaving family and coming to a strange town to find treatment for the little girl. How could someone accuse her of abuse? He hoped they could find out where the accusation had come from, but he doubted the actual accuser was ever brought to light in such cases.

When everyone was seated at the kitchen table, Sheila poured Hailey a glass of milk and gave her a chocolate chip cookie. "I'll just put this plate of cookies here on the table, and the adults can help themselves. I've got tea or coffee on the counter."

Tom and Sheila got coffee and cookies, but Caleb couldn't think about eating while his stomach roiled with self-criticism. Tara took a cookie but barely nibbled on it. He couldn't imagine her worry over this situation on top of all the other worries she had dealt with over the last few years.

Sheila leaned closer to Hailey. "Can you tell us what's been happening at school?"

Hailey shrugged with downcast eyes. "I don't know."

"You seem a little upset. Is there anything you'd like to tell me?" Sheila patted Hailey's arm.

Hailey looked up, a wary expression in her eyes. "Can I tell you a secret? Just you?"

"Would you like the others to leave?" Sheila glanced around the room, then back at Hailey. "The two of us can talk here in the kitchen."

Hailey nodded silently.

Caleb took in the exchange and wondered what Hailey's secret was. He glanced at Tara to see her reaction, but she had none. She stared straight ahead as if she were in shock. What was going through her mind? Despite her denials, was she guilty of something? He couldn't keep the negative questions at bay.

Without warning, Tara jumped up from the table and started for the door that led to the living room. "I'll be glad to go into the other room."

Caleb looked over at his dad, who nodded toward the door as he got up. They quietly followed Tara into the other room. She didn't say a word but paced back and forth in front of the window. Caleb wanted to comfort her somehow, but he didn't have the slightest idea what to do or what to say. That seemed to be the theme of the evening.

Caleb's dad went over and stood in front of Tara, placing his hands gently on her shoulders. "This will all work out. It seems bad right now, but you aren't guilty of anything."

Tara licked her lips. "But DCF can make my life miserable. They don't play fair. They take children away from parents without just cause."

"What makes you say that?" Tom knit his eyebrows.

"One of the women I worked with at the inn told me about how they took her kids away when she wasn't guilty of abusing them in any way." Tara sniffled as she swiped at her tears. "They want to take Hailey away. They just can't do that."

"And we won't let them." Tom squeezed Tara's shoulders, then hugged her. "You're like a daughter to us, and we will stand by you and fight this thing."

Tara looked in Caleb's direction. "Do you believe I'm innocent?"

"Yes. Absolutely." The words tumbled from Caleb's mouth as he took in her unstated doubts about his belief in her. Her reservations pricked his heart. Could he ever explain his struggle between the present and the past? Probably not without hurting her even more. But this whole episode made him realize that he did believe in her when it came to Hailey. Tara loved that little girl and would never do anything to harm her.

A tentative smile curved her mouth. "Thank you for believing in me."

Before Caleb could respond, Hailey bounded into the

room and threw her arms around her mother. "Mommy, Ms. Sheila says I need to tell you something."

Tara held Hailey at arm's length. "Let's sit down over here, and you can tell me whatever's on your mind."

"Do you want the rest of us to leave?" Caleb raised his eyebrows.

Tara shook her head as she led Hailey to the couch. "If you're going to help me, you should hear this, too."

Sheila sat in the nearby chair, and Tom sat on the arm. Too keyed up to sit, Caleb leaned up against the doorjamb between the living room and the kitchen. Hailey looked over at Sheila as she settled on the couch, her little legs sticking out. For a few seconds no one said a thing. The silence bore down on Caleb almost as if a large stone sat on his chest. He held his breath while he waited for the little girl to say something.

"Go ahead, Hailey. Tell your mom what you told me," Sheila said.

Hailey bit her lower lip and scrunched her face up as if she were in pain. She let out a heavy sigh. "Mommy, promise you won't be mad at me."

"Hailey, just tell me what's troubling you."

The little girl hung her head. "You know how I begged to wear my new outfit to school, and you didn't want me to?"

"Yeah." Tara's attention was focused on her daughter. "So what does that have to do with what's going on here?"

Hailey still didn't lift her head. "At recess today I tripped and fell on the playground and tore a big hole in the knee of my pants and the elbow of the shirt."

"And why did I not know about this?"

"Because I didn't tell you." Hailey twisted her hands in

her lap.

"I didn't see any ripped clothing when you came to the office after school today."

Hailey finally looked at her mother. "That's 'cause I changed at school and kept my coat on so you wouldn't notice the different clothes. My teacher has some spare clothes for accidents. I have to take them back."

"What did you do with the ruined clothes?"

"They're in my backpack." Hailey hung her head again.

Tara let out a harsh breath. "When were you going to tell me about this?"

"I don't know." Hailey shrugged, then looked at Sheila. "Would you tell my mom the rest?"

"If it's okay with her." Sheila motioned toward Tara.

Tara hesitated as if she was weighing the request. Caleb couldn't help admiring the way she had so calmly talked to her daughter. The situation had to be tearing her apart.

"If Ms. Sheila is willing to do it, she can finish for you, but I may need to ask you some questions, too." Tara glanced at Sheila, then back at Hailey. "Okay?"

Hailey nodded and crossed her arms over her midsection, relief painting her little face.

"You did a good job so far." Sheila reached over and patted one of Hailey's arms, then looked at Tara. "Well, Hailey had to go to the nurse to get her scrapes cleaned and bandaged. When Hailey took off her torn clothes, the nurse saw the big bruise on Hailey's thigh where she fell that day when we got back from the apple orchard. The nurse asked questions about it."

Shaking her head, Tara brought her hands up and covered her mouth, a horrified expression on her face. She let her hands fall to her lap. "Hailey, what did you say to the nurse?"

"I told her I fell, but she kept asking me if I got hurt some other way." Misery etched itself across Hailey's features. "She asked me if you ever got mad at me, and I told her you would be mad because I tore my new clothes."

Tara gathered Hailey into her arms as the little girl started to sob. "It's okay, sweetie. You just told the truth."

Wiping her eyes, Hailey extracted herself from her mother's embrace. "But I should've told you about the clothes instead of keeping it a secret. Then those people wouldn't have come looking for you."

Caleb wondered whether Hailey had any inkling what the visit from "those people" actually meant. Would the explanation scare the child? Tara and Hailey shouldn't have to go through this. He knew for a fact that Tara's assessment of DCF was correct. They took children away from parents for no good reason.

"It will all work out with God's help." Tara seemed to be reassuring herself as well as her child. "The best thing is that we've all learned that telling the truth is most important. Isn't that right, Hailey?"

The little girl nodded. "I promise I won't hide stuff from you again, Mommy."

"That's good to know." Tara leaned over and hugged Hailey. "And I want you to know that when you tell the truth, you won't be in trouble."

Hailey nodded, and Tara stood and glanced around the room as she pulled the little girl up from the couch. "It's time to head home. We've bothered you enough for one evening."

Tom stood. "You're never a bother."

Caleb stepped forward. "Let me walk you back to your

place just to make sure no one is lurking in the dark."

Tara gave him a frightened look. "Do you think they're still around?"

"No, but it's better to be safe than sorry." Caleb started for the door. "Besides, I have to walk home myself. I might as well make sure you get home okay, even though it's right next door. I'd take you through the breezeway connection, but Mom has made it her storage area. No telling what we would trip over."

Sheila chuckled. "Okay, no need to make fun of my pack-rat tendencies."

"You should have Tara organize that area like she has the office." Caleb shrugged into his coat.

"Good idea." Sheila nodded with a smile and gave Tara and Hailey a hug. "You take care, and this will all work out. We can all be praying."

"Thank you." Tara took Hailey's hand as she stopped in the doorway. "I appreciate your prayers. Good night."

Caleb followed Tara and Hailey out into the night, their breaths making clouds in the cold air. They walked silently across the yard. Tara unlocked the door and ushered Hailey inside.

"Please go brush your teeth and get ready for bed. I'll be there in a minute."

"Aaah, do I have to? Can't Mr. Fitz read me a story?"

Tara shook her head. "Not tonight."

Hailey trudged away as Tara remained on the porch. As they stood there face to face, Tara threw her arms around Caleb. "Thank you for understanding. Thank you for being so kind to Hailey. Thank you for being on my side."

Caleb felt her tremble in his arms. "I didn't really do anything."

Tara jerked back and looked back at him and put a hand over her mouth. "I'm so sorry. I shouldn't have done that. I was just so relieved that you were watching out for me. It's been a very stressful night."

"It has." Caleb gave her a lopsided smile. "That's okay. I understand."

"Thank you again."

Caleb looked down at Tara, the porch light illuminating her pretty face. For one instant, he almost gathered her back into his arms and kissed her. But the image of Amy's face flashed through his mind. She'd done the same thing when he'd helped her father. She'd thrown her arms around his neck and thanked him profusely. The next thing he knew he was kissing her. The similarities scared him. He stepped back, almost careening off the porch. He grabbed the railing. "No problem. Good night."

"Good night." Her soft voice echoed after him.

Caleb sprinted toward his house as if running could separate him from his troubling memories. He was torn in two. One minute believing that Tara was a victim of overreaching authorities. The next, thinking that she was good at playing the helpless victim the same as Amy had done.

So many innocent people didn't know not to let the authorities into their residences. Had she known that because of her talk with the woman who'd had her kids taken away? Why did he have to be suspicious? He knew the answer. Amy had taught him not to trust. Was that lack of trust going to be his downfall?

CHAPTER ELEVEN

As Tara left the church building, her nerves were still on edge. She thought about how close she'd come to having those people take Hailey away. Grateful for the conversations with her friends from the women's shelter at the Hawthorne Inn that gave her an insight into dealing with DCF, she let the sunshine warm her face and tried to think of the good things in her life. That didn't come easily.

Even while she'd been getting ready this morning, she worried that someone would show up to take Hailey from her. How could she send the child to school tomorrow? She feared the authorities would come to school and take her daughter. Something similar had happened to one of the women Tara had worked with at the inn.

Taking a deep breath, she tried to push away her worry as she zipped her jacket against the cool breeze that whipped a strand of hair across her face. God was in control, but sometimes that was hard to remember after she'd spent the last two years helping her daughter fight a deadly disease.

"Hey, you ready for a great lunch out at the Hawthorne Inn and your meeting with Nick?" Heather came up beside Tara.

Tara smiled, wishing so many people didn't know her business. But wasn't that what friends were for—to come alongside and help? She should be happy she had so many people who cared about her and Hailey and wanted to help. But sometimes Tara felt as though she were a failure because she couldn't handle her own problems without always asking for assistance.

"It all makes me a little nervous."

"Believe me. Nick will put you at ease." Heather patted Tara's arm.

"That's what Molly and Sheila said, too." Tara glanced at Hailey, who was playing with Eric and Emily. "It'll be a fun time for Hailey. She enjoys playing with the twins."

"We'll see you out at the inn." Heather waved as she joined Max on his way to their car.

"Yeah." Tara headed toward the spot where Hailey was playing.

Molly approached the kids at the same time. "Hey, we're excited to have everyone over for lunch, and my kids want Hailey to ride with us."

Tara nodded. "She still needs a booster seat."

"We've got it covered. We always keep one in the back of the SUV." Molly motioned toward their vehicle parked nearby. "We'll see you at the house."

Tara watched them go, Hailey barely bothering to say good-bye as she skipped off with her friends. As Tara turned, she nearly bumped into Caleb.

"You've got to watch where you're going." Grabbing her by the shoulders, he grinned. "Mom and Dad are ready to leave. You ready?"

Tara heart thumped against her rib cage, and she hoped Caleb didn't have any idea how much his presence affected her. She swallowed hard. "Yeah. Hailey's going with the Jansens."

"Good." Caleb headed toward his parents' car.

On the ride to the inn, Tara said very little. She hadn't talked with Caleb about the incident Friday night, even during yesterday's work on the fundraiser. It was as if no one wanted to mention it, but the episode was never out of Tara's mind. The thought of losing her child terrified her. She had dealt with the possibility of losing Hailey permanently to cancer. Now another threat lurked on the horizon. Trying to leave it all in God's hands was hard, but it shouldn't be. Why was it so difficult for her?

After Tom parked the car near the inn, Tara walked toward the Jansen's residence. The colonial house with the white clapboards and black shutters at the windows sat at the back of the property, nestled among the tall Norway spruce trees and the bare-branched hardwoods. Molly often bragged on Kurt, who had built the house after they were married. They had overcome a lot of adversity to find love. Tara wondered whether she would ever find love again.

She glanced at Caleb. He was a dead end when it came to love. Even though she had an inexplicable attraction to the man, she recognized that he was as wary of love as she was. What would it take to get the people around them to understand that? Even today, when the reason for the meeting involved the very serious subject of her court summons, her friends were playing matchmaker.

But Tara intended to make the best of this day no matter what transpired. She would trust God to see her through. The sermon this morning had been directed right at her and her doubts. The Scripture from Hebrews couldn't have said it better. She let the words roll through her mind and settle in her heart. *I will never leave you or forsake you.* She needed to believe in God's promise. He would see her through this trouble.

"You're very quiet." Caleb looked her way.

"I have a lot on my mind." Tara didn't want to say that one of those things was him.

He nodded. "I just want you to know that I'll help you in any way I can."

Tara forced a smile. "Thanks. You and your parents have been a big help already."

Caleb acted as though he was about to say something else, when Hailey came running toward them. He greeted her with a smile as she grabbed their hands and started pulling them toward the back of the colonial. "You have to see what Eric and Emily have."

Tara trotted along with Hailey as they rounded the corner of the house. "You have to slow down, or I'll wind up flat on my face."

Hailey laughed. "No, Mommy. You're a good runner."

"But the shoes I'm wearing today aren't made for running." Tara glanced down at her low-heeled pumps. "I need sneakers for running."

Hailey let out an exasperated sigh. "Oh, all right. I'll be slow just for you."

Tara stifled a smile as she looked over at Caleb, who was doing the same. Moments like these made her want to throw away her restraint regarding Caleb and see what might happen with this very kind man, but she promised herself to keep caution at the forefront of all her decisions. It was safer that way. Safety trumped everything.

"Is there any chance you can give us a clue as to what we're going to see?" Caleb asked.

"It's a surprise." Hailey grinned from ear to ear as she pointed toward the screened porch that ran along the back of the house. The twins, who were standing inside, waved.

"Come on, Mommy. Mr. Fitz is in a hurry to see, too." Hailey pulled on Tara's arm.

As they drew closer, a tiny bark sounded from the porch. Tara had no doubt they had a puppy in there. She feared that Hailey would want one, too. One more thing she couldn't have. Tara didn't know how many times she could continue to say no when Hailey asked for something.

Before they reached the back door, Hailey let go of Tara's hand and raced ahead. Caleb turned to Tara with a knowing look. "A puppy. You know what that means."

Nodding, Tara sighed. "She can't have a puppy. You can give her the doll to soften the blow."

Caleb let out a halfhearted laugh. "Even though she wanted the doll, somehow I don't think that can substitute for a puppy."

"I know, but that's the reality. I can't afford to feed another mouth, even if it's only a puppy. That doesn't count vaccinations and all the other stuff that goes along with having a pet." Tara pressed her lips together in a firm line. Surely he would understand.

"Yeah, it's a tough call." Caleb chuckled as he opened the door for her and moved aside so she could enter the porch.

"Mommy, come and see." Hailey motioned toward the crate in the corner.

Reluctantly, Tara looked inside. A squirming bundle of fur jumped at the sides. The cute little brownish-tan puppy threatened to melt Tara's resolve, but she steeled herself against any collapse in her determination not to give way to her daughter's unspoken wishes.

Anticipation painting her features, Emily looked up at

Tara. "Would you like to hold her?"

"Can we? Can we?" Hailey clapped her hands while she jumped up and down.

"Okay." Tara leaned over and picked up the puppy, which almost wiggled out of her grasp and licked her face.

Caleb leaned closer. "Hard to resist."

Tara nodded. Not only was the puppy hard to resist, but so was the man standing next to her. "But I will." *On both accounts.*

"Looks like you've met the newest member of our family." Molly joined the group and petted the wriggling little dog.

"Does the newest member have a name?" Tara handed the puppy to Molly.

Molly stroked the puppy's back as she settled down on Molly's shoulder. "Ginger."

"And how does Smoky like Ginger?"

Molly grinned as she set Ginger on the ground. "So far, so good. Although I have to say that Smoky more or less tolerates the new addition."

"So when did you decide to get a dog?" Tara watched Hailey play with the puppy, which thumped its tail against the floorboards.

"We were in town last week when the local animal shelter was having a pet adoption, and Kurt caved to the kids' begging." Molly shrugged as she shook her head. "You should get a puppy for Hailey."

"Don't say that too loudly. I'm afraid she may already have that idea, and it's just not something we can do right now."

"Yeah, I understand." Molly glanced over at the kids, then back at Tara. "Hailey can come over anytime to play with the kids and have some puppy time."

Tara sighed. "I know, but it seems like the days fly by, and I don't make time for that since we moved."

"We'll have to make a better effort to arrange that time. I know my kids miss having Hailey around, especially Emily." Molly motioned toward a car coming down the drive. "Looks like Nick and Allison are here."

Tara looked at the couple who emerged from the fancy sports car. She stood rooted to that spot as Molly hurried to greet them. Hailey's interest in the puppy had made Tara forget for a few minutes the real reason she was here.

***

During the meal, Caleb watched Tara. She barely picked at her food. He guessed that she was nervous about her meeting with Nick. Caleb wished he could reassure her that she had nothing to worry about. She had done nothing to hurt Hailey. He wished there was some way he could lighten her mood, but he had no idea how it really felt to have the threat of losing your child hang over you like a large boulder ready to fall and crush you at any moment.

He hoped he would get the chance to have a little talk with her before the afternoon was over. Once everyone else had arrived, she spent her time talking with everyone except him. Was she avoiding him? The tension between them jumped out to grab him just like Smoky pouncing on the unsuspecting Ginger.

When Molly called everyone into the kitchen to get dessert, Caleb made his way toward Tara. As he stood in line behind her, he leaned forward. "I was thinking about Hailey and that puppy."

Tara turned to him with a frown. "Didn't I make my thoughts on that subject very clear?"

"You did, but I was thinking of a compromise solution—maybe one that can make all of us happy."

Tara put a hand on one hip. "And just what would that be?"

Caleb gave her a lopsided grin. "I thought I could adopt a puppy, and we could share."

Tara eyed him, skepticism radiating from her eyes. "And just what does sharing involve?"

"It involves as much as you want."

"You mean as much as Hailey wants, and that will definitely be more than I want."

"How do you know unless you ask her?" Caleb raised his eyebrows.

Tara let out a heavy sigh. "Let me think about it."

"Molly says the shelter is having another adoption day this coming Saturday at the fall festival." Caleb grinned. "It'll be the perfect time to find the perfect dog."

"You're welcome to pick out a dog. You don't need me or Hailey to help you."

"Come on, Tara. Be a sport."

"You're not going to guilt me into this."

Caleb shrugged, holding out both hands. "If you're feeling guilty, you only have yourself to blame."

Turning away, Tara picked up a dessert plate and fork, then helped herself to a piece of Molly's coconut cake. "This is my favorite."

"So I'm in for a treat?" Caleb placed a piece of cake on a plate. He would give her time to think over sharing a puppy, just as she had asked. He was making peace with himself and the past, but peace about Tara eluded him.

Next weekend was the fall festival and Max's celebration—two big events. Tara's life was so intermingled with his these days that he was sure to share the festivities with her, but did he want more? He kept asking himself that question, but he never answered it. Besides, right now Tara had a lot on her plate. She had to get through this hearing. He was sure the outcome would be in her favor, but there was always an outside chance something could go wrong. Sometimes the justice system was anything but just. He thought about Kurt's unjust conviction. Caleb didn't know whether he would be able to forgive those who had wronged him, as Kurt had done. Maybe that was the reason Caleb had struggled to get over Amy's betrayal. Shouldn't he forgive instead of letting someone who wasn't even around keep him trapped in the past?

As Caleb finished his cake, his heart was lighter. He wouldn't let the past keep him from living in the present. He would work on forgiving Amy, even though she wasn't here to receive his forgiveness. After Tara had her court appearance, he would ask her on a real date, not one that involved their fundraising or someone else's attempt to push them together.

He glanced over at Hailey, who was having the time of her life with the twins and their new dog. Could he convince Tara that her daughter could use at least a part-time pet? And could he convince Tara to go out with him when he hadn't been very welcoming in their first encounters?

"What are you doing over here in the corner?" Max clapped Caleb on the back.

Caleb held up his fork. "Just enjoying this cake."

"I hope you're still planning to attend my anniversary celebration."

"Wouldn't miss it." Caleb nodded. "And I even have a date. Little Ms. Hailey."

"You've stolen my best girl." Max chuckled.

Caleb laughed in return. "She's so full of life."

"Now she is." Max grimaced. "Heather told me that Hailey had a couple of rough years. It's good to see her healthy, but I think Tara still worries about Hailey."

Caleb nodded. "She does, probably the same as Heather worries about you."

"True. It's a burden caring for someone with cancer." Max looked over at Heather. "Heather was my lifeline even when I didn't know it. She loved me even when I wasn't very lovable."

"We can all be unlovable, and it's good to have friends and family who will stick by us during those times." Caleb wondered whether Tara could see beyond his faults. He was determined to find out.

While Caleb talked with Max, Tara and Nick disappeared into a room down the hallway from the kitchen. Caleb wished he could be there with her and help her, but he didn't know the first thing about dealing with the court system in a situation like this. The only thing he could do was pray. *Lord, give Nick the wisdom to advise Tara.*

"You're awfully quiet all of a sudden." Max gave Caleb a speculative look. "Worried about Tara?"

Caleb let the question rattle around in his mind for a few seconds. Did he dare confide in Max? After all, Caleb didn't know Tara's friend that well. "Aren't we all?"

Max nodded, the conjecture still showing in his look.

"But you have a special interest in her."

Was there any point in denying it? Caleb took a deep breath as he stared at Max, who appeared interested in only one thing—a straight answer. Caleb wasn't sure he had one. "Would you understand if I said I'm still trying to figure that out?"

Max chuckled. "Absolutely. Heather and I didn't exactly have smooth sailing when we first met. It took us a while to recognize what we were feeling for each other."

Caleb shrugged as he smiled. He wasn't about to explain his trust issues. That was the bottom line. He was still afraid to trust his heart to another woman. But hadn't he decided to push his fear aside and ask Tara out? He had to hang on to his courage.

"I think I should let her get this court thing behind her before I act on my interest."

"That might be a good idea, but I'm the last person to give relationship advice." Max shook his head. "Heather was just kind enough to let me muddle through. Thankfully, I convinced her to marry me."

"It doesn't take much to see she loves you." Caleb wished he had a clearer vision of how Tara viewed him.

"And I'm amazed every day that she does." Max glanced over at Heather, who was talking to Molly and Sheila. "Heather's always on the go. Don't get in her way when she's planning something."

"I know she's been a big help to Tara in the fundraising efforts."

"Heather is the queen of fundraising."

"I figured as much when she said I should be on your PMC team almost a year in advance." Caleb glanced down the hallway and wondered what was happening with Tara.

He wished he could be the one to ease her burdens, but all he could do was stand by and pray that the authorities would see the truth.

As Caleb finished the last of his cake, his mother appeared at his side. "Would you like me to take your plate back to the kitchen?"

"If you'd like to." Caleb handed it to her with the suspicion that she wasn't here to relieve him of his plate. She wanted to know what he'd been talking to Max about.

Sheila took the plate and slid it under hers as she put the forks on top. "Seems you and Max were having a serious discussion."

"We were. Tonight's kind of a serious night for Tara."

Sheila nodded. "For all of us. Your dad and I can't believe what has happened."

"None of us can." Caleb hoped his mom would leave the conversation at that as he glanced over at Hailey, who seemed unaffected by the adult concern around her. "At least Hailey's having a good time with Emily, Eric, and that puppy."

Smiling, Sheila turned toward the three children, who took turns using an old sock to play tug-of-war with the puppy. "I'm glad she's having fun."

Caleb nodded. "Mom, I'm thinking about getting a dog from the shelter. What do you think?"

"Does this have anything to do with Hailey?"

"Yeah. I'm quite sure she'd love to have a dog, but Tara nixed the idea when I brought it up."

"So you're going to let Hailey play with your dog?" Sheila chuckled as she raised her eyebrows.

"That's my thought." Caleb shrugged. "Do you and Dad object?"

"You're asking our permission to have a dog? You're a grown man with his own house, so you can do what you want." Sheila laughed. "Are you worried that Tara will see through your plan?"

Caleb sighed. "I just don't want to do anything to alienate her or make her worry more."

Sheila laid a hand on one of Caleb's arms. "Son, I'm sure it's no surprise that your dad and I think the world of Tara, and—"

"And you're trying to push us together."

Sheila gave him an innocent look. "Did I say that? Must be on your mind."

Taking a deep breath, Caleb didn't disguise his annoyance as he stared at his mom, even though he had finally come to a point where he didn't care that his parents were trying to be matchmakers. "Tara and I have discussed your schemes to push us together."

"And did you decide that we have a good idea?"

"I'm not going to tell you about our private discussions."

"That must mean your dad and I are making progress."

Before Caleb had a chance to comment on his mother's statement, Tara and Nick walked into the room. Caleb couldn't tell from Tara's expression whether good results had come from the discussion. Would Nick or Tara say anything to the group? She glanced his way, and his heart thudded against his rib cage like the puppy's tail thumping against the floor. But she looked away almost as quickly as she had caught his gaze.

Hailey rushed forward and grabbed Tara around the waist. "Mommy, I've been playing with the puppy. She's so fun."

"Puppies are fun, but they're a lot of work, too. You have to train them so they are well behaved." Tara patted Hailey on the head.

Hailey looked up at her mother with anticipation. "I can be a real good trainer if I had a puppy."

"I'm sure you would. You can help Eric and Emily whenever you come over to play." Tara looked down at her daughter.

"But it's not the same." Hailey pouted.

"I know, but that's the way it has to be for now." Tara hugged Hailey. "Run along and play with the twins and that puppy. Get your fill of puppy time before we have to leave."

Hailey trotted back toward the kitchen, where Emily and Eric were still entertaining Ginger with that sock. Would she or Nick give the gathering any information about the upcoming trial, or was their meeting completely between attorney and client?

Stepping closer to Tara, Caleb searched her face. "I hope your meeting went well."

Tara gave him a tentative smile. "I think it did. Nick's going to say something about it in a minute."

Caleb stood there while Tara joined Heather and his mother. He wished he knew what Nick was going to say. Tara didn't appear troubled, just uncertain. After talking with Max, Caleb couldn't deny that he had come to care about Tara more than he had realized. His concern for her was abundantly clear. Still, he worried about making another wrong choice. He was trapped in the prison of his own doubt.

While Caleb stewed, Nick stepped to the middle of the living room and let out a sharp whistle. Everyone turned to look at him. He motioned for Tara to join him. She moved to his side, her arms crossed at her waist. Caleb couldn't help feeling her anxiety.

Nick surveyed the room. "As you know, Tara and I discussed her upcoming court appearance, and there are still a lot of unknowns in this case. I will be getting more information tomorrow, and most likely I'll be asking many of you to testify on Tara's behalf. For right now, I'd like to take this time for prayer. Psalm thirty-four seventeen says, 'When the righteous cry for help, the Lord hears, and rescues them from all their troubles.' I believe that promise. If you feel led to pray aloud, please do. I'll start."

Nick held out his hand to Allison, and the group quickly formed a circle, even the children. Caleb's protective instincts kicked into high gear as Tara placed her hand in his. Bowing his head, he wondered whether she could hear his thundering heart. Caleb closed his eyes as Nick's voice rose above the ticking of the mantel clock.

After Nick finished his prayer, several other adults prayed. Caleb wanted to pray for Tara, but he wasn't used to praying aloud in a group. He should be listening to the other prayers rather than worrying about how he should pray.

Finally, during a pause, Caleb opened his mouth to pray, but a sweet little voice filled the silence. Hailey's high-pitched tones were unmistakable. "Dear God, please help the judge to know my mommy loves me and is the best mommy in the whole world. Amen."

Hailey's earnest prayer twisted Caleb's heart. This little girl shouldn't have to worry about judges or anyone separating her from her mother. He would do whatever it took to make sure that Tara and Hailey didn't have any trouble.

After Tom said the final prayer, Tara pulled Hailey into her embrace and held her tightly for several moments. "Thank you for your prayer, sweetheart."

"God will make everything right." Hailey smiled brightly at her mother, then scampered away to play with the puppy.

Conversation swirled around Caleb as he let his thoughts linger on Hailey's statement. He should take a lesson from her. He'd let Amy's betrayal smash his faith instead of embracing it when trouble came. Tara and Hailey were showing him how to live.

CHAPTER TWELVE

The following week, the judge entered the courtroom as the occupants stood. Tara had never been in a courtroom before and was surprised that the place was so Spartan. She'd expected something like she had seen on TV, where the judge sat at a huge ornate desk at the front of the room, which sported dark wood paneling, tables, chairs and benches. Instead, the small space reminded her of a high school classroom, with its chrome-and-wood chairs and tables.

Tara took a deep breath, hoping to calm her nerves. Kurt had talked to her about his day in court and had reassured her that the judge would see reason in this situation, even though Nick had told her this judge was often sympathetic to DCF. Surely the judge would see the truth.

After further meetings with Nick, Tara understood how her refusal to let the DCF social worker into her home had probably saved her from having Hailey taken from her at that time. The thought of being separated from her daughter for an indefinite amount of time made Tara shudder. But she wouldn't dwell on something that didn't happen.

She was grateful God had provided her with a calm sense of purpose during her encounter with the DCF officials. Looking back, she knew her composure was something she hadn't managed on her own. Most of all, she was thankful for a good attorney. Nick had advised her on how to prepare a note for the school, indicating that Hailey was not to talk to anyone from an outside agency unless Tara was present. That had helped to ease her worry about sending Hailey to school. Tara took a deep breath and prayed God would see her through this, too.

As the court proceedings went forward, Tara listened with trepidation as the DCF lawyer called the social worker who presented testimony about Hailey's account of the day she had fallen on the playground and ruined her clothes. When the woman described Hailey's injuries and concluded that the child was afraid to give a truthful statement about what happened, Tara wanted to jump up and tell the woman she was wrong. Instead Tara grasped the arms of her chair and took a deep breath.

Although these people were wrong about their conclusions that Tara abused her child, Tara understood their perspective and their desire to protect children. She prayed the judge would see the fallacy of their judgments.

The testimony of her friends, who talked about Tara's watchful care of Hailey during her cancer treatments, warmed Tara's heart. God had provided her a wonderful set of friends in this place so far away from her Montana home. She had a lot of people on her side.

Their steadfast support had her rethinking her plans to go back to Montana. Her grandparents were about the only reason to return to her birthplace. She felt a kinship with the people she had known here for only a few years. The thought of leaving them behind saddened her. But Montana was definitely a less expensive place to live, and she couldn't rely on the Fitzpatricks forever. She had to strike out on her own.

Tara's outlook brightened as she continued to listen to the statements her friends gave, especially Caleb's. When he left the stand, their gazes met. Tara's pulse quickened when he smiled. Was Caleb's presence a big part of her reason for reconsidering a move back to Montana?

She couldn't make a decision based on her attraction to him. Their relationship had come a long way since the day he'd taken her to lunch and grilled her about her employment in his parents' office. He was always looking out for her and Hailey, but did that translate into something more than friendship? Tara couldn't hope too much for that. No matter how tempting, living her life to please a man was a mistake she wouldn't make again.

Once all the testimonies and statement were finished, Tara ventured a look at the judge as he appeared to be looking at something on the desk in front of him. She wished she could read his expression, but it gave no clue to what he was thinking. She twisted her hands in her lap.

Finally the judge looked up and surveyed the courtroom. "I am ready to make my ruling at this time about this matter. After listening to all the witnesses, I have come to the conclusion that there is no support for this claim of abuse against Tara Madsen." The judge looked her way. "You are free to leave, Ms. Madsen."

After that statement, the judge banged his gavel, then rose and left the courtroom. In the next few seconds, Tara's friends surrounded her as they hugged her and expressed their happiness about the judge's decision. For a moment, she felt as though she were on the outside looking in at her life.

Tears pricked her eyelids as she realized everything was going to be okay. She blinked them back as she covered her mouth with her hands, then clasped them in front of her. "Thank you, everyone. You helped me so much today."

"We were glad to set the record straight." Heather gave Tara another hug.

Tara turned to Nick. "I can't thank you enough for taking my case."

Nick smiled. "I like to see justice done. That's why I became a lawyer."

At just that moment Hailey, who had been waiting outside the courtroom with one of Nick's aids, rushed through the doors and down the aisle. She launched herself into her mother's arms. "Mommy, Ms. Sheila told me we're going to have a party because the judge says you're the best mommy ever."

Hunkering down, Tara hugged her little girl with all her might as she fought back more happy tears. She thanked God for this little girl and all of their friends.

Hailey extracted herself from her mother's embrace. "Let's go to the party."

Sheila clapped her hands. "Okay, everyone. You heard Hailey. You're all invited over to the office for a little party."

"Won't that ruin your business day? You've already spent part of your morning here." Tara looked from Sheila to Tom and back again.

"We have no pressing appointments today, and we intend to have a celebration for our receptionist." Sheila grinned. "You are coming, aren't you?"

Tara hugged Sheila again. "You're too good to me."

"You deserve it." Sheila motioned Tara out into the aisle that led to the courtroom door. "We're ready to get the party started."

"Mommy, let's hurry." Hailey grabbed Tara's hand and started to pull her mother into the aisle.

"Sounds like someone's eager to get the celebration under way."

Still holding Hailey's hand, Tara turned at the sound of Caleb's voice. Nodding, she swallowed hard as she looked up at him. He'd been a steady rock of reassurance through this whole ordeal. He shouldn't make her so nervous. She finally managed to find her voice. "Yeah, your parents are really sweet to do this. Hailey's excited about missing a whole day of school, too."

Caleb grinned down at Hailey and extended his hand for a high five. "And I'm excited to miss a whole day of work."

As they walked out to the parking lot, Tara held Hailey's hand and didn't look back. Tara wanted to wipe this trouble from her mind and look forward. But the future was almost as scary as the past because the days ahead were an unknown quantity. This latest trouble reminded her that nothing about life was certain, especially with Hailey's health. She had to have faith that God would continue to give her the help she needed.

When they neared the place where the cars were parked, Hailey dropped Tara's hand and raced ahead to join Sheila and Tom.

"It appears that my parents have made your daughter their honorary grandchild." Caleb stepped up beside her and gave her a knowing look that morphed into a grin. "I think that makes me her honorary uncle."

Tara gave him a sideways glance and wondered where this was leading. "And just what does being an honorary uncle entail?"

"I think it entails making sure she has a puppy."

"I hope you haven't said this to her." Tara pressed her lips together as she eyed him.

"I haven't said a word, and I know you said she couldn't have a dog, but—"

"And that's what I meant. Please understand."

"I do." He put an arm around her shoulders as he slowed his pace.

"Then please don't press the issue." Tara's heart raced. She didn't want to feel this way. Did he have any idea how his touch affected her? To him, it was probably just a brotherly gesture, as an uncle to Hailey, but Tara couldn't deny her attraction.

He stopped and turned her so she was facing him. "I'm going to get a dog, and I want Hailey to share in that. Is that okay with you?"

Tara looked at him, her heart still racing. "So you're saying the dog is yours, and Hailey will share how?"

"She can come over anytime to play with the dog. She can take the dog for a walk. Whatever she wants as long as it's okay with you." Caleb lifted his eyebrows as he gazed back.

Tara didn't know how she could object to his plan. "Okay, but stuff with the dog can't interfere with her homework."

"Good." Caleb's smile spread across his face. "We can make it a rule that she can't do anything with the dog until her homework's done."

"A good incentive not to delay it."

"I'd like for you and Hailey to help pick one out during the fall festival." Caleb held out his hand. "Shake on that?"

Tara stared at his extended hand and steeled herself against the reaction she would have when their hands touched. She'd been married, widowed, and dealt with the grave illness of her child, but she didn't know how to deal with her reaction to this man. She definitely didn't want to read anything into his attention.

When his large hand closed around hers in a firm handshake, she took a deep breath and let it out slowly. "Don't let Hailey talk you into a dog you don't want. After all, it'll be your dog."

"We can definitely work together to pick out the perfect pet. You, too." Caleb grinned as he let go of her hand. "For someone who should be extremely happy, you seem a bit serious. I don't want this dog thing to ruin your celebration."

Looking up at him, Tara swallowed hard. What would he do if he knew his presence was the reason for her subdued attitude? "I don't like to get too excited about anything because I've learned that today's happiness might not last."

Caleb didn't say anything for a moment. He just looked at her with sadness in his eyes. "I wish I could make everything better for you."

Wishing she hadn't opened her mouth, she lowered her gaze. Now he would think she was a truly negative person. "I'm sorry. I didn't mean to undermine your celebratory mood."

He stepped closer and put an arm around her shoulders again. "You haven't done that. Besides, it's your celebration. I just want you to be happy."

Caleb's nearness took Tara's breath away, but she finally managed to speak. "Thank you. Really, I'm happy—happy that all this court stuff is behind me and Hailey's treatments have gone well. She's happy, and that's all that counts."

"I have to admit that your little girl has captured my heart. I want her to be happy too." Caleb dropped his arm from her shoulders and shrugged. "That's why I'm getting a dog."

"I shouldn't let you spoil my child, but I won't stand in your way." Tara couldn't keep a smile from escaping as she looked at Caleb. She wished she could capture his heart, too.

The realization that she had let herself care too much for this man scared her. Was she afraid that he would never feel the same, or was she afraid that a new relationship might end in disaster because the course of her life was a true roller-coaster ride?

Every time she hit an emotional high, an emotional low waited in the wings. Caleb said Hailey had captured his heart, but would he stick by her if her health failed again? Tara wished she knew. She wanted a smooth road—or maybe she only wanted someone to help her smooth out the bumps.

***

The forecast for above-average temperatures in the sixties and clear skies boded well for the fall festival. Caleb loaded the back of his SUV with the boxes filled with the Christmas decorations that the church youth had made. As he shoved the last box in, a giggle caught his attention. He turned just in time to see Hailey sprinting toward him.

"Mr. Fitz, I'm ready for the festival." She waved a cloth bag in the air. "Mommy says I can collect candy at the booths and put it in here."

"Your mommy is always well prepared." Caleb smiled as he looked over Hailey's head to see Tara carrying another box, following close behind her daughter. "Get buckled into your booster, and we'll be on our way in a minute."

While Hailey scrambled into the backseat, Caleb took the box from Tara, trying to ignore the way the accidental touching of their hands set his pulse racing. He turned quickly and stowed the box away, then closed the hatch. "Guess we're ready to go, unless you have to get something else."

Tara gave him a subdued smile. "Ready."

"My folks are already in town, helping Kurt and Molly with their booth." Caleb opened the door for Tara. "We can drive right up to the booth to deliver this stuff as long as we get there before eight o'clock."

"Thanks." Tara gazed up at him, then back at Hailey. "She's so excited about today, but I haven't said anything about the you-know-what."

"When would you like to tell her?"

"Is it okay if I play it by ear?"

"Absolutely. It's your call."

She smiled again, broader this time. "I appreciate that."

While Caleb drove into town, Hailey jabbered on about the festival and her big plans. He could hardly wait to let her know about the dog. He hoped she would be as enthusiastic as he was. He and his brother had had a dog when they were kids, but Sparky had been hit by a car.

Caleb had never quite recovered from that, and they had never adopted another dog.

Then he wondered when he was going to get up his nerve to ask Tara out. Maybe today. Or maybe not today. Today his priority was looking for the right opportunity. Prayer would have been a good idea, but he hadn't done that either. He wasn't sure why. But he knew why he put off asking her. He was afraid she would be as reluctant to go out with him as she was about letting Hailey have a pet.

Caleb cast a look in Tara's direction. She sat there staring out the window. Did he dare ask what she was thinking? She was always rather quiet, and Hailey was just the opposite. Was the little girl like her father? There was a lot about Tara that he didn't know. Would that prove to be a problem, like it had with Amy?

He pushed the thought away. If he wanted a relationship with Tara, he was going to have to banish the past from his mind. Easier said than done. It cropped up at the most inconvenient times.

"Mr. Fitz, are we almost there?"

Caleb chuckled at Hailey's question. "Almost. Count to three hundred, and we'll be there."

Hailey started to count, and Tara looked over at him with a smile. "You know you're going to be in trouble if she gets to three hundred and we aren't there."

"I've driven this route so many times that I have it down to a science." Caleb tapped a finger against the steering wheel.

"Sure of yourself, aren't you?"

"Of course. What did you expect?" He grinned at her.

"Two hundred eighty-eight. Two hundred eighty-nine…"

"Ten seconds." With raised eyebrows, Tara looked over at him.

"You see where we are?"

Tara nodded. "Yes. We're on Main Street."

In a matter of seconds, Caleb parked his vehicle near the booth. He rolled down his window and greeted Kurt and Molly as Hailey scrambled out of the car and ran to join Eric and Emily without a backward glance.

With Tara's help, Caleb unloaded the boxes. "Have you thought anymore about you-know-what?"

Tara gave him a look that was half frown and half smile. "It hasn't even been an hour since you asked me that question. Please give it some time."

"Okay, but I can't get it off my mind."

"I'm beginning to think you're more ecstatic about the prospect of getting a dog than Hailey will ever be." Tara grinned.

"I don't know about that. I imagine she'll be plenty excited."

"I suppose you're right."

"I know I am." Caleb opened a nearby box. "Do you want one of each item out for display?"

"I do." She reached into the nearest box and brought out some placards. "These have descriptions and prices. I'll set these out, and you can place the appropriate item next to them."

"At your service." Caleb saluted as he went to work.

After they finished displaying the items they had for sale, Caleb checked with Kurt to see if he needed any help.

Kurt shook his head as he motioned toward the spot where Molly, Tom, and Sheila were working. "I've been here since six this morning getting everything ready. Molly was back at the inn cooking, and she arrived about the same time as your parents. Tara's going to watch the kids while we finish here. So we're good, but thanks for asking."

With no other job, Caleb decided to make the most of his freedom. He moseyed over to where Tara stood beside a table that formed the left side of the booth. The early morning sun made her blond hair sparkle like spun gold. Her pretty features held a serious expression as she instructed the children. She wasn't only pretty, but she had a tender heart.

He stopped and watched, his insides giving him that crazy butterfly feeling. He'd been fighting his reaction to her for weeks. Today he was going to quit fighting and start living. Today was going to be a good day. He would find a way to ask Tara on that date.

Tara motioned toward the row of boxes sitting at the back of the booth. "When someone wants to buy something, you can find the items in these boxes. Each box has a label on it."

Standing behind the table covered in a blue cloth, Hailey nodded. "Do we put them in bags?"

"If the customer wants one." Tara pointed to a pile of plastic bags sitting on a box under the table.

"I can hardly wait till we can start." Hailey gave Emily and Eric each a high five.

Tara laughed. "The event doesn't start until nine o'clock. So while you're waiting, you should take a few minutes and grab a bite to eat."

The kids helped themselves to one of Molly's muffins. Caleb grabbed one and handed it to Tara. "Eat up. You need your nourishment."

She laughed. "As delicious as these are, they probably aren't the healthiest breakfast."

Caleb took another bite, then studied the muffin. "I don't care what you say. This is the best muffin I've ever tasted."

"I didn't say they aren't delicious, but even Molly admits that there are much more nutritious things to eat for breakfast." Tara peeled the wrapper off her muffin and took a bite.

Caleb could read the pleasure on her face as she ate. He hoped he'd see that expression when he asked her out. His stomach churned. Surely she wouldn't turn him down.

Once the festival started, Caleb stayed in the booth with Tara, Hailey, Eric, and Emily until some of the high school kids from the church youth group arrived. After Tara gave them instructions, she took the younger children around to the different booths to play games and collect the goodies folks were giving out.

When lunchtime rolled around, Tara herded the kids back to Molly and Kurt's booth. Caleb tagged along like a lost pup. He couldn't get dogs off his mind, but Tara didn't give him any opportunity to pursue that topic. He didn't want to force something on her. Even though the dog would be his, he feared his desire to share the pet with Hailey was overstepping his bounds.

Caleb let the troubled thought roil through his mind while he ate in silence. The kids' chatter gave him an excuse not to talk. They were talking about Ginger. When Hailey lamented about not having a dog of her own, Caleb glanced in Tara's direction. She gave him a knowing little smile. Was that a good sign?

After they finished eating, Tara gathered up the

children's trash and headed for the nearest garbage container. Caleb followed close behind. Tara dumped the stuff in the can, then turned around. She let out a little gasp when she almost ran into him.

He grinned. "So what do you say? Are you ready to pick out a dog?"

Staring at him, she let out a heavy sigh. "Yes, after I make sure we're all set with people to take care of our sales station."

"Good. I'll wait right here. Bring Hailey with you when you come back."

Without another word, Tara returned to the booth, and Caleb watched Hailey playing a game of tag with Eric and Emily. Finally, Tara leaned over and said something to Hailey, and her gaze swung to Caleb. Grinning, he waved.

Hailey charged over and stopped in front of him, her blue eyes wide with anticipation. "What's my surprise?"

"I want you to help me pick out a dog from the shelter."

Hailey's eyes grew even bigger. "You're getting a dog?"

Caleb nodded. "Do you want to help?"

"Yeah." She jumped up and down, then hugged Caleb.

He laughed and gave Tara an I-told-you-so look. "I think someone's excited."

"You don't have to convince me."

Caleb looked down at Hailey. "Ready to go?"

Nodding, Hailey grabbed Caleb's hand and trotted beside him as they made their way down the block to the booth where the local animal shelter had dogs ready for adoption. As they drew nearer, Hailey tugged on his arm, and he quickened his pace.

When they reached the booth, Caleb surveyed the group

of dogs—small, large, and in between. Puppies and adult dogs. Caleb favored a puppy, but he wanted to stand back and observe the dogs' reactions to Hailey and her reaction to the animals.

"Are you interested in adopting one of our dogs?" A lady stepped out from the booth. "Your little girl looks like she's ready to find one."

Caleb didn't know whether to correct the woman or let her statement ride, but he didn't have time to do either. Hailey made a beeline for a black-and-white puppy with fur sticking out in every direction as the dog chased its tail around in circles.

"I like this one. He's funny."

Tara stepped forward. "Hailey, this is going to be Caleb's dog, not yours. So you let him choose."

"Tara, it's okay if she wants to give her opinion. After all, I did tell her that I want her to help me pick out a dog."

Tara shrugged, "It's your choice."

When Caleb turned back to look at Hailey, she had already moved on to another dog, whose fur made him look like a huge black bristle brush. The dog licked her hand, and Hailey smiled up at Caleb. "Maybe I like this one better. Which one do you like, Mr. Fitz?"

"I don't know. It's hard to choose. Let's look at some others." Caleb wanted to let Hailey choose, but he didn't want a small furry dog, the kind that seemed to attract Hailey. A little fur ball of a dog didn't strike him as very manly. He would have to put his wants in second place and consider himself the caretaker for Hailey's dog.

As Caleb accompanied the little girl around the booth, looking at each dog, Tara hovered in the background, then stepped closer to him. "How are you going to decide?"

"With my gut. Sometimes, you just have to go with your instincts."

"And what does your instinct tell you?"

Tara's question caught Caleb off guard. She was talking about picking out a pet, but he couldn't help thinking about his instincts where she was concerned. He'd made a snap judgment about her, but that had proved wrong. Still, he had a hard time putting the thoughts aside. He teetered on the edge of throwing aside every doubt. Then something like the police showing up at her door brought them all to the surface again.

"Mr. Fitz." Hailey tugged on his arm. "I got one picked out."

With a knot in his stomach, Caleb looked down at the little girl. Did he dare look where she was pointing? He forced a smile. "You do?"

"Yeah, it's the one in the corner of the pen."

Caleb trudged over to the pen on one side of the booth. His heart sank when he saw four furry pups frolicking in the straw lying on the ground. He forced another smile. He'd asked for this, so he had to accept the outcome. "Show me which one you like the best."

Hailey stepped closer to the pen and pointed to the far corner. "That tan-and-white one with black spots."

Caleb's mood brightened as he observed the pup that reminded him of his childhood pet. The dog's sleek tan coat gleamed in the sunlight. As if the dog knew it was under observation, it pranced over and looked at Hailey with soulful brown eyes. The pup let out a howl that made Hailey giggle. She held out her hand for the animal to sniff, then petted it until it lay on its back.

"She wants you to rub her tummy."

"How do you know it's a girl?" Hailey looked up at him.

Panic clicked in Caleb's mind as the child's big blue eyes stared at him with expectation. The birds and bees. Not a topic he was prepared to discuss with a little girl. He swung around to look for Tara. She stood behind him with a twinkle in her eyes and a knowing smile curving her mouth. Was she going to save him or let him stew?

She stepped up beside him. "Need some assistance?"

"Yeah." He chuckled with relief. "I'd appreciate it if you'd explain about boys and girls."

"Okay." Tara hunkered down next to Hailey and quietly talked to her child.

Caleb couldn't hear the conversation, but Hailey kept nodding as Tara went through the private instructions.

After Tara finished, Hailey pranced over to Caleb. "My mommy's really smart. She told me how to tell the girl dogs from the boy dogs."

"Yes, your mommy is very smart." Caleb glanced at Tara over the top of Hailey's head. "You're a lucky girl to have such a good mom."

"Do you mind having a girl dog?"

Caleb hadn't thought about whether that mattered. "I don't."

"Good." Hailey patted the pup's head. "I like her. Do you?"

Caleb reached down and let the dog sniff his hand. Immediately, the little dog pushed her nose under Caleb's hand. He rubbed and scratched her back, and she rolled over for another belly rub.

"Mr. Fitz, she likes you, too." Hailey looked up at him with eagerness brimming in her eyes. "Do you want to get her?"

Before Caleb could answer, one of the shelter workers came over. "Did you find a dog you would like to adopt?"

Caleb wasn't sure how to answer. Hailey liked the little dog. He was drawn to her, too, but was this a good breed for a child? "Maybe. What can you tell me about this pup? Do you think she'll be good with children?"

"This dog is a beagle, Jack Russell terrier, and pug mix. These breeds are usually good with children, but each dog is different." The woman scratched the pup's head. "I will say that this type of dog usually needs lots of attention, which includes walks and playtime. So if you can provide those, this will probably be a good dog for your family."

There it was again. Family. Caleb smiled at the woman, then at Hailey. "I guess we have a winner."

"Yippee!" Hailey jumped up and down. "She's perfect."

Caleb had expected Hailey to correct the woman about the family thing, but the little girl remained silent. Tara didn't say a word either. Maybe they figured it was easier not to have to explain. But today seemed like a family day. Caleb couldn't banish that thought.

He looked at the woman. "What do we need to do now?"

The woman motioned him over to a table at one side of the booth. "There's a little paperwork that you need to fill out."

"We're involved with a festival booth. May I leave the puppy here until I'm ready to go home?" Caleb started to look over the papers.

"Certainly." The woman smiled at Hailey. "I'll take good care of your puppy until you come back for her."

"What are we going to name her?" Hailey knelt down

and stroked the puppy from the top of her head to the end of her tail, which wagged with delight.

"That's something we'll have to figure out." Caleb finished reading and signing the papers, then handed them to the woman. "You be thinking of some names."

"I'm going to think of the best name ever." Hailey grinned from ear to ear. "I can hardly wait to take her home."

As Hailey skipped between the two adults, Tara looked down at her daughter. "You'd better remember that this dog is not yours. She belongs to Caleb. He's just letting you have a part-time stake in taking care of her."

"I know." Hailey slowed her pace.

Caleb's heart wrenched at the sadness in the child's voice. She desperately wanted a dog of her own. He would do his best to make sure she had as much time as possible with the puppy. This dog would surely further cement his involvement in Hailey's and Tara's lives. He wanted that, and he had to grab what he wanted without having second thoughts.

CHAPTER THIRTEEN

"Someone's not happy." Tara raised her eyebrows as she looked over at Caleb.

He maneuvered his SUV onto the main road toward his house, the headlights beaming into the darkness. "Maybe I'll let that pup spend the night at your place."

"Can we, Mommy?" Hailey jumped into the conversation.

"No." Tara wasn't going to let Hailey or Caleb change the plans for this puppy. "Mr. Fitz is going to keep that dog at his house tonight."

"But, Mom—"

"No 'but moms.'" Tara nailed her daughter with a pointed look. "In the beginning, a pet needs to get used to its new home and surroundings. So it's best to let her stay with Caleb. And sometimes, puppies cry just like babies."

"But she'll be so sad." Hailey frowned.

"True, but she'll soon get used to her new home." Tara steeled herself against Hailey's attempt at manipulation. "Have you thought of a name? That's something you can do."

Hailey huffed as she continued to frown. "Did you ever have a dog, Mommy?"

"No, just the stray cats that Grandma and Grandpa fed when we lived with them in Montana. Do you remember them?"

"Sort of. But they only showed up when they wanted to be fed. They were no fun." Hailey leaned forward in her booster seat. "Mr. Fitz, did you have a dog before?"

Caleb nodded and turned into the drive that led to his house. "When I was a kid, my brother and I had a dog named Sparky."

"Where's Sparky now?" Hailey asked.

"Dogs don't live as long as people." A muscle worked in Caleb's jaw as he stared straight ahead. He stopped his vehicle in front of his garage and pushed the button that opened the garage door. Light flooded the interior and spilled out on the SUV.

"Does that mean I'll live longer than this dog?"

Caleb looked her way, a bit of unease in his eyes. "That's what happens when you have a pet. You have to know that one day you'll lose them."

Tara suspected that the loss of that dog had affected Caleb in a deep way. So getting a new dog may not have been so easy for him. Some folks jumped right in and got a new dog when their beloved pet died. Others found it hard to ever replace a pet and elected not to get another one. This man had likely set aside his own feelings to give Hailey a chance to share in the experience of having a pet.

Caleb hopped out of the SUV and hurried to the back, as if he was trying to avoid any more discussion of lost pets. Tara couldn't blame him. Talking or thinking about the death of a loved one—humans or pets—didn't make for the best conversation. Hailey was too young to remember the death of her own father, and Tara rarely mentioned it. She had lived with the constant threat of losing her only child for too long. She wanted to think about living, not the prospect of death, even though it was part of life.

Hailey unbuckled her seat belt and scrambled out of the car. Without waiting for Tara, the little girl sprinted around the SUV and joined Caleb where he stood in the dim glow coming from the yard lights along the drive. He lifted the carrier from the back. The puppy whined and pressed her nose to the side.

Caleb looked down at Hailey. "Will you help your mom bring in the supplies?"

Hailey nodded as she raced to Tara's side. "Let me carry the bag."

"Gladly." Tara handed the bag filled with dog supplies to Hailey. "I'll get the puppy food."

Hailey skipped ahead with the bag swinging by her side, her breath leaving a trail of vapor clouds in the cold night air. She got to the door inside the garage at the same time as Caleb, and she opened the door for him before he said anything. Soft puppy sounds continued from the carrier as the two went inside. Tara sighed as she followed them. Hailey had not only adopted Caleb, she had adopted his puppy, too.

Here she was getting drawn further and further into Caleb's life, thanks to her daughter. A little knot of worry twisted her insides. Her own experience had led her to be cautious with relationships. None of them seemed to last.

When Tara stepped into Caleb's kitchen, she glanced around. She'd never been in Caleb's house. They had always interacted at the office, his parents' house, or her tiny apartment. This place reminded her of her grandparents' kitchen, with the dark cabinetry, white appliances, cream-colored Formica countertops, and wallpaper sporting flowers in shades of smoky blue and rose. Caleb and Hailey knelt on the floor together, beside a wire cage. The puppy sat inside, seemingly unsure about the whole thing.

The skepticism in Hailey's expression mirrored that of the dog. "Mr. Fitz, does she have to be in a cage?"

"She likes it in there. It gives her a feeling of safety. It's like her den."

"Then why is she still whining?"

"Because you haven't given her a name."

"I don't know a good name. I've never had a dog or any kind of a pet before." Hailey stared up at Caleb while her eyebrows knit in a little frown. "What was the name of your dog?"

Caleb let out a harsh breath, but he still managed to smile at Haley. "Sparky."

"That's a good name."

"But she needs her own name, not a hand-me-down one."

"Yeah, I know." Hailey looked Tara's way. "Mommy, do you have any good names?"

Tara shrugged. "I wish I did, but I don't. You'll have to think of one."

Hailey pressed her lips together and wrinkled her nose. "I think we should name her Sadie. Remember Great-Aunt Sadie? I think she would like to have a dog named after her. She loved dogs."

Tara couldn't believe Hailey even remembered Aunt Sadie, Tara's grandmother's sister. She had only visited a couple of times, bringing her menagerie of dogs with her. Although Tara liked the name, she remained silent. Caleb should be the one to agree or disagree.

Caleb plucked the pup from the cage and cradled her in his arms as he stroked her head. The puppy snuggled against him. "What do you think, little lady? Does that name suit you?"

As if the dog understood the conversation, she let out a high-pitched bark followed by a howl. Hailey laughed and wrapped her arms around Caleb's arms as he continued to hold the dog.

When Hailey sat back, she grinned from ear to ear. "She likes that name."

"Then that's what we'll call her." Caleb set Sadie on the floor and stood.

Tara looked down at Hailey. "Now that you've given the dog a name, it's time to head home."

With soulful eyes, both Hailey and Sadie gazed up at Tara. "Do we have to leave now? I didn't get to play with her."

Tara didn't want to overstay their welcome. "You'll have time another day."

Caleb reached down and scratched behind the puppy's ears as he glanced up at Tara. "It's okay if Hailey wants to stay, but it's up to you."

Tara looked over at the clock on the microwave. "Half an hour. Then we have to go home."

Hailey let out a loud whoop and retrieved a dog toy from the bag. "Come on, Sadie. Let's play."

Tara stepped closer to Caleb. "You know you're going to spoil my child. She'll want to spend all of her time over here with that dog."

Caleb motioned toward the doorway leading to the living room. "Would you like to discuss a schedule?"

"You mean for her to play with the dog?"

"That's kind of what I had in mind." Caleb grabbed a pen and paper from the kitchen desk. "I wouldn't want to get in trouble with you. I might be already."

"You're not." Tara turned to Hailey. "If you'd like, you can stay in here to play with Sadie."

"I'll take good care of her." Hailey petted the dog's head. "She likes to play tug-of-war just like Ginger."

"Then you should have fun while Mr. Fitz and I talk over some stuff." Tara glanced at Caleb.

"We'll be in the living room if you need anything." Caleb tapped Hailey on the shoulder. "I know you'll do a good job with her."

Hailey smiled as she nodded her head vigorously. "I will. You'll see."

Tara hoped this whole thing wouldn't be a fiasco as she followed Caleb into the living room. He indicated she should sit on the floral-print couch sporting the same smoky-blue and rose colors as the kitchen. None of the furnishings looked like a man had made the choices. She could only guess that the house contained his grandparents' things.

This house's interior made Tara momentarily homesick for Montana and the smells of her grandmother's chocolate chip cookies. But she didn't have time to wish she were back there. She had a life here. Her dreams of returning to her childhood home seemed far, far away, lost in the realities of her life now.

"What did you have in mind for a schedule?" As she settled on the edge of the couch, she stared at Caleb, who sat at the other end.

"That's up to you. I leave it in your hands. You know what's best for Hailey."

Tara shrugged. "I thought we'd already agreed that she would have to finish homework before she could do anything with the dog, and that will vary from night to night."

Caleb set the pen and paper on the dark-oak coffee table with more than its share of nicks and dings. "I'm going to leave the entire thing up to you. I really wanted to ask you something else."

"What?" Tara's voice squeaked as her stomach did a flip-flop. Had she done something wrong? He was always kind to Hailey, but he looked at her as if he wasn't pleased with what she did. Today especially. Why did he have to make her so nervous?

He scooted forward on the couch and placed one hand on the arm, as if he wanted to run instead of talk to her. "I want to ask you something."

Tara nodded, afraid to speak again for fear that her voice would show her nervousness. Whatever he had to say, it must be bad, because he was having trouble saying it.

"You know I admire the way you handle all that stuff with DCF..." Caleb's voice trailed off.

"Thanks." A moment of relief washed over Tara. Maybe he wasn't going to say anything bad after all, but was a qualifier coming?

"You do a great job with Hailey."

"Thanks again. I appreciate the compliments." Tara sensed this praise was leading up to something. "You said you had a question to ask me, but you haven't asked me anything."

He gave her a lopsided grin. "Yeah, I know. I was trying to get on your good side before I asked."

Was he looking to ask her a favor, and all these compliments would make her look ungrateful if she turned him down? "You've flattered me enough. So ask away."

"It hasn't been flattery. I mean it."

"Then what makes this question so difficult?"

Caleb took a deep breath.

"Mommy. Mr. Fitz. Come quick."

Tara jumped up from the couch and raced into the kitchen. With a pained expression on her face, Hailey stood next to a puddle on the oak hardwood floor. "Sadie had an accident. I couldn't get her outside before it happened."

"That's okay. She'll learn. I'll have to make a better effort." Caleb strode across the room and picked up the dog and her leash. "It's my fault. I should've made sure she went out before I left you two to play. I'll take her out now."

"Would you like me to clean up the mess?" Tara asked.

"No. You shouldn't have to clean up after this dog." Caleb snapped the leash onto the puppy's collar, then shrugged into his jacket. "Hailey, you want to come with?"

Hailey glanced Tara's way. "Is that okay?"

"Sure." Tara helped Hailey into her jacket, then watched as that puppy strained at the leash, pulling Hailey toward the door.

While Caleb and Hailey were outside, Tara used some paper towels to blot the puddle. She puzzled over Caleb's question. Would he continue their conversation when he came back? Did she want him to? Maybe this thing with the dog would sidetrack him, and he would never get around to asking it. She threw the paper towels in the trash.

A few minutes later, Hailey, Caleb, and Sadie burst through the door. As soon as Hailey removed the leash, the puppy danced in a circle, her tail wagging and her ears flapping. Tara's daughter laughed with delight, and the sound warmed Tara's heart. This puppy was good for her child, and Tara had Caleb to thank.

Everything about today brought with it a sense of accomplishment. The only downside, if she could call it that, was her growing attraction to Caleb. She looked over at the man who was slowly but surely making her see him in a different light. She was losing count of the number of ways he had made her life better.

As Caleb hung the leash on a hook near the door, he glanced around, his gaze stopping on Tara. "You cleaned up the mess?"

"Yeah, I didn't see any point in letting it sit there. It could've ruined the floor." Tara shrugged. "You'll want to do a better job. I just blotted it up with paper towels."

"Thanks."

While Hailey played with Sadie, Tara debated about mentioning their previous conversation and decided against it. If he wanted to bring it up, he would. The half hour Tara had said they would stay had come and gone. She couldn't keep Hailey out any longer, or she would be too tired in the morning.

"Hailey, time to say good-bye to Mr. Fitz and Sadie." Tara gave her daughter a pointed look.

"Okay." Hailey gave Sadie a hug. "You be good for Mr. Fitz. No more accidents."

Caleb chuckled. "I hope she obeys."

Tara slipped into her jacket. "Thanks for all your help with the fundraiser today."

"Glad to do it." Caleb smiled at her, not a hint that he even remembered he had wanted to ask her something.

"Good night. See you in the morning at church." Tara ushered Hailey to the door that led to the garage. "Hope you have a good night with that pup."

"Me, too." Caleb opened the door for them. "I'll walk you home."

"Not necessary."

"Maybe not, but I'd feel better if I did. I can give Sadie a little more exercise that way, too."

"Okay." Would he ask his question now?

The two adults, one child, and one little dog traipsed down the lane, the yard lights casting their shadows across the darkened landscape. They walked in silence, their footsteps crunching on the gravel. When they reached Tara's place, she quickly ascended the steps and unlocked the door.

Hailey gave Caleb a hug before she bounded up the steps, then darted back down and gave the puppy one more hug. "You be good for Mr. Fitz."

Tara chuckled as she waved to Caleb. "Thanks again for everything."

"You're welcome. It was a good day." He waved in return as he headed home.

Tara stood in the doorway and watched him go with the puppy loping by his side. The day had been productive, but it ended on a note of worry on her part. Obviously, whatever he had wanted to ask wasn't urgent, so she should forget it and not make something out of nothing.

Despite his attention, she still sensed he held something against her. Did it have to do with the hurtful relationship in his past? She'd like to ask, but it wasn't her place to do so. His interest in her and Hailey probably didn't go beyond friendship, and she would be wise to keep it that way. Tomorrow was another busy day with Max's party on the agenda. Tara promised herself that she wouldn't worry.

She would remember that God was in control.

CHAPTER FOURTEEN

··

Clouds obscured the moon and stars as Caleb drove his SUV toward his parents' house. A cold front had brought frigid temperatures into the region, so he left his car running as he hurried to their front door. As he stepped onto the porch, his parents came out the front door.

"You're right on time." Sheila adjusted the scarf around her neck. "I don't want to stay in this cold any longer than I have to."

"Go ahead and get into the car. It should be warm." Caleb accompanied his parents down the steps. "I'll get Tara and Hailey and be right back."

As Caleb made his way to Tara's door, he berated himself for letting Sadie's accident keep him from asking Tara out. The moment had been lost, and he didn't know how to recapture it. Or maybe he'd been chicken. He wasn't sure she would say yes. It was kind of like stepping out on the pond in the winter and hoping the ice would hold. He didn't see tonight as a good opportunity to ask her out. Too many other people around at Max's celebration. Or was he still being chicken?

If he hadn't hemmed and hawed around last night, he would have already asked her for a date. Caleb wished he didn't always zig when he should zag when it came to women.

As Caleb knocked on Tara's door, he heard Hailey's

high-pitched voice.

"Mommy, are you almost ready? Mr. Fitz is probably knocking on the door."

"Almost." Tara's voice sounded muffled. "Please get the door."

The door swung open. "Hi, Mr. Fitz. Mommy isn't ready yet."

"You look like you're ready." Caleb grinned, hoping Tara might be primping for him.

Hailey twirled around, the frilly ruffled skirt of her dress flaring out from her waist in a circle. "Do you like my dress, Mr. Fitz? Your mom bought it for me. I love it."

"I do like your dress." Caleb helped Hailey with her coat.

Tara entered the living room and grabbed her coat from the back of the nearby chair. "Sorry I'm late."

"You're not late." Caleb couldn't tear his gaze from Tara. The blue dress with the flowing skirt brought out the blue in her eyes. His heart thudded. "You…that dress looks great on you."

"Thanks." She blushed as she picked up her purse. "So I guess we're ready."

Caleb opened the door and stood aside as Tara and Hailey went out. Key in hand, Tara turned to lock the door. They hurried to the SUV, their breaths making clouds in the cold night air. He opened the door for Tara, then helped Hailey into her booster seat. He couldn't help thinking of this as another family moment, but he was letting his thinking get way ahead of reality. He hadn't even worked up enough nerve to ask Tara on a date.

Hailey settle in her seat. "Mr. Fitz, I hope Sadie isn't going to be lonely tonight."

Caleb buckled his seat belt. "She'll be fine. She needs to get used to being by herself. She was playing with one of her toys in her kennel when I left."

"It's too bad dogs can't come to the party."

After Hailey's statement, a collective chuckle rolled through the car.

"We don't need dogs at the party," Tara said.

"We could have a dog party sometime," Hailey said.

Caleb laughed. "I'll let you plan it."

"Yippee." Hailey pumped her fist. "I'll invite Ginger and Eric and Emily, too."

On the drive to the venue, chatter about a dog party filled the vehicle, but Caleb didn't join in. His mind played through a half-dozen scenarios of how he could ask Tara out. He planned at least that many date ideas and discarded them all. He had to come up with something good, but first he had to manufacture some courage.

"Mr. Fitz, are you going to dance with me?" Hailey's question shook him from his thoughts.

"Are you going to save a dance for me? You might be so popular that you won't have time for me."

"Who will dance with me besides you?" Hailey's voice held a hint of worry, like the worry that filtered through his mind when he thought about asking Tara for a date.

"I'm sure Heather will let Max dance with you."

Hailey giggled. "Max let me dance on his toes last year."

Caleb loved the sound of Hailey's laugh. "He did? Is that the way you want to dance with me?"

"Can you dance with me on your toes?"

"If Max can do that, so can I." For a moment, Caleb felt silly for trying to compete with the other man, who wasn't even here, for the affections of an eight-year-old.

"Do you always let your dance partners step on your toes?" Tara's voice hinted of suppressed laughter.

"Only the eight-year-olds." Caleb caught Tara's gaze in the rearview mirror, and his heart did a little dance of its own. "Looks like we're just about there. I'll drop you all off, then find a parking spot so you don't have to walk through the cold."

"That's quite thoughtful of you, dear." Sheila patted him on the shoulder.

After Caleb found a parking place, he strode toward the entrance, the cold penetrating his coat. He was thankful the frosty weather had waited to arrive until after the fall festival. As he entered the building, warm air took away the chill. Could it break through his ice-bound cowardice when it came to Tara?

While he searched for Tara, Hailey, and his parents, he took in the large wood-paneled room. Ornate chandeliers cast light on the round tables covered in white tablecloths that sat along three walls. A dance floor occupied the center, with a stage at the far end. Drums, a keyboard, and guitars sat on the stage. Folks milled around the tables as conversation floated through the room.

"Mr. Fitz, we're over here." Hailey's voice sounded above the crowd.

Caleb smiled as he made his way toward the table where she stood waving her hands above her head. "Thanks for finding me."

"I saved a place for you right here." Hailey patted the table next to the chair where Tara sat.

Caleb nodded. "I appreciate that."

"You get to sit between me and my mom."

"That's a very special place." Caleb smiled at Tara, hoping she knew how much he meant that statement.

Tara nodded as she returned his smile. "We'll make sure he behaves, won't we?"

Hailey scrunched up her face. "Do you think he might be bad?"

Caleb laughed. "I intend to be very, very well behaved tonight."

"That's good because I wouldn't want you to be in trouble with my mom." A serious expression painted Hailey's features.

"I'll keep that in mind." Caleb looked at Tara to see her reaction to her daughter's statement. Tara's countenance told him nothing. His activities apparently weren't much of a concern to her. He, on the other hand, was very aware of her actions.

"Where's the guest of honor?" Tara glanced around the room. "I haven't seen Max or Heather since we got here."

"Me neither, but the Jansen family has just arrived." Caleb nodded his head toward where people were checking their coats. "And my folks have wandered across the room to greet some people they know."

Hailey tugged on Tara's arm. "Will I be able to play with Eric and Emily?"

"Maybe later." Tara took Hailey's hand. "We can go over and say hi to them."

Following Tara and Hailey, Caleb took in the joy of the folks that had gathered to celebrate with Max. Caleb didn't know many of the people in attendance, but his parents appeared to know a good number of them. Were they folks his parents had met through their fundraising efforts?

Fundraising had always been a part of the Fitzpatrick

family dynamic. He'd been dragged into their do-gooder world as a youngster and had hated every minute of it. Then Amy had come along and made him bitter about the whole idea, but Tara was changing his outlook. Helping people could be rewarding. He didn't want to lose that attitude. He prayed he wouldn't be disappointed again. Or stay bitter about what happened with Amy. Moving forward meant forgiving her. If he wanted a new relationship with Tara, he had to forgive Amy. He could see that now, but he could only do it with God's help.

While he and Tara talked with the Jansens, more guests arrived. The place hummed with conversation and laughter. Suddenly someone flickered the overhead lights, and the conversation died down.

A tall gray-haired gentleman in a suit walked onto the stage and picked up a microphone. He tapped it, and a thumping sound reverberated through the room. "Hello, everyone. I hope you're ready for a celebration to beat all celebrations. Please find a seat, because I have a big surprise for everyone."

A murmur swept through the crowd as folks found their way to the tables situated around the dance floor. When everyone was seated and most of the talking had ceased, the man motioned to someone off stage. In a moment, a petite dark-haired woman in a flowing green dress came to his side. He looked at her and smiled. "Many of you know us, but for those who don't, I'm Robert Harkin, and this is my wife, Nancy. We're gathered here with friends and family to praise God for bringing our grandson Max into our lives and also for seeing him through his battle against cancer. I'd like to open this evening with a prayer."

While Robert prayed, Caleb prayed also. He'd been

feeling sorry for himself while others were suffering much more than he ever had. He prayed for a positive attitude and a forgiving heart. He prayed that God would lead him to make the right decisions where Tara was concerned.

After Robert finished praying, he looked over at his wife and grinned broadly. "Now for the big surprise. I'm going to let Nancy announce this."

Nancy took the microphone. "We're not only here tonight to help Max celebrate the one-year anniversary of his transplant, but we're going to celebrate with Max and Heather as they get married."

As a cacophony of voices and applause filled the room, Nancy tapped on the microphone. When the room quieted again, she made a sweeping gesture with her hand. "I know this is quite unexpected, but with family and friends gathered together, Max and Heather decided it made perfect sense to get married now instead asking people to make another trip back here in a few months for their wedding."

Robert put an arm around his wife and leaned into the microphone. "So let's get this celebration underway."

Hailey pulled on Tara's arm. "What's that man talking about?"

"That's Max's grandfather. Do you remember him?"

Hailey shrugged. "Maybe, but what's he saying?"

Tara leaned closer. "Max and Heather are going to get married tonight. Isn't that exciting?"

Hailey sat up straighter in her chair. "You mean she's going to have a wedding dress and veil and everything?"

Tara smiled. "I guess so. We'll see in a few minutes."

As a low buzz of conversation swirled through the venue, Caleb watched Tara explain the situation to Hailey.

The two of them made him smile. It had been a long time since he'd been this happy.

Tonight's event had taken on a new twist. He couldn't help remembering the conversation he'd had with Max just weeks ago about love and romance. Had he known then that they would get married today? Maybe life's uncertainty made them decide not to wait.

Caleb was afraid he'd let too many opportunities pass him by because he'd been mired in self-pity and bitterness. He looked over at Tara and Hailey again. He wanted to be a part of their lives. He hoped they would let him in.

While Caleb thought about the direction of his life, soft music floated through the room. He finally noticed the group of musicians who had quietly taken their places on the stage.

"Mommy, is that Amanda?" Hailey pointed toward the band.

Tara nodded as a puzzled look came over her face. "How do you remember Amanda?"

"She played guitar and sang at Max's last party, and she went to the baseball game with us." Hailey sat taller in her chair. "I want to learn to play a guitar like her."

"Maybe when you're a little older. Right now the guitar would be as big as you are." Tara patted Hailey on the head, then turned to Caleb. "Amanda's the woman playing the keyboard. She's also Max's cousin of some kind."

"Cousin of some kind?" Caleb gave Tara a curious glance.

"Yeah. Stepcousin maybe."

Before Caleb could make another comment, Max and one other guy, both dressed in dark suits, took their places at the end of the dance floor closest to the stage.

"There's Max," Hailey whispered. "Where's Heather?"

"Shhh." Tara put her finger up to her lips. "She'll be here soon enough."

Hailey strained to see as she pressed her little lips together in anticipation. A moment later a woman wearing a light-brownish dress that flowed around her stepped onto the dance floor. She carried a bouquet of red, yellow, and orange flowers as she walked down the center of the dance floor.

Caleb leaned toward Tara. "Who's that?"

"That's Emma Butler. She's a nurse and works with Heather at the clinic. Emma and her husband ride on the PMC team." Tara turned her attention toward the back of the room. "There's Heather."

"Who's the man with her?" Hailey asked as the notes of the traditional "Wedding March" filled the air.

"I suppose that's her dad. Fathers usually walk their daughters down the aisle." Tara smiled at Hailey as they stood along with the rest of the crowd.

Her little brow wrinkling, Hailey looked up at her mother. "Who will walk me down the aisle?"

Leaning over, Tara pulled Hailey close and whispered something in her ear. Caleb had no idea what Tara had said, but it brought a smile to Hailey's face. The little girl's question had him thinking he could be that man. That thought was way ahead of the here and now, but the idea rooted itself in his mind and wouldn't go away.

Crazy.

He hadn't even asked Tara on a date yet. He had to get his thoughts in check, but the whole wedding thing did nothing to evict that idea from his head. The way Max smiled at his bride made Caleb want to find that kind of love. Could he find it with Tara?

They had shared a lot in the past few weeks. He had gotten to know her and care about her. A lot. He adored Hailey. Could this all translate into something for his future? He was going to take measures to find out.

"Heather's beautiful!" The awe in Hailey's voice made Caleb smile.

"She is." Tara stared after Heather as she made her way toward Max.

Caleb watched Tara as Max and Heather exchanged their vows and rings. Tara's faraway look made Caleb wonder if she was remembering her own wedding or the loss of her husband. How did weddings affect a young widow?

At the end of the ceremony, the minister reminded everyone of what Max and Heather had been through together in the last year as they prepared to do a unity ceremony. The best man placed a small table covered in a lace tablecloth in front of Max and Heather, who each held a small beaker filled with clear liquid. A larger beaker sat on the table. Heather and Max stood with the table between them.

The minister stepped behind the table and looked out at the gathering. "Today, Heather and Max are going to commemorate their marriage with a unity ceremony. Instead of a candle or sand, they have chosen to use something that relates to their lives. Max has spent many years working in a lab, and Heather, as a nurse, has seen her share of lab equipment."

A collective chuckle rolled through the room.

The minister smiled. "This ceremony symbolizes their union, which is something new and beautiful."

Heather and Max held their beakers and poured the contents into the larger one. As the liquids combined, they changed from clear to pink. Oohs, aahs, and applause came from the crowd.

"Mommy, that was so cool." Hailey clapped her little hands as she squirmed in her chair. "How did they do that?"

"You'll have to ask Max." Tara winked at her daughter. "I'm pretty sure he knows how that was done."

"When are they going to kiss?" Hailey asked.

Caleb grinned as he looked at Tara over the top of Hailey's head. "Sounds like you've got a romantic there."

"I think she's read too many princess stories."

Caleb laughed and wondered whether he could help one little princess and her mother find a happy ending.

The minister said some final words, then looked at Max and Heather. "I pronounce you husband and wife. You may kiss the bride."

As Heather and Max kissed, spontaneous applause filled the air. When they ended the kiss, they faced the crowd. Their smiles lit up the room as they stood hand in hand.

The minister gestured toward the guests. "I now present to you Mr. and Mrs. Reynolds."

Applause and the recessional music echoed as Max and Heather made their way to the doorway at the back. Robert Harkin took the stage once again and motioned for the happy couple to join him. The applause continued as they made their way onto the stage.

When they reached the stage, Robert gave them each a hug, then stepped forward as he held the microphone. "Max and Heather have an announcement."

Max took the microphone with one hand while he put

his other arm around Heather and drew her close. "We'd like to thank everyone who is here to share our special day. We know this ceremony was a surprise to many of you. Instead of wedding gifts, we request that you make a donation to one of the cancer charities that we have listed for your convenience on the cards the servers will bring to the table with your meals. We also have a table set up near the door, where you can buy Christmas ornaments and wreaths made by local youths. All the proceeds go to the cancer charities."

Max handed the microphone to Heather. "I want to thank everyone, too. Please be sure to sign our special guest book. It's a puzzle. Pick a piece and sign on the back, then put it in the box. Thanks again and enjoy your evening."

As the guests applauded again, Robert took the microphone and said a prayer of thanks for the meal. Within minutes a group of servers began bringing food to the tables while soft recorded music played.

Caleb looked over at Hailey. "Well, what did you think?"

Wide-eyed, Hailey looked at him. "It was supercool. I've never been to a wedding before."

"You picked a good one to attend."

"But I didn't pick. It picked me."

Caleb laughed. "It picked all of us, and it's the best wedding I've ever been to."

"Have you been to a lot of weddings?" Hailey cocked her head as she looked at him.

Yeah. He'd been to a lot of weddings over the years, as one by one his friends and relatives got married, including his brother. Early on he was glad to avoid the wedding fever that seemed to sweep through the men he hung out with. Then they started their families, and Caleb began to feel like an outsider.

Was that why he'd fallen so quickly and so hard for Amy? He wasn't sure, but he couldn't let that bad memory dissuade him from his quest.

"Are you trying to count them all?" Tara's question made him look her way.

"No. I was just thinking back to all the different ones I've been to." Caleb shrugged. "I was best man in my brother's wedding."

"And that wasn't your favorite?" Tara gave him a puzzled look.

"As best man, I had too many responsibilities to enjoy it." Caleb chuckled.

Tara shook her head. "I've never been in a wedding."

"You were in your own." Caleb raised his eyebrows.

"We eloped. So there wasn't a real wedding. No wedding dress. No special ceremony. Just me, Blake, the judge, and a couple of witnesses. No family. No friends." Tara lowered her gaze as she twisted her hands in her lap.

She didn't appear to be happy about those circumstances, but that was what she'd chosen at the time. Did she regret that decision? "Eloping saves a lot of money."

A little smile curving her lips, she glanced up at him. "Yeah. That's a good way to look at it. We definitely didn't have any money. He was a poor rodeo cowboy, and I was a waitress right out of high school. You do crazy stuff when you're young and in love."

Before Caleb could make another comment, servers brought food to the table. As everyone started eating, he contemplated Tara's statement. He hadn't been that young, but he'd been in love. He'd let love cloud his judgment. He had to guard against doing so again. He shook away that thought. A constant battle with himself over whether he could trust Tara would do him no good.

The meal ended, and the bandleader announced the bride and groom's first dance. Then Heather danced with her father and Max with his mom. By the time all the specialty dances were over, Caleb was wound up in knots over the thought of asking Tara to dance. He continued to stare at the dance floor as other couples joined the newlyweds. Where had all of his confidence gone?

"Mr. Fitz, are you going to dance with me?" Hailey tapped him on the arm.

Caleb smiled at Hailey. "I thought you'd never ask."

Hailey giggled. "You're supposed to ask me, silly. That's what the prince does in Cinderella."

"Oh, I guess I didn't know I was the prince." Standing, Caleb held out a hand. "May I have this dance?"

Hailey hopped out of her seat and walked with Caleb to the dance floor. As he held the little girl's hand, that familiar protective feeling took hold of his heart. He wanted to make her happy. He wanted to make her mother happy.

Her expression full of expectation, Hailey stared up at him. "Am I going to dance on your feet?"

"Is there any other way to dance?" Caleb held both of her hands and let her step on his shoes. She was so slight that he barely knew she was standing on his toes as he waltzed her around the floor.

She gazed up at him. "You're a good dancer. Are you going to ask my mommy to dance?"

"Would you like me to do that?"

Hailey nodded, a shy little smile curving her mouth. "You should dance with her a lot."

"I'll see what I can do."

"I know she'll say yes."

Caleb hoped that was the case. He didn't know why she wouldn't, but even Hailey's reassurance didn't untie the knots in his stomach. While he gave himself a mental pep talk, Max approached.

He tapped Caleb on the shoulder. "May I cut in?"

Caleb let out a sigh. "I suppose, but you'd better take care of my best girl."

"Don't worry. I will." Max grinned as he took Hailey's hand. "Now you can ask her mother to dance."

Caleb gave Max a knowing smile. The other man was playing matchmaker right along with a little girl. "You're the second person who has suggested I do that."

"Well...what are you waiting for? Get to it." Max danced off with Hailey, who was giggling and having the time of her life.

Caleb glanced back at the table where Tara sat alone. Here was his chance, not only to ask her to dance but to ask her on a date. As he approached, she looked his way and smiled. His heart danced right along with the music.

"Someone stole my partner." Caleb stopped next to Tara's chair. "Would you care to dance and help me drown my sorrows?"

She smiled up at him. "Do you think I could possibly do that?"

The question hit Caleb right where he lived. Could she? Could she take away the hurt from the past? He held out his hand. "Let's give it a try."

"Okay." Standing, she put her hand in his.

As he led her to the dance floor, his heart thundered. He was thankful that the music surely drowned out the sound. As he took her into his arms, the song ended.

"That was bad timing."

"That's okay. I'm sure they'll play another song." She stepped back and looked over to where Max and Heather were talking with Hailey. "What do you suppose my daughter is talking about?"

"She's probably telling Heather how pretty she is."

Tara nodded. "Yes, that's something Hailey would do. She's always been a people pleaser just like her father."

Had Tara's late husband been on her mind all night? Should he comment or let her statement slide right on by? This was no time to let her past or his past get in the way. The next song started, and Caleb held out his hand again. She didn't say anything, just let him lead her through the dance.

He liked the way she fit into his arms. He liked the way she smiled up at him. He liked everything about her. He swallowed hard, Dancing with her shouldn't make him this nervous, but it did. They had spent hours together during the past few weeks. She was his friend, but he wanted more. He needed a little small talk to break the ice and settle his nerves.

He took a deep breath. "Did you enjoy the surprise wedding?"

She nodded. "I don't know how they pulled it off."

"I imagine Max's grandparents had a lot to do with it, since they already had the party plans in place."

"You're right. It was lovely. Probably better than if they'd had months to plan it."

He'd already run out of small talk as they continued to dance to the slow, romantic tune. So now what did he say? Obviously this was the time to ask her out. "We've been pretty busy lately with all the stuff that's been going on."

"We have. I'm kind of glad we get a breather." Tara sighed. "I just want to sit home on the weekend and relax for a change."

Caleb forced a smile. Did that mean she wouldn't be interested in going out with him? *No excuses. Ask her out.* "I'm sorry to hear that."

She puckered her forehead as she gazed up at him. "Why?"

"Because I was kind of hoping that you'd go out with me next weekend."

"Just kind of?" She gave him an impish smile.

"No. Not kind of. I definitely want to take you on a date." Caleb held his breath.

"In that case, I'd really like to go out with you."

Releasing his breath, Caleb smiled. "Good. Is there anything special you'd like to do?"

Tara shook her head. "I'll be happy to do whatever you'd like."

"Then I'll plan something special."

"Oh, what about Hailey?" Tara put a hand to her mouth.

Caleb chuckled. "My mom will be over the moon to watch her."

"Shouldn't we ask her first?"

"We can, but I doubt that it's necessary."

Tara stepped out of his arms. "I'd feel better if we do."

"Okay, we can do it now." Caleb took her hand and led her toward the spot where his parents were just leaving the dance floor. "Mom, could I speak with you for a moment?"

Sheila turned and glanced from Tara to Caleb. "Sure. What's going on?"

For a moment, as Caleb gazed at his mother, he feared she would jump up and down and cheer when he mentioned this date with Tara. "Would you be willing to watch Hailey this coming Saturday night so Tara can go out with me?"

A smile spread across Sheila's face, and her eyes sparkled as she clasped her hands in front of her. "Of course. I'm so happy that you two are finally going on a date."

"Thanks for agreeing to watch Hailey," Caleb said.

Sheila gave Caleb a hug, then hugged Tara. "I should be thanking you. You've just made my day."

"Glad I've made you happy." Caleb took Tara's hand again and hoped his mother wouldn't put too much stock in this one date. "Now we're off to dance some more."

Sheila waved them away. "Your dad and I will keep an eye on Hailey while you dance."

Tara motioned toward the dance floor. "She's having the time of her life dancing with Max and his cousins. She's basking in the attention."

"I can see that." Sheila nodded. "I see Eric and Emily out there, too. They're all having a good time. You two run along, and don't worry about her."

"You don't have to convince me." Caleb twirled Tara onto the dance floor as the band struck up a lively number. "So we're all set. I knew my mother would jump at the chance to watch Hailey."

"Your parents have been more than kind to me, and I'm so grateful," Tara said.

"Not as grateful as they are that you've agreed to go out

with me." Caleb chuckled.

"So you're saying that we've given in to their matchmaking?"

Caleb nodded. "My mom's been pushing for this almost since the day I returned home."

"Are you just doing this to please her?" Tara's eyes filled with concern.

"No. I'm doing this because I like you and your daughter. I like having you as part of my life, and I want to see where that might lead." Caleb grimaced. "I hope that doesn't scare you off."

Tara shook her head. "It doesn't."

Caleb pulled Tara close as the sounds of another slow number filled the room. He'd probably said way too much, but he didn't care. Taking this step with Tara was a big part of putting all the bad things from the past behind him. His future looked brighter than it had in months. He promised himself that he wouldn't let old hurts stand in the way of this new happiness.

CHAPTER FIFTEEN

Rain splatted against the window as Tara looked out at the darkened landscape. Rain had dominated the weather the day she'd met Caleb. How appropriate that the same kind of weather would accompany their first date. She just hoped it didn't turn into snow before the evening was over. He still hadn't told her about his plans, but he had said to dress in business casual.

As the headlights of a car beamed into the darkness, Tara smoothed her navy slacks and shrugged into her matching blazer. Her nerves zinged, and her stomach churned. She hadn't been on a date since before Hailey's illness. She hoped her nervousness didn't show as she opened the door for Caleb. He ducked inside, and she quickly shut the door.

Rain dripped from his umbrella as he closed it and looked down at the puddle on the floor. "Sorry about that. It's coming down in buckets out there. You got something so I can wipe that up?"

"Sure." Letting a bit of calm take over, Tara hurried to the kitchen and pulled an old rag from one of the drawers, then returned to the living room. "Here."

"Thanks." Caleb smiled as he grabbed the rag and wiped.

"You're welcome." Tara's heart beat in rhythm with the rain pelting the window. Why was she talking to him as if he were a complete stranger?

After he wiped up the water, he stood and held out the rag. "Done."

When she took it, their fingers brushed. Her pulse raced. She took a deep breath as she turned back to the kitchen. She thought she'd won the battle of nerves, but she was still as jumpy as the minute he'd walked through the door.

This was Caleb, the guy she'd come to depend on for so much help. They worked in the same office and attended the same church. He lived right down the lane and shared a puppy with her daughter. He shouldn't make her tense.

But tonight was something new. A date.

"So is Hailey all settled?" Caleb ran his fingers through his curly wet hair as he gazed at her.

Tara nodded. "She's already enjoying her evening with your parents. She was so excited about getting to spend the night with them."

Caleb chuckled. "Almost as excited as my parents are to have her."

Tara's mouth was as dry as the weather outside was wet. Tension zinged between them as they stood in front of the door. She should be used to that by now. Besides, the tension wasn't all bad. It was the kind that made her heart race and made her wish for things she wasn't entirely sure she should be wishing for. She wanted a whole family again—a father for Hailey. Was Caleb the type of man who was willing to take on another man's child who might require more medical attention in the future?

Tara tried to shake away the question. She reminded herself that this was only a date, not a mandate for her future life. She should've learned to live one step at a time by now. Hailey's treatments had required that kind of thinking, but now that they were over, Tara just wanted to live again without worry. She wanted to throw open the gates and let joy in and not worry about the future. Could Caleb help her do that, or was she asking too much of this young relationship?

"Hey, are you okay?" Caleb looked down at her.

Tara forced a smile. "Yeah."

"I hope you don't mind, but this rain has ruined my plans." Caleb grimaced as he motioned toward the outside. "I was going to take you to downtown Boston, but the weather's only supposed to get worse. They're saying the rain is supposed to change over to snow in a couple of hours. I didn't want to chance it."

"Oh, sure. I understand." Did she dare ask about his plans? "So what did you have in mind?"

"I know this is a very lame idea for our first date, but I brought over some videos. Your choice." He reached into his jacket pocket and pulled out several DVD cases. "I also brought popcorn."

Tara smiled as the tension drained from her body. "That sounds perfect to me. I like the idea of just relaxing after my busy, busy week."

"Perfect." He handed her the DVDs. "I'll make the popcorn while you decide on the movie."

"Okay." Tara went to the couch and sat down as she studied the description of each movie. He had chosen quite a variety. It had been a long time since she'd seen any movie except those on TV that were a few years old. She'd very seldom allowed herself to indulge in the time it took to watch a movie. She had too many other things to occupy her time.

Pop, pop, pop. The sound floated from the kitchen, and Tara still hadn't picked a movie. She didn't want to select something he wouldn't like, and some of these looked like chick flicks he'd picked to please her.

When Caleb returned carrying two bowls heaped with fluffy-white kernels, he set them on the table. "Got the movie picked out?"

"You really didn't have to bring so many." Tara shrugged.

"I wanted to make sure there would be something you liked."

"I've narrowed it down to three. So you make the final decision." Tara handed him the three finalists.

"Oh, no." Caleb shook his head. "You have to decide, even if it means playing a little game."

Tara laughed. "What kind of game are you going to make me play?"

"You'll see." He made his way into the kitchen and returned a minute later with three of the colorful hot pads Hailey had made. "Turn around and don't look."

Turning her back, Tara wondered what he was doing. Maybe this was exactly what she needed. A little fun. Something less serious.

"Okay. You can turn around."

Tara whirled around to find Caleb smiling as he stood next to the dark wooden coffee table. The three hot pads sat side by side. "So what do you want me to do?"

"There's one movie under each pad." He grinned as he made a sweeping gesture. "Tara Madsen, which do you choose? Hot pad number one, number two, or number three?"

Tara giggled. "What if I pick the wrong one?"

Caleb frowned. "How can you pick the wrong one if these are the three you made your final choices?"

"I don't know." Tara shrugged. "I'm just afraid you won't like what I pick."

Caleb came over and put an arm around her shoulders and drew her close. "You can't make a wrong choice as far as I'm concerned."

Tara's pulse pounded all over her body. She swallowed hard. "Number three."

He stepped away and picked up the third hot pad on the table, revealing the movie Bridge of Spies. "A wicked-good choice."

"Wicked?" Tara stared at him. "How can it be wicked and good at the same time?"

Caleb let out a belly laugh. "You've lived around here long enough to recognize that expression, haven't you?"

Tara searched her mind. "Yeah, I have, but it's still very foreign to me. How can wicked mean very or really?"

"Got me. It's an expression I've used all my life. I realized how provincial it is when I went to Florida, and most people didn't understand it unless they were from this area." Caleb grinned as he took her hand and led her to the couch. "You sit there while I get this movie going. Help yourself to the popcorn."

Still standing, Tara gazed back at him. "Do you want something to drink? I have pop."

"Pop?"

"Yeah, you know, like cola, et cetera."

"You mean like soda or tonic? Seems that we have somewhat of a language barrier here." Caleb laughed again.

Chuckling, Tara took a step toward the kitchen. "What

would you like?"

"Cola is fine." He turned toward the small entertainment center that held the TV and the DVD player. "I'll get this going while you get the drinks."

Tara poured the drinks, the rest of her anxiety lifting away like the bubbles of carbonation in the colas. Why had she been so nervous? The answer: She wanted Caleb to have a good time with her. She wanted to take away that sometimes-disapproving look forever. Taking a deep breath, she picked up the two glasses. Tonight was going to be a good night.

When she walked into the living room, Caleb was sitting on the couch with the remote in his hand. He looked her way. "Should I start the movie?"

Tara nodded as she set the drinks on the coffee table. "Sure."

With a flick of the remote, the movie sprang to life. Caleb patted the space next to him on the couch. "I've reserved your spot."

"Thanks." Tara smiled and settled beside him. He handed her a bowl of popcorn.

"You're more than welcome." He placed his popcorn bowl in his lap and put an arm around her shoulders while the opening scene flooded the screen. "My parents said this is a good movie."

"So your parents have seen this?"

"Yeah. They saw it with my maternal grandparents, who actually remember the events that this movie is based on." Caleb squeezed her shoulders. "I always loved history in school. What about you?"

While her pulse raced, Tara wondered whether she should confess that history had always seemed boring.

Maybe movies would have made it more interesting. Would he care if she hadn't been the best student in the world? Now that she was an adult, she wished she'd taken her education more seriously. She'd loved art, but she'd let that interest slip away when she married Blake. Why was she thinking about that stuff now? She should just watch the movie.

Caleb leaned closer. "I guess your silence means I should be quiet and pay attention to the show."

Nodding, Tara turned to him with a smile. That should get her out of having to answer his question. He would never have to know that she hadn't been very studious. Would a well-educated man like him still be interested in a woman like her if he knew her report card had been filled with Cs? Pushing her worries away, she settled in to watch the movie as she munched on the popcorn and savored having Caleb's arm around her shoulders.

When the final movie credits rolled on the TV, Tara stretched her arms over her head. "That was really, really good. Your parents were right. I wish my history teachers in high school would've made things more interesting, like this movie."

Caleb removed his arm from around her shoulders and gathered up the empty bowls. "So you're saying that you didn't like history?"

Tara slapped her fingers against her mouth. "You weren't supposed to know that."

Caleb chuckled. "That's okay. I was considered a nerd because I liked it."

"I can't imagine you as nerdy."

Standing, Caleb laughed again. "You should see my high school yearbook. On second thought, you shouldn't."

"Does anyone love what they looked like in high school?" This time Tara laughed.

"Some people." Caleb started for the kitchen.

Tara followed. "True, but I was just glad to be done when I graduated."

Tara blew out a harsh breath. She had done it again—said too much. She wanted Caleb to like her for who she was now, not the girl she'd been in high school. But he was making her feel those same fluttery feelings of that silly high school girl who had run off and married the handsome cowboy without thinking about what she was really doing.

She didn't want to get too tied up in how Caleb made her feel. That was what she'd done with Blake, and it hadn't turned out to be everything she'd expected. She needed to take things slowly with Caleb and make sure she didn't let her heart rule her head. She had Hailey to think about now. That was the most important thing.

But didn't Caleb adore Hailey? And she certainly idolized him.

As Tara put the dishes in the kitchen sink, she glanced out the window. "It's snowing, and it's really coming down hard."

Caleb stepped closer and leaned over to look out. "It sure is. Looks almost like a whiteout. Good thing we decided not to go into Boston."

Tara turned to him. "Let's go outside."

"And play in the snow?"

Caleb's smile made Tara's heart skip a beat. "Not play in the snow. Just go for a walk down to the lake. I love the snow here. It looks like those Currier and Ives pictures."

"If you want to go out, put on your coat and boots."

Tara giggled. "You sound like my grandmother."

"That can't be good." Caleb rubbed a hand across the back of his neck. "Are you saying I sound old?"

"Oh, no." Tara stared at him, wishing she wouldn't keep putting her foot in her mouth. Better not to say another thing about him. "I do need to get my coat and boots and hat."

Caleb grabbed his coat from the back of the living room chair and shrugged into it. "I've got boots in my car. I can get them when we go out."

A few minutes later, Tara, bundled up in her coat, hat, and gloves, followed Caleb to his car, where he put on his boots. She looked up into the night sky. White flakes filled the air. The snow was already sticking to the bare branches of the deciduous trees that dotted the landscape. The branches of the huge Norway spruce in the distance already sported a coating of white.

Stillness surrounded Tara and Caleb as they walked hand in hand down the path that led to the lake. Even through her gloves, the warmth of Caleb's hand surrounding hers made her feel warm inside. His presence brought a sense of security ever since the night that DCF had almost taken Hailey. She pushed the troublesome memory away. Good things would fill this night.

When they reached the edge of the tiny lake nestled among the trees, Caleb put an arm around her waist and pulled her close. "It's peaceful here."

"When we first met, I remember you telling me about how you liked to fish on the lake."

"I do."

"Do you ever ice skate?"

Caleb shook his head. "We're never sure the ice is safe. We don't want someone falling through."

"That's too bad. I like to ice skate." Tara sighed. "Back in Stockton, the small lakes like this always froze over. You could even drive cars on them."

"That doesn't happen here." Caleb started walking. "But I promise to take you and Hailey to skate at the Frog Pond in Boston."

"That sounds like fun. Thank you." Tara trotted alongside Caleb as they made their way around the lake.

"Should we make that our next date?"

"So you're asking me for another date?"

"Yeah, if you'll go." Caleb's gaze didn't waver as he stared at her.

"Yes. That'll be fun. I know Hailey will love it. Thanks for including her."

Tara tried not to get too excited that he wanted to have another date. This one had been very low key, and she liked that. The next one would include Hailey, and that was even better. As a young widow with a child, she had dated too many men who weren't interested in sharing anything with her daughter.

Caleb stopped and put an arm around her shoulders again. He stood there for a moment without saying anything. Then he looked down at her. "This is the spot where my grandpa and my brother and I would come to fish and camp out on summer nights. This place holds a lot of good memories."

Caleb's statement brought her grandparents to mind. She wondered whether they missed just being grandparents, since they had raised her. For the first time in a long time, she thought of her mom and dad. What were they doing? Did they ever think about her? She didn't need to go there. Reflections about them would only make her sad and worried that if she got too close to Caleb, something would separate them just like she'd been separated from everyone else she had loved, except Hailey. And that had almost occurred.

"You're awfully quiet all of a sudden. Something wrong?"

Tara gave him a little smile, not wanting to tell him her worries, especially since they involved him. "Just taking in the beauty of the night and the snow."

"I only see one beauty." Caleb dusted the snow from her shoulders.

Her heart racing, she looked up at him. Snow had collected on the shoulders of his jacket, stocking cap, and the hair that stuck out from under the cap. Was he going to kiss her?

She didn't have to wait for an answer, as he leaned closer and gently brushed his lips against hers. She let him pull her closer as he deepened the kiss. The world faded away, and Tara didn't want the moment to end. She hadn't been kissed like this in forever.

When he ended the kiss, he stepped back. Tara stared up at him. What did she say after a kiss that made her pulse pound? Nothing.

He smiled. "One more good memory to add to this spot. It's one I'll take home with me."

"Me, too." Her voice came out in a whisper.

He took her hand. "We'd better head back to the house."

"Would you like to cap off the evening with some hot chocolate?"

"That sounds great."

Tara let Caleb lead her back to the house as they

traversed the slippery terrain. The whole time she relived that kiss. It would be hard to get off her mind.

When they reached the front steps, Caleb paused and looked at her. "You know this is the first snowfall, and it always calls for at least one snowball."

Tara gave him a sideways glance. "Are you challenging me to a snowball fight?"

"Would I do something like that?"

"I don't know. Would you?" Tara stealthily scooped a handful of snow off the porch railing and hid it behind her back. "I've got a pretty good aim."

"Not as good as mine."

"Should we see?" Tara lifted her arm and flung the snow she had compacted in her hand. It landed with perfect precision on the front of Caleb's jacket.

He grinned as he made a snowball. "This is war, and I'm going to win."

"Oh no, you're not." Tara ran behind a nearby tree and made herself another snowball.

"You think that tree is going to protect you?"

"Yeah. You can't hit me now."

With his arm raised, Caleb raced toward the tree. Tara moved around the tree in an effort to keep out of his range. Finally, he circled around to her backside and threw his snowball. It grazed off her right shoulder.

"Not a square hit," Tara shouted as she darted away.

"Don't get too cocky."

Tara made another snowball. "Me? Never."

Caleb charged toward her. "You're going down in defeat."

Tara darted away, laughing. Without warning, she slipped in the snow and landed on her back with a thud.

Caleb grinned down at her. She held her hands in front of her face. "Mercy."

Caleb rubbed his chin with his free hand while he held a snowball in the other. "You want mercy?"

"Please?"

Caleb held out his hand. "No mercy. There's a price to pay for not getting hit with a snowball."

"What's the price?"

"Take my hand and find out."

Tara weighed her options. Taking his hand meant surrender. Why was she even debating? This was only a silly game. She smiled as she held up her hand. "Okay. You win."

"I certainly do." He pulled her to her feet, then took her in his arms and kissed her again.

Tara returned his kiss. Surely the snow beneath her feet was melting. When the kiss ended, he held her in his arms for a few moments as the snow fell silently around them. She drank in the warmth and security of his embrace.

Hoping to put the brakes on her emotions, she stepped out of his arms. "Let's get that hot chocolate."

Caleb nodded as he put a hand to her back and guided her toward the house. "Tomorrow we can build a snowman with Hailey."

"She'll like that." Tara smiled up at him.

Was she falling in love too quickly again? She was afraid so, and she didn't know how to stop it from happening.

***

Hailey skipped across the snow-covered yard without a

care as she made her way toward Caleb's house for Thanksgiving dinner. "Mommy, hurry up. Everyone's waiting for us."

"I think you mean you can't wait to play with Sadie." Tara chuckled as she carried the pumpkin pie with care. She didn't want to fall down and wind up with her face planted in it.

"No. Everyone's there except us." Hailey pointed to the cars parked along the lane.

"You don't know that for sure."

Hailey made a disgusted face. "That doesn't matter. I want to see Caleb and Sadie."

"You see them almost every day."

"It would be so much better if we lived with Caleb and Sadie."

Hailey's statement shocked Tara.

Before she could gather her muddled thoughts, Hailey put her hands on her hips as she planted herself in front of Tara. "Are you and Caleb going to get married like Max and Heather?"

Tara nearly dropped the pie. To Hailey, living with Caleb meant having a father, something she'd never really known.

Balancing the pie in one hand, Tara hunkered down to eye level with Hailey. "Sweetie, we're not ready to make a decision like that."

"When will you be ready?"

How could she explain adult love to her child who just wanted a father? *Lord, give me wisdom.* Tara put her free hand on Hailey's shoulder. "I can't tell you that. It might never happen."

"Don't you love Caleb?" A little frown marred Hailey's

expression.

Tara wished Hailey would stop asking questions—questions that made her examine her own feelings. "We both love Caleb as a friend. That's not the same as the marrying kind of love."

"I think you should love him more, so we can have a real family." Hailey let her lower lip protrude as she turned and marched toward the house.

With a heavy heart, Tara trudged behind Hailey and prayed that her child wouldn't make such a pronouncement in front of Caleb or his family.

The Fitzpatrick clan was gathered at Caleb's house for Thanksgiving, and Hailey hadn't stopped talking about it since they'd been invited. On the other hand, Tara's stomach roiled at the thought of meeting Caleb's brother, aunts, uncles, and cousins, even more now that Hailey had made her desire for a family known. Would Caleb's family like her? She didn't know why she was worried. Tom and Sheila approved of her relationship with Caleb.

The past three weeks had flown by. True to his promise, Caleb had helped Hailey make a snowman, not only the day after the first snowfall, but after the two subsequent snows that had occurred over the next three weeks. The area looked like a real winter wonderland. He'd also taken both of them to the Boston Common Frog Pond, where Hailey had tried her hand at ice skating. With every passing day, Tara's efforts not to fall in love slowly slipped away like a slow glide on a skating rink. Had Hailey sensed the change? Is that what had prompted her growing wish for a family? Tara added that to all her other worries.

Thanksgiving with all the Fitzpatricks meant Caleb's house would be overflowing with people. She wasn't used to large holiday gatherings. During her childhood, Thanksgiving dinner usually consisted of her grandparents and her grandmother's widowed sister and maybe someone from Stockton who didn't have anyone to share the day with. Last year she'd had Thanksgiving with the women and children at the shelter, and the year before in the hospital with Hailey. Today she prayed for wisdom. She wanted to make a good impression.

When she reached Caleb's house, she stomped the snow off her boots as she made her way up the steps onto the front porch. Before she could knock, Caleb opened the door.

He grinned. "My two best girls."

"Caleb, Mommy made the best pumpkin pie."

"I'm sure she did." Caleb patted Hailey's head, then smiled at Tara. "You want me to take that into the kitchen?"

Observing the crowd gathered in the living room, Tara swallowed a lump in her throat. The thought of being left in a room full of strangers petrified her. "No, I'll take it and say hi to your mom."

"Sure. When you come back, I'll introduce you to everyone in here. Mom will introduce everyone in the kitchen." Caleb helped Hailey out of her coat. "Hailey can stay here with me and get to know my niece and nephew."

"Okay." Tara hurried away, expecting to see more strangers in the kitchen. She stepped through the doorway and surveyed the group of women gathered around the kitchen table in the middle of the room. "I've got the pumpkin pie. Where would you like me to put it?"

"Hello, Tara." Sheila hurried to Tara's side and held out her hands. "Looks delicious. I'll just stick it in the fridge."

"I can do that." Tara stepped toward the refrigerator.

"After you do, I want you to meet everyone."

Tara nodded and found a spot in the overcrowded refrigerator, then turned back to Sheila. "Wow! You've got a lot of food in there."

"Takes a lot to feed this crowd." Sheila propelled Tara toward the center of the room. "Hey, everyone. I'd like to introduce you to the young woman who is our receptionist. This is Tara Madsen. She and her daughter live in the in-law suite at our house."

Tara pasted a smile on her face and gave a little wave. What did it say about her relationship with Caleb that Sheila didn't mention it? Maybe she was leaving that for Caleb. No sense in reading anything into Sheila's introduction.

"Hi, everyone."

Sheila went around the room giving the names of the ladies there. Her two sisters, Sharon and Silvia. Her three sisters-in-law, Linda, Mary, and Janet, and a couple of their daughters. There were too many names to remember. Lastly, Sheila introduced her daughter-in-law Melissa, a pretty brunette with a ready smile that put Tara at ease for the moment.

As the ladies chatted, Tara learned that the families had traveled from as far away as North Carolina and as close as western Massachusetts. She couldn't help wondering whether she could fit into a big, happy family like this one.

Tara looked at Sheila. "Is there something I can do to help with the preparations?"

Before Sheila could answer, Caleb rushed into the kitchen and gently tugged on one of Tara's arms. "She's not helping with anything. She's coming with me."

That statement was followed by a lot of teasing and laughter on the part of the ladies. With a helpless expression, Tara turned to the group. "Is that okay?"

"Yes. Absolutely." Sheila waved them away with a wink. "We just like to tease. You'd better get used to it."

As Caleb ushered Tara back into the living room, he leaned close. "My mom's right. This family is big on teasing. So take what they say with a grain of salt. Keep your sense of humor handy."

"Okay." Tara tried to smile, a feeling of dread coming over her. She hoped she could get through this day. She should be grateful for having someone to share the holiday with. After all, it was Thanksgiving.

When they entered the room, the adults turned in Caleb and Tara's direction. One of the older men stepped toward them. "Who do we have here?"

Tara tried not to let the group intimidate her as Caleb nudged her farther into the room.

"This is Tara Madsen. She's our receptionist and lives over in the in-law suite. You've met her little girl, Hailey."

The man chuckled. "Yes, she's one livewire. Cute kid."

"She keeps me on my toes."

"That's a kid's job, you know." The man laughed again.

Caleb gestured toward the jovial man. "This jokester is my uncle Frank."

"It's nice to meet you, Tara." Frank winked at her. "Caleb always goes for the blondes."

Caleb didn't respond to the remark, but a muscle worked in his jaw, as if he was biting back a retort. He hadn't introduced her as his girlfriend. Did he not want his relatives to know they were dating, or was he trying to spare her more teasing? Caleb's old girlfriend was probably a blonde. Tara didn't know what to think about that either. She cautioned herself not to overthink. Caleb had warned her about the teasing. She guessed this was part of it.

In the next few minutes, Tara met the rest of the clan, including Caleb's other uncles—Danny, Sean, Michael, and Phil. At the end Caleb introduced her to his brother, Joshua.

Waggling his eyebrows, Joshua grinned. "I'm happy to finally meet the woman who is putting a smile on my big brother's face."

Tara didn't know how to respond to that either. Should she acknowledge their relationship, since Caleb hadn't mentioned it? This was getting more awkward by the minute.

Caleb put an arm around her shoulders and drew her close. "She does that for sure."

"I see that my kids are having a great time with your daughter and that puppy." Joshua motioned to the other side of the room.

Tara glanced over to where Hailey was helping the smaller children play with Sadie. "That pup is going to be spoiled by the end of the day."

"Sadie's already spoiled, thanks to your daughter." Caleb smiled down at Tara. "She sneaks treats to that dog all the time."

"I have a pretty good idea that she has some help from Sadie's owner." Tara gave him a look that dared him to deny it.

"Okay, you got me there."

The jovial mood continued as the men made sure the TV was tuned to the station with football. Tara wasn't sure why she was the only woman not in the kitchen. How could she excuse herself and not give the impression that she was trying to get away from Caleb? While she was trying to find a solution, Sheila rescued Tara and took her back into the kitchen.

Sheila shook her head. "I don't know what Caleb was thinking when he dragged you in there with all those guys."

"He just wanted me to meet everyone."

"That's fine, but he shouldn't have left you there." Sheila chuckled. "We have better things to talk about than football."

Feeling less intimidated, Tara joined the other women as they worked on the final preparations for the meal. When everything was ready, everyone bustled into the dining room and gathered around the table that had been stretched to its full length by adding every available leaf. It filled the entire room, with barely enough room for the chairs. Even the children who would sit at a smaller table set up in the living room on the other side of the foyer joined the adults for the Thanksgiving prayer as they joined hands in a big circle.

Tom motioned for quiet as he looked over the group. "It's our tradition that the host or hostess start the prayer. Then we'll go around the circle, and each person will give thanks for at least one thing as part of our Thanksgiving prayer. Then I will end the prayer."

Caleb stood next to Tara in the circle. He took her hand, and his smile warmed her heart. She was so thankful for his presence in her life, but she wasn't going to say that out loud in the group.

The deep timbre of Caleb's voice played across Tara's

heart as he started to pray. "Lord, we thank You for the people gathered here today. Thank You for the new friends who are here to share this day with us." Caleb squeezed her hand. "Please bless this group as we praise You for your many gifts."

As the prayers of thanksgiving went around the circle, Tara closed her eyes and thought about all the things besides Caleb that she was grateful for. The prayers of the others reminded her of more things for which she should be thankful.

When Hailey's turn came, she held tight to Tara's hand. "Dear God, I thank You most for my mommy. She takes care of me."

Her child's simple prayer brought tears to Tara's eyes. She wasn't sure how she could say her own prayer with a large lump sitting there clogging her throat. She swallowed hard. "Dear Lord, I want to thank You for bringing me here where doctors could help Hailey and bringing me friends here who could lend me support. Thank You for healing my little girl."

Tara fought back more tears and sniffed as Caleb squeezed her hand again. Tears threatened to roll down her cheeks. Without a free hand to wipe the tears away, they trickled down her face despite her efforts to blink them back.

Tom closed the prayer, giving thanks for the food. A collective amen sounded through the room as the circle dispersed, and people lined up to go through the buffet line assembled in the kitchen.

As Tara hung back and wiped her eyes, Caleb came to her side and put an arm around her shoulders. "Hailey's prayer was touching."

Tara smiled up at him as she let out a harsh breath and placed a hand over her heart. "I just got those tears under control. Don't you make me cry again!"

Caleb raised his eyebrows as he looked at her. "What can I do to make you laugh?"

Tara let out a chuckle. "You just did. Thanks."

"Any time you need a laugh, just call on me." He gave her a silly smile.

"I will." Tara proceeded through the food line and tapped Hailey on the shoulder. "Make sure you take something besides mashed potatoes and gravy."

Turning, Hailey frowned. "Oh, all right."

Caleb leaned over Tara's shoulder and whispered, "I had no idea she was so fond of mashed potatoes."

"You hadn't noticed that she's a picky eater?" Tara whispered back.

"No. I always thought she ate pretty good for a kid."

Tara sighed. "I guess she really does. I just want to make sure she has the proper nutrition to keep her healthy."

"I know you worry about her health." Caleb nodded. "That's why she was thankful that you take care of her."

Tara waved a hand in front of her face. "I don't know what's wrong with me today. I seem to be a little weepy. That's not me."

"But as my mother would say, 'It's good to let out your emotion.'"

Nodding, Tara wondered whether that had anything to do with the woman who had broken Caleb's heart. Did that old romance ever cross his mind now that they were dating? Tara pushed the question away. She shouldn't worry about Caleb's past love life, but she knew her relationship with Blake still colored her thoughts about falling in love again. But today was Thanksgiving—a day to be happy and grateful for the good things in her life. Caleb was exactly that—a good thing.

CHAPTER SIXTEEN

"Are you ready to go Christmas tree hunting? The first Saturday in December is my family's traditional tree-hunting day." Caleb grinned at Hailey, who was definitely dressed for the excursion in black boots that came almost up to her knees, bright-purple leggings, her pink-and-purple ski jacket, and a purple stocking cap.

Nodding, Hailey clapped her gloved hands. "I'm going to pick out the best tree ever. This will be the first Christmas tree that is just for mom and me. Are your mom and dad coming, too?"

Caleb shook his head. "Not this year. Both of them have a bad cold, so they're going to have me pick out a tree for them."

"That's too bad. I'll miss them."

"Me, too. Will you let me help decorate your tree?" Caleb eyed the little girl.

Hailey screwed up her face as she pretended to think hard. "If you're really good."

"I thought that's what your mom always says to you." Caleb raised his eyebrows. "Are you the one who's going to decide if I'm good?"

"Yeah." Hailey nodded as she pressed her lips together in a firm line as she appeared to think again. "You'll be good to put the stuff on the top of the tree."

Caleb laughed out loud. "At least I'll be good for something."

"What's so funny?" Placing a beret-like knit cap on her head, Tara emerged from the bedroom.

"Your daughter has plans for me."

"What would those be?" Tara glanced at Hailey, then back at Caleb.

"She says I can put the ornaments at the top of the tree."

"Definitely, and I'm hoping you'll help with the lights."

Caleb saluted. "At your service, ma'am."

Hailey giggled and grabbed Caleb's hand and pulled him toward the door. "Let's go."

"Okay. We'll get this show on the road." Caleb raced Hailey to his vehicle.

"I win." Hailey raised her hands in triumph as she skidded to a halt in the snow beside the SUV.

Caleb opened the door for Hailey. "You sure did. Now hop into your seat."

"You let an eight-year-old beat you?" Tara chuckled as she hurried to the passenger side.

"Sad, but true, but I love her energy."

"Me, too." Tara sighed. "It's such a contrast from the way she used to be. I just pray she'll continue to be healthy. She gets more like the precancer Hailey every day."

"I'm glad she continues to improve." Caleb hopped into the driver's seat.

"Why the trailer? Are you planning to buy a huge tree?" Tara buckled her seat belt.

"Not a big one, but we're going to purchase four. Two smaller ones for my place and the office, and we're going to get yours and one for my parents."

"Wow! I had no idea we were shopping for so many. That should make Hailey extra happy, right, Hailey?"

"Super. Duper!" Hailey called from the backseat.

Caleb glanced in the rearview mirror. "Everyone ready?"

"Ready." Hailey gave him a thumbs-up sign. "How long will it take us to get there?"

"Not long." Caleb leaned across the console and whispered, "Are we going to hear that famous phrase, *are we there yet?*"

Tara smiled. "Probably."

Caleb drove his SUV onto the main road. The week following Thanksgiving had brought warmer weather that had melted much of the snow cover. Still, plenty of the white stuff, which in many cases was now a dingy gray, remained piled on street corners and in the shady areas along the road and on the north side of many buildings.

Within minutes Hailey asked when they were going to get there. Caleb and Tara exchanged a knowing look. He couldn't help thinking this felt so much like family—a family he wanted. Even though he and Tara had been dating for only a month and had known each other for barely two months, it seemed much longer. Was he rushing their relationship? He couldn't shake the niggling doubt that resurfaced all too often.

Today he would seek to have fun and take in a lot of Christmas cheer, not let doom and gloom dominate his thinking. He wanted to give Tara and Hailey a festive day.

The sun peeked through the clouds as they arrived at the Christmas tree farm. The place was filled with families looking for the perfect trees. The big red barn with the festive decorations dominated the landscape.

"Do we get to cut our own?" Hailey pranced beside Caleb as they got out of the car.

"Not this time." Caleb motioned toward the rows of trees in the distance. "The cut-your-own trees here are too big, but they have plenty of already cut trees that we can search through. And they have hot chocolate."

"Yippee!" Hailey skipped ahead.

"I hope she doesn't get too excited, like the night of the pumpkin disaster." Tara's eyebrows knit in a little frown.

"I think she's learned her lesson, and she's not going to be hauling trees." Caleb put an arm around Tara's shoulders and pulled her close. "She'll be fine. If a kid can't get excited about Christmas, when can they get excited?"

"Yeah." Tara grimaced. "I should quit being a worrywart."

Caleb squeezed her shoulders. "You're the cutest worrywart I've ever known."

"And you make me smile."

"That's a good thing. Now let's find ourselves some trees."

Caleb took Tara's hand and forged ahead to the barn, where Hailey waited at the door. The interior was filled with trees of every shape and size. Hailey glanced around, wide eyed.

"We need to make a plan." Caleb looked at Tara. "What size tree do you want?"

"Probably about a six-footer."

"Okay. I need to get another six-footer for my parents and a little smaller tree for my place."

"What about the office?" Tara asked.

"A small one we can put on that table in the corner."

Caleb guided them toward the six-foot trees. "We'll pick yours out first."

"The selection here is amazing." Tara ran her hand down a branch. "These are so fresh."

"That's why I brought you here."

Caleb held up each tree while Tara and Hailey stepped back to look and give their opinions. They dismissed many until he wasn't sure they'd find one that suited both of them. He picked up another tree, without much hope of pleasing them.

"I want that one. It's the best." Hailey scurried toward the tree with her arms open wide.

"Hailey, what are you doing?" Tara called after her child.

Hailey stopped and turned around. "I was going to hug it."

Tara chuckled. "Please don't. You might hurt the branches."

Hailey made a disgusted face. "All right, but this is the tree I pick."

"So that's the one we'll get." Tara nodded. "I agree with your choice."

"Good. I thought you would never find one you liked." Caleb smiled and asked for a Sold sign to be placed on the tree.

During the next half hour they picked out the other three trees. They drank hot chocolate and looked at wreaths and bows. With every activity, thoughts of family collected in Caleb's mind. Contentment filled his heart. He couldn't ask for anything better. He only hoped Tara would eventually share his feelings, but he didn't want to push and scare her away.

He hoped it was a good sign that she was now looking at his mother's matchmaking with a smile. When it had first become obvious, Tara was right there with him, hoping to ignore it. He didn't want to worry about it. He should just enjoy the day and be happy that Tara and Hailey shared it with him.

On the drive home with the trees secured in the trailer, Hailey chattered on about how she was going to decorate the tree. After a little while, quiet came from the backseat. Caleb glanced in the rearview mirror. The exuberant Hailey slept as her head lolled to one side.

Caleb glanced at Tara. "Your daughter has dozed off. Will she be too tired to decorate your tree?"

"Probably not." Tara shook her head as she smiled. "She takes after me. I can remember how my grandparents always visited someone after church on Sunday. It would be a long day. On the drive home, I would always fall asleep. When we got home, I was suddenly wide awake."

"So you're saying she'll be ready to go when we get back?"

"Absolutely." Tara gave him a little frown. "She's not going to miss out on decorating a tree for anything."

When Caleb pulled his SUV to a stop in front of Tara's front door, Hailey's voice sounded from the back. "Are we there yet?"

Caleb laughed along with Tara as he turned to look at the little girl who had captured his heart. "We are. Are you wide awake now and ready to decorate a tree?"

Hailey nodded and yawned widely at the same time. "Do I get to put the angel on the top?"

Caleb opened his door. "I'll make sure you get to do that. Right now you can hop out and help your mom with the wreaths and bows while I take my parents' tree to them."

"Tell your mom and dad we hope they're better soon," Tara called after him.

Whistling a Christmas tune, Caleb hoisted the tree over his shoulder and trudged to his parents' front door. Tara and Hailey scooted by him as they headed for their end of the house. They disappeared inside just as his mother came to the door.

"Got your tree." Caleb laid the tree on the porch "How are you feeling?"

"Not much better." His mom held a tissue to her nose. "Thanks for getting the tree. You'd better not hang around here. We don't want you to get sick, too."

"Is the tree stand in the garage?"

His mom nodded. "I'll open it so you can go in. I'll put water in the stand after you're gone."

"Okay." Caleb waved. "After that I'm going over to Tara's."

Sheila sniffled. "Is there a chance that a wedding might be in our future?"

Caleb let out a sound that was half laugh and half groan. "Mom, don't make more of our relationship than you should. Please don't start looking too far ahead. It won't make things good for any of us."

"Okay. Have a good evening." She closed the door.

While he took care of his parents' tree, his mother's words paraded through his mind. She was making it more difficult not to think of the possibilities in his relationship with Tara. But he didn't want to long for something that might not come to pass. He had to temper his thoughts with reality. Their relationship was too new to be thinking in terms of marriage.

But was it?

His brother, Joshua, met his wife when he took a new job in North Carolina. A month later they were engaged, and six months later they married. Theirs was definitely a whirlwind romance. Why couldn't he have one like that?

Caleb carried Tara's tree toward her front door, where Hailey waited, her eyes bright with excitement.

"Hurry. Mommy has the stand ready."

"Hey, munchkin, this tree's heavy. There's no hurrying."

"But you're big and strong."

Caleb laughed at Hailey's comment as he brought the tree through the door. She knew how to butter him up. "Be sure to close the door behind me."

Tara appeared from the bedroom, her coat, hat, and boots gone. "The stand's right over here in front of the window. I'll help you put the tree in."

"Thanks." He held the tree up as she hunkered down and helped guide it.

With great efficiency, they had the tree in the stand in seconds. Tara straightened from the position where she had tightened the bolts in the stand and looked him in the eye. His heart hammered, and he swallowed hard. Her presence in his life made it so much better. Should he tell her how he felt?

"I'll get water, and you can start with the lights." Tara motioned toward the sofa, where she had strings of lights already laid out.

Hailey began gathering the ornaments she had made. She walked over to the tree and held one up. "I like this one. I'm going to put it on first."

"That's fine, but you have to wait until I have the lights on the tree." Caleb looked down at her.

Hailey smiled up at him, her eyes wide with excitement. But she waited patiently to place her ornament on the tree. Tara put on some Christmas music, and humming along, Caleb made quick work of placing the lights on the tree. Tara plugged them in and switched off the living room lamps.

The multicolored lights sparkling in the darkness reminded Caleb of how Tara brought a sparkle to his existence.

Hailey clapped her hands. "Isn't it beautiful?"

"It is." Tara gave her daughter a hug. "In a few minutes it will be even more beautiful when we put the garland and ornaments on it."

Next, Caleb and Tara worked together to place the silver garland on the tree. Then Hailey handed him her treasures to put at the top of the tree while she put hers near the bottom. Tara filled in the middle. Teamwork. Another reminder of how they fit together. Love overwhelmed his heart. His mother's words trickled through his brain. *Is there a chance that a wedding might be in our future?*

The question hung there like an ornament on the tree. It dangled in front of him and tempted him to grab it, but he needed to take the advice he'd given his mother. *Don't think too far ahead.*

"We're done!" Hailey raised her arms in a triumphal pose. "Except for the angel, and I get to do that."

Caleb stared down at her. "Would you like some help?"

She looked at him with the wide-eyed expression she'd had all day. "Are you going to lift me up?"

"If that's what you want."

Hailey nodded as Tara handed the angel to her child. "Okay."

As Hailey clutched the angel, Caleb lifted her high with no difficulty. She giggled as she reached out and placed the angel on the top of the tree and nestled it in place.

"Is it in place? Are you good to let down?" Caleb asked. "Yes."

Caleb set Hailey on the floor, and they both stepped back. "What do you think?"

"I think it's perfect."

"I do, too." Caleb gave her a high five.

"I have potato soup in the Crock-Pot, if you'd like to stay for dinner." Tara gave him a little smile, almost as if she was worried about extending the invitation. Was she still not completely comfortable around him? That idea didn't put his thoughts at ease.

Before he could answer, Hailey rushed up to him and grabbed his arm. She pulled him toward the kitchen. "He wants to stay, don't you?"

Caleb laughed. "Yeah, but first I have to take care of Sadie. She needs to be let out and fed."

Hailey put a hand to her mouth, then pulled it away. "Oh no. We forgot about Sadie."

"She's fine, but we do need to take care of her now." Caleb glanced at Tara. "Hailey and I can take care of the dog while you get dinner ready?"

Tara nodded. "That works. The soup will be on the table when you get back."

Caleb drove his SUV down the lane to his house. Hailey bounded to his front door as he took both small trees from the trailer and placed one over each of his shoulders. After they got inside, he placed the trees in the stands he had prepared earlier that morning. He let Sadie out of her kennel. Whining and wiggling, she licked Hailey's hands and face. They could barely get the leash snapped to her collar.

Caleb let Hailey take the dog outside to do her business as he poured water into the tree stands and filled Sadie's bowl with food. When the child and the dog scrambled back into his kitchen, Sadie barked at the trees.

"Why is she barking?" Hailey asked.

Caleb shrugged as he shook his head. "I don't know. She must think they are strangers who have invaded my house."

Hailey giggled. "She's your protector."

"Not yet. She's too little." Caleb chuckled. "I'm going to put her back in her kennel so she doesn't decide to attack them."

"That would be bad." Hailey frowned.

"Yes, it would." Caleb laughed again. "Now that we've taken care of Sadie, let's go back and get some of that soup."

When they returned, Tara had everything ready. Caleb said a blessing for the food, then took a big spoonful of the creamy liquid. "This is phenomenal."

Tara smile. "It's my grandma's recipe. I always loved it."

"Me, too." Hailey slurped her soup.

"Is that polite?" Tara frowned at Hailey.

Hailey shrugged. "It's good, but I'll try to eat quiet."

Caleb held back his laughter. He was sure Tara wouldn't appreciate it if he laughed at her daughter's antics. Sitting around the kitchen table with Tara and Hailey was just one more thing that made him want this as a permanent part of his life.

After dinner Caleb helped Tara clean up the kitchen while Hailey got ready for bed. When she was ready, she read a story to Caleb. Then he read a story to her. He stood beside Tara as Hailey prepared to say her prayers.

"Dear God, thank You for my Christmas tree and Sadie and my mom and Caleb. Help us to have a good Christmas and remember about Jesus being born. Amen."

"Amen. I liked your prayer." Tara gave Hailey a hug and kiss as she tucked her into bed.

Hailey reached up. "I have a hug for Caleb, too."

Caleb leaned over and hugged the little girl, his heart overflowing with emotions. There was nothing like a hug from a child. With each passing day, he could see himself as a daddy to this little girl, but would her mother agree?

Tara tiptoed out of the bedroom, and Caleb followed, leaving the door open just a crack. "Does she usually fall asleep right away?"

Tara turned to him, a thoughtful expression on her face. "Why do you ask?"

"I think she was asleep before we left the room."

"She's had a big day." Tara pressed her lips together and blinked as if she were holding back tears. "Thanks for making this a fun day for her."

"You're welcome, but no thanks needed. I enjoyed every minute. It was fun for me, too." Caleb took in Tara's smile while his heart raced. Surely this was the right time to confess his feelings. "I adore your little girl."

"And she adores you." Tara placed a hand over her heart.

Taking a deep breath, Caleb reached out and took her hand. "And I adore her mother. These last few weeks have been incredible."

Tara looked up at him, her eyes brimming with tears. "For me, too."

Caleb gathered her into his arms and held her close as her hair tickled his cheek. Where was this relationship going? Could he trust his heart? Could he trust her? Why were these questions still plaguing him even as he confessed his feelings? Tonight he would cast aside his doubts and not look back.

"What's this?" Caleb picked up a small bag from the end table by the couch.

Shaking her head, she held it up. "Mistletoe. Hailey insisted that we buy some."

"And why does she need mistletoe?" Caleb laughed.

"She thinks you should kiss me under the mistletoe because that's never happened to me." Tara made a face that was half grimace and half smile.

"We'll have to remedy that." He took the sprig of greenery with the little white berries clinging to it and held it over her head. With his other arm, he pulled her close and kissed her. She was everything he wanted in his life. He had to be brave enough to let her know, but not tonight. When the kiss ended, he stepped back. "Now you can say you've been kissed under the mistletoe."

She gave him a little smile, then stood on her tiptoes and kissed his cheek. "This has been a perfect day."

"It has." He motioned toward the door. "Guess I'd better be going."

"You don't have to leave yet, unless you want to."

"Do you want me to stay?"

She nodded. "I wouldn't have asked if I didn't. I want some time to talk, just the two of us."

"Okay." Caleb wasn't sure whether to be happy or concerned about her request. Her serious expression gave him an uneasy feeling. "You want to sit down?"

"Sure." She plopped onto the couch.

He joined her. "Is there something specific you wanted to talk about?"

She took a deep breath. "I...I don't want to be presumptuous, but..."

"But what?" he swallowed hard.

"I don't know how to say this."

Caleb took her hand. "Just tell me what's on your mind."

"I have Hailey to think about. She's the most important thing in my life, and I don't want to do anything to hurt her."

Caleb puzzled over her statement. "You're a wonderful mother. How could you hurt her?"

"By being involved with you."

Her words were a punch to his gut. Everything had seemed so perfect. She had said it was perfect, but now she was pulling the rug out from under him with this pronouncement. "What do you mean?"

"I'm sorry. This isn't coming out very well." She shook her head. "We haven't been dating very long, but I need to know where you think our relationship is headed, because Hailey's clearly attached to you already. You say you adore me, but I don't know what that means."

Caleb put an arm around her shoulders and drew her close. When she didn't pull away, he breathed a sigh of relief. "I'm thinking we are headed toward a serious relationship. I care a lot for you and Hailey. Is that what you wanted to know?"

Biting her lower lip, she nodded. "I guess I'm afraid of a new relationship. I rushed the first time with Blake, and I didn't want to do that again because there's more than just me to think about this time. I've got Hailey and her feelings to consider."

Caleb didn't say anything for a moment. Was she saying her marriage to Blake wasn't a good one? He wasn't sure he could ease her worries. Love had no guarantees. "I wish I could say everything was going to work out, but I can't. You lost your husband in a terrible accident. Someone I loved betrayed me. Neither of us saw these things coming."

A pained expression crossed Tara's beautiful face. "I'm not saying you should guarantee anything."

"Then are you telling me we shouldn't see each other anymore because it could hurt Hailey if things didn't work out?" Caleb hoped that wasn't the case.

"No, I just want you to know my worries and fears." Tara pulled her hair back with one hand and held it there, the pained expression still in place. "I don't know how to deal with these feelings."

"I don't know either." Caleb shook his head, hoping he could ease her fears enough that she didn't make a quick decision to end their relationship just when he was starting to figure out his own feelings. "Can we keep on dating?"

Closing her eyes, she let out a little sigh. Her eyes blinked open, uncertainty evident in them. "I want to, but I'm scared of doing the wrong thing."

Caleb took both of her hands in his. "Should we pray about this?"

"Aloud?"

"Yes. I'll pray, and you can, too, if you want to."

"You go." She bowed her head as they continued to hold hands.

Caleb let a moment of silence surround them as he also bowed his head. "Lord, thank You that we can talk to You about our concerns. Be with us in our relationship and help us to know the way forward. You know our hearts, and You know what is best for us. Lead us in that path and our decisions. Be with Hailey and continue to keep her cancer-free. In Jesus' name we pray. Amen."

Tara squeezed his hands as he finished praying. "Thank you."

Caleb looked up. "That was the problem with my previous relationship. I forgot to pray about it. I'm glad we did this."

Her eyes sparkling with unshed tears, Tara smiled at him. "You make me happy."

"Does this mean you're good to go on another date?" He took a deep breath. "I was thinking the three of us could go into Boston again to skate at the Frog Pond and look at Christmas lights."

Tara blinked rapidly and smiled. "Okay. Hailey will like that."

"Will you?"

She nodded. "I just want to proceed with caution."

"I understand." Caleb returned her smile, but he wasn't sure he was being completely truthful with himself. Did he understand? He didn't want to make a mistake this time, but he also had that same urgency to make this relationship work. He had to have the patience to follow God's plan and not his own.

"Good." Tara stood.

Caleb figured that was his signal to go. "Thanks for a

great day."

"Thanks for helping us decorate our tree." Tara walked with him to the door.

"You're welcome. It was my pleasure." Stepping outside, Caleb decided a good-night kiss was something for another time. "See you in the morning."

Tara waved as she closed the door. Caleb trudged back to his house along the lane. The yard light illuminated the patches of snow that still hadn't melted. He hunched into his coat as a gust of wind rattled the bare tree branches nearby. The cold blast made him think of how his life would be without Tara and Hailey in it. Despite his eagerness to make them a permanent part of his life, he had to take things at a measured pace. He wouldn't find that easy.

As he climbed the steps to his porch, he glanced up into the night sky sparkling with stars. God's handiwork. God was in charge. Caleb had to remember that. He'd prayed for God's guidance. Now he had to seek that very thing first and put his own wishes aside, no matter how painful. God's way was best—a hard principle to follow—but Caleb promised himself that he would, for his sake and Tara's.

Everything about today was perfect—at least, almost perfect until the end. He had no doubt he'd fallen in love with Tara Madsen. Could he convince her that her life was here and not in Montana? Could he convince her to make him part of her family? Could he convince her to trust him with her love?

CHAPTER SEVENTEEN

The following Saturday evening, Tara held one of Hailey's hands while Caleb held the other as they made their way out of the T station at Government Center in downtown Boston. The cacophony of noises coming from an orchestra warming up and the sounds of conversation, shouts, and laughter filled the cold evening air, creating a sense of anticipation.

"That was cool." Hailey looked up at Caleb. "I've never been on the subway before."

"I'm surprised, since you've lived in the area for a couple of years." Caleb looked over the top of Hailey's head at Tara.

"We always took cabs, or someone drove us to town. Most of the time Hailey was not well enough to take the T." Tara didn't want to remember that time—the time when she didn't know whether Hailey would ever be healthy again.

"Then I'm glad she could have that experience now." Caleb dropped his gaze to Hailey. "You're gonna love these Christmas lights. It's a spectacular show."

Hailey looked up at him, her eyes full of excitement as she skipped along between them. "I can hardly wait."

Jostling with the crowd, they made their way to Faneuil Hall. Joy radiated throughout the area. Tara thought she could almost reach out and touch it. She wished she'd kept her mouth shut and not said anything to Caleb regarding her uncertainties about their relationship. Even though they were on another date, she sensed a distance between them that wasn't there before. A week of self-examination had made her regret the things she'd told him, and she feared there was nothing she could do to change things now.

"Let's go this way. It doesn't seem quite so crowded." Caleb steered them toward the edge of the walkway.

"I see the tree." Hailey pointed ahead. "It almost reaches to the sky."

"Wait until you hear the music and see the tree all lit up." Caleb guided them toward the open plaza.

Frowning, Hailey gazed up a Tara. "Mommy, I don't think I can see everything cuz I'm short."

"I can solve that." Caleb picked up Hailey and hoisted her onto his shoulders.

Hailey giggled. "I'm really tall now, and I can see everything."

Tara touched Caleb's arm. "Are you going to be okay like that?"

Caleb nodded. "She'd not that heavy, and the show starts in a few minutes."

"Mommy, don't make him put me down."

Tara smiled indulgently at Hailey. "He's spoiling you, you know."

"That's okay." Hailey grinned down. "This is cool up here."

Caleb chuckled. "She has the best seat in the house."

Tara nodded. She wished she could back up time and undo last weekend's conversation. But they had prayed about things going forward. She should enjoy their time together and not worry about where it would lead. God would guide them. She had to believe that.

When the show started, lights danced everywhere as Christmas music filled the air. Awe painted Hailey's features. Her eyes filled with wonder, and Tara's thoughts overflowed with happiness for her child. The brightness and beauty of the colorful lights reminded Tara that being with Caleb brought brightness and beauty to her world.

He put an arm around her shoulders and pulled her closer as the lights blinked from tree to tree around the plaza. The beauty and the wonder of Christmas reflected on the faces of the people in the crowd. For a moment contentment settled in Tara's heart until she thought about Hailey's one wish for Christmas. A family.

Tara wondered why she ever thought a bicycle was the one thing that would make her daughter happy. The bicycle had been on layaway for weeks. Just a couple more payments and the bicycle would be hers, but the one thing Hailey wanted Tara couldn't give her. The thought robbed Tara of any joy, but she manufactured a smile and remembered the reason for celebrating Christmas. It wasn't all about the gifts for each other, but the greatest gift of all—the Savior who had come to earth to save the world from sin. That should bring her joy of the greatest kind.

When the show was over, Tara, Caleb, and Hailey wandered through the market area and looked at the carts where folks were selling all kinds of things. Caleb bought a bottle of hot sauce for his dad, a wind chime for his mom, and a toy for Hailey.

The gift bag swinging by her side, Hailey romped a few feet ahead as they made their way back to the T station.

Caleb leaned closer. "I hope I'm not in trouble for buying that little trinket for Hailey."

Tara let out a sigh. "You always ask after you've given her something."

"So I am in trouble."

Tara let out a halfhearted chuckle. "No, I appreciate everything you do for Hailey. Really."

"Okay. I'll take you at your word." Caleb took her hand and squeezed it. "You and Hailey are very important to me. I don't want to do anything to jeopardize our relationship."

"You haven't." Tara wanted to reassure Caleb. She needed to talk with him when Hailey wasn't around. She doubted that would happen tonight. It would be too late when they got home. He had to take care of Sadie, and she had to get Hailey into bed.

"So what's on your Christmas wish list?"

Tara glanced up at him. Was he trying to figure out what to get her for Christmas? She didn't want him to spend money on her, because she didn't have money to buy a gift for him. She planned to make something for everyone on her Christmas list. "I don't have a wish list."

"There must be something you'd like to have."

"Sure. There are lots of things, but I also know I don't have to have any of them."

"Just indulge me and name one thing."

"Okay. I saw the most beautiful nativity set in one of the stores in downtown Hawthorne. I would love to have it, but it's way too expensive—an extravagance. I like to go by the store and just look at it in the window." Tara sighed as she slipped her arm through Caleb's. She wanted to tell him not to even think once about buying it for her, but that would be presumptuous. So she kept her mouth shut.

On the way home, Hailey talked and talked about the Christmas lights. Tara thought for sure Hailey would fall asleep, but she kept up her nonstop chatter until Caleb pulled his car to a stop in front of his parents' house.

"Mommy, can I go with Caleb to walk Sadie?"

Tara should've anticipated that request. "Not tonight. It's late, and you have to get in bed. Tell Caleb thanks for taking us to Boston."

A pout forming on her face, Hailey mumbled her thanks.

Caleb nodded as he opened the car door. "You can help me tomorrow."

"Okay." Hailey hopped out of the car and raced to the steps.

"Thanks again for taking us to Boston. It was a fun day." Tara smiled at Caleb as he rounded the front of his SUV. There was so much she wanted to say to him, but she still didn't see this as a good time.

"You're welcome." He took one of her hands in his as she stopped on the bottom step. "I'm just thankful that you agreed to go."

Tara looked up at Hailey, who stood at the door. "Here's the key. Let yourself in, and go brush your teeth."

Hailey's bottom lip protruded again, but she took the key without saying a word. Breathing a sigh of relief when her child obediently went inside, Tara glanced up at Caleb. Could she at least say she was sorry for her attitude last weekend? "I'm just glad you offered to take us. I'm really sorry about what I said after our last outing. I—"

Caleb put a finger to her lips. "No need to apologize. I understand. It's good to be truthful, and it's not always easy to figure out relationships."

"Thank you for understanding." Tara wished she had the courage to tell Caleb how much he meant to her, but the words just wouldn't come. Maybe this was enough for now. "And thanks again for a great day, a great evening."

Caleb nodded as he took both of her hands and held them. "Would you like to ride with me to church in the morning?"

"Hailey has to be there early because of practice for the children's Christmas program."

"No problem." He smiled as he leaned a little closer.

"Sure." Returning his smile, Tara nodded, her heart thundering. Was he going to kiss her?

"Great. See you in the morning." He gave her a peck on the cheek, then rushed back to his vehicle.

Tara stood there as she watched him drive away. Despite his declaration that he understood her feelings, his hasty exit did little to change the distance he had created between them. Could she blame him? He probably had reservations, too. He said it was good to be truthful, but was she really being honest with herself and with him?

Being honest meant acknowledging that she had fallen in love with Caleb Fitzpatrick. That was why she was so worried about what would happen in the future.

This love wasn't the teenaged, gooey-eyed infatuation she'd had with Blake. This love came from respect, caring, and understanding. Yeah. There were still the heart-racing, pulse-pounding sensations when she was with Caleb, but it was so much more. He listened. He made her look on the positive side of life. He encouraged her. She had to grab on to this and never let go.

***

The children's Christmas program brought out smiles,

laughter, and applause from the congregation. Caleb squeezed Tara's hand as he took in the joy on her face. He wanted her to be happy more than anything, and he wanted to be the one to make her smile. Today was all about making some progress toward that goal.

After the closing prayer, as the congregation spilled from the pews, he leaned closer to Tara. "Hailey's quite a performer."

Tara turned to him, little smile curving her mouth. "I'm so glad she did well. She's come a long way from the little girl who faked being sick when we first moved to Hawthorne, and you have a lot to do with that."

"You know I think she's special."

"You spoil her."

"After all she's been through, she deserves to be spoiled a little."

"I suppose."

"Anyway, I'm glad I could have a part in her life." And yours. Not daring to express his feelings for Tara, Caleb's heart swelled with a myriad of emotions. He wanted to be there to see Hailey be the best she could be. To see her grow up. To see her make the most of life. He wanted to share that with Tara. She had recanted some of her worry about their relationship. He hoped that meant he could make his dream a reality.

"Me, too." Tara let out a contented sigh. "You make our life better."

"And you mine."

Before Tara could respond, Hailey bounded toward them. "Mommy, can I go home with Emily and Eric?"

Tara raised her eyebrows. "Whose idea was this?"

"All of us."

"And who is all of us?"

Hailey scrunched up her little face. "Me, Emily, and Eric."

"What about Emily and Eric's parents?" Tara glanced around the room.

Caleb nudged her. "Kurt and Molly are near the side door."

"Yes, I see them." Tara took Hailey's hand. "Let's go over there."

Before Tara had taken two steps, Molly turned and headed their way. Tara gave a little wave as they met in the center aisle. "Hailey's asking to go home with your kids. Is this something they cooked up on their own, or are you on board with this?"

Molly chuckled as she glanced down at Hailey. "They did cook it up, but I'm okay with it as long as you are."

"I'm good with that."

"Yippee!" Hailey pumped her fist above her head.

Molly chuckled again. "Eric and Emily are looking forward to it, and we'll drop Hailey at home on our way to my mother's. She invited us over for dinner."

"I appreciate you letting her come over." Tara tapped Hailey on the head. "Now you behave yourself."

"I will." Hailey gave her mother an annoyed look.

As Emily, Eric, and Hailey scrambled down the aisle toward the door, and Tara and Molly made the final arrangement for the afternoon, Caleb hoped this spelled an opportunity to have some alone time with Tara. He loved having Hailey with them, but he wanted a chance to talk to Tara and let her know how much he cared about her. He wanted to make sure she understood how important their relationship was to him.

Tara turned back to him. "Well, Hailey's set for the afternoon. Are you ready to go?"

"Looks like you're stuck with me for the afternoon." He gave her a lopsided grin.

"Does this mean Patriots football?"

Caleb laughed. "You mean you're not a fan?"

"I didn't say that."

"But you thought it." Caleb recalled the recent Sunday afternoons and several evenings when he'd watched football with his dad while Tara and his mother pretended an interest. Hailey loved to cheer and always asked a ton of questions about the game.

"You and my mom never pay attention to the game." Caleb raised his eyebrows as he waited for her to deny it.

Tara grimaced. "I just thought it wouldn't be polite to ignore your mom and watch the game."

"You're so sweet." Caleb put an arm around her shoulders and pulled her close. "Mom would've done her own thing if you'd wanted to watch."

"Are your mom and dad going to be watching the game today?"

"Nope. They have other plans." Caleb grinned. "It's just you and me. Can you handle that?"

Tara laughed. "You, me, and football. Sounds like a winner if you throw in some hot wings."

"Got it. I know just where to get the best wings." Everything Caleb had learned about Tara in the last few minutes made him realize that he didn't know as much about her as he thought he did.

With Hailey off to the Jansens and the aroma of hot wings filling his SUV, Caleb pulled to a stop in front of his house. His breath forming a cloud in the cold December air, he hurried to the door as Tara carried the bucket of wings. He unlocked the door, and she scurried inside.

"Put the wings on the coffee table, and I'll get celery and ranch dressing." He didn't wait for her response as he strode into the kitchen.

"A bachelor who has celery in his fridge?"

Caleb glanced up to find Tara standing in the doorway. "Is that a problem?"

She gave him an impish smile. "No. I'm just impressed with any man who has veggies in his fridge."

"I'm glad I can impress you with vegetables." He chuckled, wishing he could impress her with so much more.

"Can I get the drinks?"

"Sure. I'll take a cola. You can grab what you want." He hastily washed the celery and cut it into shorter pieces that he placed on a tray. After he poured dressing into a small bowl, he held them up. "Ready for some good food?"

"I'm starved." Tara carried a glass in each hand as she led the way into the living room.

With the food and plates on the coffee table and the TV tuned to the football pregame show, Caleb settled beside Tara on the couch. "So now that I know you like football, we'll have to make this a regular thing."

"I'd like that."

Her declaration made him believe that things could work out between them. She was giving him a chance to show her that she could trust their relationship. "I'll give thanks for the food, then we can settle in to watch the game."

Tara nodded, then bowed her head. Caleb reached over and took her hand before he started to pray. Her hand felt so right in his as he gave thanks for the food aloud and prayed silently that God would guide him to do and say the right things when it came to Tara. After he finished the prayer, he squeezed her hand, and she looked up at him with a smile. His heart did a little stutter-step, and he resisted the urge to kiss her. He couldn't push this relationship, or could he?

"I'm ready for the game to start." She picked up one of the small plates and helped herself to wings and celery.

"Me, too." Caleb turned up the volume just as the players took the field for the kickoff.

For the next few hours, they cheered for their team's good plays and groaned at the miscues while they devoured the wings. As they shared the fun time, Caleb wondered why he had allowed so many weeks to pass without doing something about his feelings for Tara.

The answer wasn't a mystery. His fear of repeating a mistake made him pull back every time she drew him in. Then discovering that she had fears of her own about their relationship put a further damper on his burgeoning feelings. Like the football players he was watching, could he rush through her defenses and scores some points with her?

When the game ended with an interception that sealed the victory for the Patriots, Caleb gave Tara a high five. "That was an exciting game!"

"And the right team won." Tara jumped up from the couch and started picking up the plates. "I'll take these to the kitchen."

Standing beside her, Caleb touched her arm. "You don't have to do that. You're a guest."

"Technically, yes, but I feel right at home here."

Caleb took the plates from her hands and put them back on the coffee table.

Tara frowned at him. "Why did you do that? Just because you consider me a guest doesn't mean I can't help clean up."

"I know." He took her hands in his. "But I have something I want to say."

She looked at him with a wide-eyed expression. "What?"

Caleb took a deep breath as he said a silent prayer for wisdom. "You said you have some reservations about our relationship, but I want you to know how much I care about you. And Hailey. I don't want to scare you away, but I can't undo the fact that I'm falling in love with you."

Her eyes grew wider. Her lips parted as if she wanted to say something, but she didn't say anything. She just stared at him. Caleb swallowed hard. Had he blown it entirely by bringing up his feelings again? Had he misinterpreted her actions? He gave her a lopsided smile. "I didn't mean to put you on the spot with my declaration."

Still staring at him, she extracted one of her hands and placed it over her heart. "You didn't put me on the spot."

"We've talked before, and you raised your concerns. What are your feelings now?" Caleb's pulse skyrocketed, and every nerve stood on end as he held his breath.

Tara dropped his other hand and stepped closer. She put her arms around his neck and gazed up at him. "I'm still trying to put my own emotions into place, but I'm glad you're willing to take a chance on me. I want to throw away all my qualms and take a chance on you, too."

Putting his arms around her waist, he pulled her closer. She lifted her face to his, and their lips met in a kiss sweeter than all the Christmas treats he'd consumed in recent weeks. The room faded away, along with everything else, except Tara. When the kiss ended, he held her close. Everything about this moment felt so right. He wanted to hang on to it and never let it go.

"Thank you for not giving up on me." Her words muffled into his chest.

Caleb wished he could guarantee a happy ending when it came to their feelings for each other. He had to have faith that she wouldn't break his heart like Amy had. Still holding her tight, he pushed the bad memory away. Why did the past still have to haunt him when he held his new love in his arms?

He'd told Tara that they didn't skate on the pond because the ice couldn't be trusted to hold anyone who dared to step out there. He couldn't shake the image of love as taking a step onto the ice of the nearby pond and hoping it didn't break.

CHAPTER EIGHTEEN

L ate on the following Friday afternoon, Tara worked alone in the office as she entered figures into a spreadsheet. Tom and Sheila had left to do some last-minute Christmas shopping. Caleb had taken Hailey home with him with the promise that he would make dinner for the three of them while Tara finished their fundraising paperwork.

Tara wanted to make sure this report was perfect for him so he could make a presentation about their fundraising efforts to a group that was interested in joining their cause. As she stared at the computer screen, the door to the office opened. A cold draft accompanied the sound of footsteps.

Tara looked up as a woman, wearing a tattered dark-gray wool coat with an equally tattered scarf wrapped around her neck, approached the desk.

"We're actually closed, but may I help you?"

"Hello, Tara."

Tara swallowed hard, her heart racing. Who was this woman? "How do you know my name?"

The woman let out a half sigh and half laugh as she pushed a strand of her graying light-brown hair from her cheek. "I don't know why I thought you'd recognize me."

"I don't." Her heart skittering, Tara wished Caleb was here. "Who are you, and what do you want with me?"

"I'm Sandra Clark, your mother."

Tara's stomach rolled over, and she swallowed hard again. She didn't know what to say as she searched the woman's face. "Why are you here? How did you find me?"

The woman's gaze dropped to the floor as she took a step closer to the desk. "Your grandmother told me where I could find you."

Tara's stomach continued to roil. "That still doesn't explain why you're here."

"I had to see you and my granddaughter before I die." The woman slowly lifted her head, sadness radiating from her eyes.

Tara frowned. "You're dying?"

"Yes. Please don't turn me away."

Tara wished some coherent thought would form in her brain. Her mother—the mother Tara had never really known—was dying. "Please explain."

"Thank you for listening to me." Sandra took another step toward Tara's desk. "May I pull up a chair?"

Tara's mind still spun as she pointed at the reception area. "Sure. Take one of those."

Sandra grabbed a chair and pulled it closer to the desk. She certainly didn't appear to be debilitated or on death's door. Why was she dying? Had Tara's grandparents known and not told her?

Silence hung over the room as Sandra sat and stared straight ahead, but her eyes didn't meet Tara's. She cleared her throat. "I know you're shocked to see me, and I know I have no rights where you are concerned, but I hope you'll—"

"Just give me an explanation."

Sandra took a deep breath. "My kidneys are failing."

"Don't they have a treatment for that?"

"Dialysis, but I'm not going to do that."

"Why?"

Sandra let out a long sigh as she shook her head. "I have numerous other health issues of my own making. I've lived a hard life and made a lot of bad choices. Prolonging my life for a couple more years, half the time hooked up to a machine, isn't what I want."

Tara didn't know how to respond. What did you say to someone who was dying, especially a mother who hadn't been part of her life? "So you're here to say good-bye?"

Silence once again filled the room. Sandra rubbed the back of her neck as she finally met Tara's gaze. "I want you to take me back to Montana."

While Sandra's request filtered through Tara's mind, she tried to shake away the shock. Did her mother not realize that Tara had a job here, Hailey's doctors here, and a life here? Or maybe the woman didn't know about any of that. How could she walk in here and make such a request of the child she had abandoned so many years ago?

"I don't see how I can do that. I have obligations here that I can't just walk away from."

Sandra closed her eyes, then lowered her head. "I know it's a lot to ask of you, because I haven't been the mother I should've been, but I'm begging you now to be my daughter."

Tara stared at the top of the other woman's head, the gray hair very evident there. Anger, bitterness, and hurt filled Tara's heart, but those weren't the feelings that God would want her to have. She closed her eyes and prayed. *Lord, You know I'm struggling to do the right thing here. Please help me to love as You would.*

Sandra looked up. "Tara, please don't turn me away. I'm asking for your forgiveness and mercy. I know it's a lot to ask of you, but—"

"But you're asking me anyway."

"I am." A tear trickled down Sandra's cheek. She wiped it away.

"We'll talk about it, but first I have a report to finish." Tara looked back at the monitor as she placed her fingers over the keyboard and started typing.

"Okay. I won't bother you."

Tara used all her powers of concentration to focus on her work. She wouldn't let her mother's presence serve as a distraction. Twenty minutes later, Tara printed off the file and closed out the program. She turned to find that Sandra had moved the chair back into the reception area, where she sat reading the Bible they kept on the table there.

Her heart full of sadness, Tara stood still as she stared at the woman who had given birth to her. Tara wondered what had happened to her father. What was her mother's relationship to the Lord? Dozens of other questions drifted through Tara's thoughts. The biggest one of all—what was she going to do with her mother?

"I'm finished, so I guess we can talk." Tara didn't really want to listen. She wanted to cover her ears so she didn't hear her mother's pleading, but she forced herself not to succumb to the childish gesture.

"Okay." Sandra motioned toward the chair on the other side of the small table where she laid the Bible she'd been reading. "Please sit here."

"Sure." Was the Bible reading a ruse? She wished she could walk out on her mother just like she had walked out years ago, but that would be wrong. *Turn the other cheek.*

Do good to those who hate you. Do not be overcome by evil, but overcome evil with good. Passages from the Bible rolled through her mind as she settled in the chair. God was reminding her of what was right. Yes, she had to do the loving thing whether she felt like it or not.

Sandra leaned forward. "I believe you were better off with your grandparents than with me and your father. The way we lived was no way to raise a child."

Tara couldn't bring herself to meet her mother's gaze. She was probably right. Being raised by Grandma and Grandpa Pitman was the best thing that could have happened. Still, a corner of Tara's heart harbored the hurt from the abandonment. Tara finally looked up. "Where's my father?"

Sandra took a deep breath and let it out slowly. "He died from a drug overdose six months ago, and I've been getting clean and sober ever since."

A sick sensation invaded Tara's thoughts as she digested her mother's words. Could she generate any sympathy for the man she had never really known? A faded photograph personified him. Tara's memories of him were as faded as the photograph. Her stomach curdled at the thought of the way her parents had lived. She should be grateful that they had left her with her grandparents.

"So you've been in rehab?"

"Not exactly." Her mother's face brightened. "I found peace through faith in Jesus—something that's been missing in my life since I took the wrong path many years ago."

Tara puzzled over her mother's statement. "So you got sober on your own?"

"No. With the help of God, my faith, and a caring

couple who work with addicts."

"Where have you been all this time?" Tara wasn't sure she even wanted to know, despite her mother's claims concerning her faith.

"Your father and I drifted and picked up odd jobs from town to town, mainly out on the West Coast." Sandra's face sobered. "We thought we were living free, but we were really in a prison of our own making—a prison that eventually killed your dad."

"How did you meet the people who helped you?"

"They came around numerous times to the area where we lived and talked about the love of Jesus. We just ignored them. But when your father died, they really helped me, and I saw the love of Jesus through them."

Tara had the inexplicable urge to reach across the table and take her mother's hand, but instead Tara clasped her hands in her lap. "I'm glad they were there to help you."

Sandra smiled, her eyes lighting up for the first time as she sat up a little taller. "Thank you for saying that. I wasn't sure how you'd receive me."

Tara frowned. "If you came from the West Coast, how did you get to Massachusetts?"

"I flew. Then took a cab here."

Tara stared at her mother and wondered how she'd gotten the money for a plane ticket and cab fare. "You could afford to fly?"

"The Cabreras gave me the ticket so I could see you."

"The Christian couple who taught you about Jesus?"

Sandra nodded. "They've done so much for me. I can only repay them by living out the last of my days at peace with God and my fellow man. That's why I want to make peace with you, and my parents, too."

"Why didn't you go to Montana first?"

"Because I don't know how much longer I have to live, and I had to see you and Hailey first."

Tara wondered how she was going to explain the appearance of her mother to Hailey. Tara had never talked about her parents, Hailey's grandparents. And how would Caleb react? "I've never mentioned you to Hailey. I don't know what she'll think."

Sadness spread across Sandra's face as she hung her head. "I understand why you didn't. I've made so many bad decisions in my life."

"I don't know how to tell my child that you're dying." Tara wished she could generate some sympathy for her mother, but hurt held Tara's heart captive. The more she thought about it, the more the situation made her uncomfortable. "And how were you getting to Montana? Do Grandma and Grandpa know you're planning to come there?"

"I mentioned that I was going out there after I met with you. I told them that I hoped you'd come with me."

"Did they tell you that we came to Boston because Hailey was treated for cancer?"

Sandra nodded. "I know that, but I thought you'd like to go back to Montana for Christmas, not permanently. I know your grandparents would love that."

A few months ago that had been Tara's plan. She'd wanted nothing more than to go back home, but Montana didn't seem much like home anymore. Caleb and their new budding relationship were here. Sheila and Tom, who had practically adopted her and Hailey, were here. Good friends like Heather, Max, Molly, and Kurt were here. Only her grandparents were back in Montana. "I can't afford to go back. I have a job here."

"Won't they understand if you take a little time off?"

Tara knew the Fitzpatricks would sympathize with her, but how much time off would she need? Was her mother expecting her to stay or just visit? And what a grim way to spend her time there—waiting for her mother to die.

"I can't stay if I go back to Montana."

"I'm only asking you to go for Christmas. I can get you and Hailey a plane ticket."

Tara narrowed her gaze. "How?"

"The same way I got mine. The Cabreras."

"I can't go begging to people I don't know." Tara lamented the way she always had to depend on someone else for the things she needed. It was bad enough to depend on people she knew. When would she ever get to stand on her own?

"They're glad to help. Their daughter has lots of airline miles to share."

Tara let out a heavy sigh as she picked up her coat and shrugged into it. "I can't make a decision now. Let me take you to my place."

Sandra got up. "Will I get to meet Hailey?"

"Yes, but I have to prepare her first." Tara escorted her mother to the door. "I have to lock up. Wait here, and I'll come around to the front and pick you up."

Sandra stepped out the front door, and Tara locked it. She checked to make sure everything was in order before she exited out the back. As she made her way to her car in the lot behind the building, her phone rang. She plucked it from her purse and stared at the screen. Caleb.

"Hi."

"Where are you? I thought you'd be here by now."

"Something came up." Tara squeezed the phone tight as she thought about this unpredictable situation. "I'll explain when I get there. I'm leaving now."

"Okay. See you in a few minutes. Dinner's ready."

"All right." Tara ended the call and wondered how she could bear to leave Caleb behind for a woman she hardly knew. Guilt assaulted Tara.

On the drive home, conversation came with difficulty. Gripping the steering wheel until her knuckles turned white, Tara didn't know what to say as helplessness welled up inside her. Somehow she would get through this evening. Somehow she would make the best of bad circumstances. Somehow she would find a solution to a complicated decision.

***

Car lights appeared on the lane as Caleb watched out the window for Tara. When her car didn't stop, he frowned. She'd told him that something had come up. Did that something mean she had to go home first?

"Was that Mommy's car?" Hailey tugged on his arm.

Nodding, Caleb looked down at Hailey. "She'll be here in a few minutes."

"I wish she'd hurry. I'm hungry."

Caleb headed toward the kitchen. A minute ago he was as hungry as Hailey, but the disquiet settling in his stomach took away his appetite. "Let's get the food on the table so we'll be ready to eat as soon as she gets here."

Hailey trotted after Caleb. "I'll get the salad from the refrigerator."

"And I'll get the baked ziti and garlic bread from the

oven."

Hailey carried the salad bowl that was almost as big as she was to the table. "We make a good team, don't we?"

"We do." Not only did Caleb think they made a good team, but they made a good family. He wanted to make that a reality. He already loved Hailey like a daughter. "Go ahead and sit down while I pour the drinks."

"May I have chocolate milk?" Hailey held up her glass.

"If I have chocolate syrup."

"You do. I saw it in the refrigerator."

"Will your mother say it's okay?"

Hailey shrugged. "She doesn't care."

Caleb wasn't sure about Hailey's statement, and he couldn't forget that Tara thought he was always spoiling the child. He opened the refrigerator and brought out the syrup that he liked on his ice cream. "You better not get me into trouble with your mom."

"You won't be in trouble." Hailey grinned. "I told you she doesn't care."

Just at that moment the back door opened, and Tara rushed through the laundry room and into the kitchen. "Sorry I'm so late."

"You said something came up. What was that?" Caleb held out a chair for Tara as she took off her coat.

"Let's talk about it after we eat, okay?"

"Sure." Caleb sat across the table from Tara, then looked at Hailey. "Would you like to pray?"

Hailey nodded and held out her hands, one to Tara and the other to Caleb. "Dear God, thank You for our food, and help Mommy to have a good rest after a long day. Thank You for Caleb, who made the food, and help Sadie be a good dog and me a good kid. Amen."

Caleb smiled at Tara as he squeezed her hand. *She's a jewel.* Mouthing the words, he handed Tara the salad.

She smiled, but the lines around her mouth told him it wasn't genuine. He sensed worry in her demeanor. What had happened at the office?

During dinner, Hailey chattered on about her plans for her time off from school. The more she talked, the more strained Tara's appearance became. Had Tara heard bad news about Hailey's health? He wished he could ask the question, but he couldn't do that with Hailey right there.

Tara picked up the plates to clear the table as she looked at him. "Is it okay if Hailey takes Sadie out for a little walk?"

"You mean by herself?"

"Yeah." Tara bit her lower lip.

"Sure." Caleb looked at Hailey. "You think you can manage that?"

"Yeah." Hailey grinned from ear to ear as she shrugged into her jacket. "I'll do a really good job."

"Stay right around the house, okay?" Tara handed Hailey the leash as Sadie wagged her tail.

"She knows when you get out the leash that she gets to go for a walk." Hailey snapped the leash onto Sadie's collar. "She's so smart."

"She sure is." Caleb opened the door for Hailey, then turned back to Tara as Hailey bounded down the back steps. "Now are you going to tell me what's going on?"

Tara nodded, a pained expression on her face. "I don't know what to do."

"What's the problem? Does it have to do with Hailey?" Caleb laid his hands on her shoulders as he looked her in the eyes. He couldn't miss the sadness there. "Just tell me."

She took a deep breath, and her eyes filled with tears. She blinked them back. "I…I had a visitor at the office just before I was ready to close up."

"Who?"

Tara took a shaky breath. "My mother."

Dread filled his heart. Dropping his hands from Tara's shoulders, Caleb didn't know what to say. She had only mentioned her parents once—the day he'd taken her to lunch when he'd first came back. "The mother you haven't seen in years?"

Tara nodded and pressed her lips together as if she was trying not to cry.

"Did she say why she was here?"

Tara nodded again, still pressing her lips together. Was she ever going to speak, or would he continually have to question her?

Finally she let out an exasperated sigh. "What am I going to say to Hailey? How can she understand?"

"I'd like to help, but I need more information, and you'd better hurry because Hailey won't be walking Sadie forever."

"You're right." A little smile tugged at Tara's mouth.

"So why is she here?"

"She wants me to take her back to Montana because she's dying. She's over at my place right now." Despite her earlier smile, a little sob escaped Tara's mouth. She covered it with a hand and looked at him with those big blue eyes.

Caleb's pulse pounded in his head. Amy's pleas to help her father played through Caleb's mind like the rerun of a bad movie. He shook the old images away. This was Tara, not Amy, and Tara needed his help. Could he give her the right advice? "Wow! I wish I could come up with an easy answer, but I don't see one. What did she tell you?"

Tara quickly recounted the conversation she'd had with her mother at the office. "Taking her back to Montana is the right thing to do, isn't it?"

Caleb wanted to shout no. *No. I don't want you to leave,* but Tara had always said she wanted to go back. How could he tell her she shouldn't take care of her dying mother or see the grandparents she hadn't seen in years? He couldn't. "You have to do what you think is best. What will you tell Hailey?"

Tara shook her head. "That's the tough part. Can she understand why she's never met her grandmother? Will she understand dying?"

Caleb pulled Tara into his arms and just held her for a moment. He feared she would get back to Montana and never come back, but he had to let her go. "Just tell her the truth. She's already dealt with a lot in her young life. She's a tough little girl, just like her mother."

Tara let out another little sob as she tightened her hold around his waist. "I'm not feeling so tough right now."

"You're tougher than you think." Caleb wanted to encourage her to step out and do what she had to do, but he was having trouble following that advice.

She gazed up at him. "Thanks for saying that. Your belief in me means a lot."

He wished he could believe in himself and that somehow, despite this latest problem, they would find a way to make their relationship work. He had to trust that if he urged her to go that she would eventually come back to him.

Before either of them could say something else, Hailey

bounded into the house, with Sadie straining at the leash. "We had a fun walk."

"Good. Did Sadie do her business?" Caleb asked.

Hailey nodded. "Mommy, why is there a light on at our place?"

Caleb glanced at Tara. Here was the moment of truth. He said a silent prayer for Tara as she motioned for Hailey to sit at the kitchen table.

"I've got something to tell you."

"What?" Hailey sat in the chair at the end of the table.

Tara sat beside Hailey and took her hand. "We have a visitor. That's why the light's on."

"So why isn't the visitor here with us?"

Tara let out a harsh breath. "Because I wanted to tell you about her before you meet her."

"Who is she?"

"Your grandmother."

Hailey frowned. "But I know Grandma Pitman. Why can't I see her?"

"The visitor is your Grandma Clark. She's my mother."

Confusion colored Hailey's expression as she wrinkled her nose. "But I thought you didn't have a mother."

A little smile escaped as Tara gazed at her daughter. "Everyone has a mother. Mine just didn't live with me when I grew up."

"Why?"

"Because...because she had some problems and couldn't be the kind of parent—mother—that I needed, so she left me with Grandma and Grandpa Pitman. She knew they would take good care of me."

"Why is she here now?"

Tara pressed her lips together, as if she was trying to

formulate an answer. "She's very sick, and she needs someone to take care of her. She wants to meet you and have us take her back to Montana for Christmas. Would you like that?"

Hailey knit her brow and shrugged as she looked back and forth between Tara and Caleb. "I don't know. I'd like to see Grandma and Grandpa Pitman, but I'll miss Mr. Fitz and Sadie."

Tara patted Hailey's shoulder. "I know. I'll miss them, too, but you'll get to know a new grandma. So that'll be nice."

"I suppose." Hailey shrugged.

Caleb took in the conversation between Tara and Hailey as he leaned against the doorjamb. He smiled at her when she looked his way for reassurance. She'd done a good job, but she hadn't closed the deal with Hailey. He wasn't sure what he wanted to happen. He was torn between keeping her here and letting her care for her mother.

"It's time that you met your other grandmother." Taking Hailey's hand, Tara stood. She looked at Caleb. "Would you like to come with us?"

The question struck Caleb like a hard-thrown snowball. It hit him with a splat—right in the heart. Was this Tara's way of including him because she cared about him, or was she using him as a buffer? Maybe she just needed his support. No matter her reason, he shouldn't turn down her invitation, even though everything inside him wanted to be far away from this woman who had the potential to take Tara away from him. "Okay. I'll get my coat."

Moments later, Caleb trudged through the yard as he held Hailey's hand. In any other circumstances, the three of them together would have felt like family, but this felt more like a death march. Loving Tara meant giving her whatever reassurance she needed.

CHAPTER NINETEEN

Gripping Hailey's hand, Tara climbed the steps leading to her front door. The trio's silence on the way from Caleb's house did little to ease Tara's mind. Even Hailey was unusually subdued.

The light shining out the window reminded Tara that God's light would lead them in the right direction. She had to hold on to that thought.

After Tara opened the door and stepped inside, she stopped for a moment. How was she going to address her mother, who appeared to be sleeping in the nearby chair?

Hailey squeezed Tara's hand and looked up at her. "Mommy, is she okay?"

"I think she's just sleeping." Tara prayed that was the case as she stepped closer to the chair and put a hand on her mother's shoulder. "Sandra?"

The older woman blinked her eyes and gazed up at Tara. "Oh, I didn't mean to doze off."

"You're probably tired from your travels." Tara gave her mother a tentative smile, then looked at Hailey. "This is Hailey."

Smiling, Sandra sat forward and held out a hand to the child. "Hi, Hailey. I'm your grandma."

Hailey shuffled forward a couple of inches, her gaze lowered. "Hello."

"You don't know me, but I'd like to get acquainted."

Sandra lowered her head as she looked at the little girl. "Do you think we can do that?"

Hailey looked up. "Mommy says you're really sick and you need our help. You want us to go to Montana with you. Is that right?"

Sandra nodded. "Would you like to help me?"

Hailey shrugged. "A doctor would be better."

"Yes, that's true, but just being with you would help me feel better."

Hailey looked over her shoulder at Tara. Her heart twisted as she observed her daughter's indecision—the same indecision she was feeling. Tara stepped forward and put her hand on Hailey's shoulder. "We don't have to decide anything tonight. Let's spend some time together. We'll think about the future tomorrow."

Sandra's shoulders slumped, and her eyes filled with sadness as she nodded. "Okay."

"I'd like you to meet my friend Caleb. He lives down the lane, and his parents are my bosses and own this house. They've been kind enough to let me live here." Tara motioned toward Caleb, who still stood by the door. "Caleb, this is my mother, Sandra Clark."

He moved closer to the chair and extended his hand as Sandra started to stand. "No need to get up. It's nice to meet you, ma'am. I hope you enjoy your stay."

"Thank you, young man." Sandra's eyes brightened as she smiled at Caleb.

"Did you find the food I mentioned?" Tara asked.

"I did. It was very good. Thank you," Sandra replied.

Tara's stomach curdled at the stilted conversation. What could she expect when her mother was a stranger? The awkward exchange morphed into an even more uncomfortable silence. Stuffing her hands into her coat pockets, Tara shifted from foot to foot. How could she go back to Montana with this woman when she couldn't even converse with her?

"What are your plans, Ms. Clark?" Caleb asked.

Sandra looked at Caleb with relief on her face. "I'm going back to Montana to stay with my parents. They raised Tara."

Caleb nodded. "Yes, Tara told me about her grandparents."

"Has she told you why I'm here?"

"She has."

Tara listened to the conversation, grateful that Caleb could talk to her mother. Tara glanced over at Hailey, who stared at her grandmother. "Hailey, you should get ready for bed."

"But it's early. I don't want to go to bed."

Sandra laughed. Everyone turned in her direction. She laughed again, and she turned toward Tara. "You used to say the same thing."

"You remember?" Tara barely remembered being with her parents. When she was a kid, she'd always wondered why they hadn't loved her enough to take her with them. Now knowing her parents' history, she understood that leaving her with her grandparents had been an act of love.

Sadness returned to Sandra's eyes. "Yes, I remember everything. It breaks my heart that I wasn't there to see you grow up—that I wasn't the parent I should've been."

Tara couldn't generate any sympathy for her mother. She'd made the decision to abandon her child. Tara wondered whether she would ever understand. Having no kindly response, Tara turned her attention back to Hailey.

"You don't have to go to bed. Just get ready."

"Okay." Hailey trotted off to her room.

"Thank you for letting me meet my granddaughter." Tears welled in Sandra's eyes.

"You're welcome." Tara wished she could make a better response, but her heart harbored a dark place where her mother was concerned.

"Thanks for introducing me to your mom, Tara. After Hailey comes back out, I'll say good night."

Tara turned at the sound of Caleb's voice. She'd almost forgotten he was here. How could she have let that happen? Her mind was in a jumble. "Caleb, I have something in the kitchen that I want to give you."

"Sure." He led the way into the kitchen, then turned to face her. "What do you have for me?"

Tara reached into a nearby cupboard and brought out a tin. "Cookies that Hailey and I made for you."

"Thanks." Smiling, Caleb took the tin. "And Hailey didn't tell me about this."

"Well, it was supposed to be a surprise that we were going to give you for Christmas, but we probably won't be here. Besides, I needed an excuse to talk to you alone, away from my mother."

"And why is that?"

"What am I supposed to do with her?"

"I can't tell you what to do, but it kind of sounds like you already have plans." He held up the tin.

Tara put a fist in front of her mouth as she blinked back tears. "Not necessarily. I wish you could give me the answer."

"It's a decision that you have to make, not me. Pray about it."

Tara dropped her hand and straightened her shoulders. "And how am I supposed to know the answer?"

Caleb shook his head. "It's not always easy to know the answer even when we pray, but let God guide you."

"What will your parents say when I ask for time off?"

"Maybe their response will give you an answer."

"Mommy, I'm ready." Sporting her pink-footed pajamas, Hailey bounded into the room and stopped short when she spied Caleb. "Mommy, how come you gave Caleb the cookies?"

"If we go to Montana, we won't be here for Christmas."

"But you should've waited for me." Hailey stuck out her lower lip.

Tara nodded. "I should have. I'm sorry I didn't wait for you."

Caleb set the cookie tin on the table and picked up Hailey. "Thank you for the cookies. Do you want me to save them until Christmas, or can I eat them now?"

Hailey giggled. "You can eat them whenever you want. They're good."

"Since you made them, I'm sure they're extra good." Caleb set her back on the floor. "Now it's time for me to get home."

"Will I see you tomorrow?" Hailey asked.

"Absolutely. You have to help me with Sadie."

"I'll be ready." Hailey tilted her head. "Do you suppose my grandma could help us?"

Caleb raised his eyebrows as he glanced at Tara, then back at Hailey. "If she'd like to."

"I think she will." Hailey looked up at Tara. "Mommy, she said she wants to read me a story. Is that okay?"

Tara nodded as Hailey raced back to the living room.

Caleb stepped closer and put an arm around Tara's shoulders. "I think you might have your answer right there."

"I suppose so." Tara tried to smile as she turned her head to look up at him. Why couldn't she be happier about Hailey's readiness to accept her grandmother? And why was Caleb so eager to join Sandra's side? Didn't he care if Tara left? What had happened to his declaration of love? Maybe she put more stock in their relationship than he did. The whole situation made her want to cry, but instead, she would put on a happy face and do her duty even though her heart wasn't in it.

Caleb guided Tara toward the living room. "You can talk to my parents tomorrow about having some time off."

"Sure." Tara stepped into the living room and found Hailey snuggled up on Sandra's lap while she read a story. Hailey's rapt attention should warm Tara's heart, but that cold, icy place didn't even begin to thaw. Could God change her heart?

***

A week later, Tara stood in her grandparents' living room. A fire crackled in the fireplace, making the room toasty warm and inviting. Multicolored lights danced and sparkled on their Christmas tree, and their faces shone with happiness as they hugged Hailey and Sandra and motioned for Tara to join the group hug.

Reluctantly, Tara moved forward and extended her arms into the group. This reunion with her grandparents had been her goal for the past year. She couldn't let her mother's presence strip her of any joy. Her emotions were on edge about her mother's reappearance, and she wasn't prepared to examine them too closely. She had to embrace this experience, not let it bring her down.

But being here in Montana confirmed the things she'd been feeling back in Massachusetts. Even though she would enjoy being with her grandparents for the holiday, Montana wasn't her home anymore. She missed Caleb, but he didn't seem to care that she'd left. He'd encouraged it, as if it didn't bother him that she might not come back. As she'd left, he didn't say one word about wanting her to return.

Everything about this trip made Tara sad except the chance to see her grandparents again. She had to make the most of this time with them. Would her mother expect Tara to stay after Christmas was over? That was what everyone here would expect. Guilt ate at her heart like a ravenous monster ready to devour every ounce of Christmas cheer. She couldn't let that happen, at least for Hailey's sake.

Tara knew she should look at her circumstances in the light of God's will. Every reason for her to make this trip had fallen into place. Hailey's doctors had cleared her to go back to Montana permanently, if they chose to do so. The Fitzpatricks had given their blessing for Tara to spend as much time as she needed with her mother. They had expressed their disappointment that she wouldn't be there for Christmas, but Caleb had not. Tara tried not to think about her own disappointment.

Hailey extracted herself from the group and ran over to the tree. "Mommy, look at the cool lights and this ornament. I made this one."

Glad for an excuse to end the group hug, Tara joined Hailey and gazed down at the little red apple ornament with Hailey's name on it. "You made that the Christmas before you got sick."

"And that one." Hailey pointed to a snowman hanging on an upper branch that she couldn't reach.

Tara lightly touched the misshapen snowman that she'd helped Hailey make out of cookie dough. The glaze and sparkles made it shine on the tree. Memories—hundreds of memories—flooded Tara's mind as she thought about all the Christmases she'd shared with Grandma and Grandpa Pitman, then Blake and Hailey. But Tara had no recall of a single Christmas with her parents. What kind of Christmas memories did her mother have? Tara wondered whether she really wanted to know.

"I've got hot chocolate and cookies waiting for you." Grandma Pitman took Hailey's hand. "Would you like to eat them in the kitchen or here by the fireplace?"

"By the fireplace. I always liked that best." Hailey sat on the chair with the worn, brown tweed upholstery.

"Wonderful. I'll bring it all in here." Grandma Pitman looked Tara's way. "Will you help me bring everything into the living room?"

"Sure." Tara followed her grandmother into the kitchen.

Her grandmother placed frosted sugar cookies of various shapes and sizes on a red-and-white Christmas plate edged with green trim. As she put the mugs of hot chocolate on a tray, she turned to Tara. "I'm sensing that you're troubled about your mother."

Tara stared at her grandmother's snowy-white hair that sat like a puffy cloud around her wrinkled face—a face that Tara loved. She nodded as she placed a hand on her chest. "My heart hurts."

Her grandmother stepped closer and gave Tara a hug.

"It'll be all right. Give your mother a chance. She wants to make things right and reconnect with her family."

"I know I should." Tara hugged her grandmother tight. "I'm so glad to see you, but I had to leave the bike I bought for Hailey back in Massachusetts. I don't have anything to give her now."

"Don't worry. It'll all work out." Grandma stepped back and patted Tara's arm. "Just take it a day at a time. I know that's clichéd, but you really need to do that. Let God guide you."

Tara smiled. Yeah, that was what everyone kept telling her. She didn't want to believe that her faith couldn't stand up to this test. She had to love as God loved her. "Pray for me, Grandma."

"I always do." Grandma picked up the tray of mugs. "Now let's have some goodies."

As Tara stepped into the living room, she found Hailey laughing with Sandra as they looked over more ornaments on the tree. Tara's heart twisted at the sight. At that moment, Tara realized she'd been harboring bitterness against her parents for years. Despite her supposed faith, she had been unforgiving.

She had to find a way to forgive and welcome her mother into her heart and life. Hailey had already formed an attachment to the woman who had abandoned Tara. Maybe the best way to see her mother was through Hailey's eyes—the eyes of an innocent granddaughter.

"Refreshments are ready." Tara set the plate of cookies on the coffee table.

Hailey scrambled back to the big tweed chair. "Grandma Sandy, come sit with me."

Sandra laughed. "You think we can both fit in that

chair?"

Hailey nodded. "We're both skinny."

Sandra let out a laugh that filled the room. "That's as good a reason as any to share that chair with you."

Hailey giggled as Sandra snuggled down in the chair beside her granddaughter. Tara gave each of them a mug of hot chocolate and held out the plate of cookies to them. As her mother took a cookie, she smiled, thankfulness in her eyes. Tara swallowed the lump that rose in her throat and promised herself that she would make this time with her mother work.

An uncertain future loomed in front of Tara, but she had to trust God to see her through. That was what she had done all through Hailey's illness. Sometimes she had doubted that God was there, but she knew now that faith was about trusting God whether things were going well or not. She would make peace with her mother and love her in the time she had left.

***

Silence surrounded Caleb as huge flakes of snow floated down from the darkened sky. He walked toward the lake, with Sadie trotting ahead of him down the lane. He missed Tara. He hadn't heard from her since she'd left. Once again he'd come in second place when it came to love.

Sure. He'd encouraged her to go. He wanted to give her space to find peace with her mother, but he feared that doing so had shoved her away. He thought he'd done the right thing when he'd insisted Tara go to Montana for Christmas. He'd made her choice easy, and she'd chosen her mother and Montana instead of him.

Why would he have expected anything else? He was selfish to think she would choose otherwise. Maybe it was that whole betrayal thing with Amy slipping back into his thoughts. It was time to forgive her and move on. And Tara had never betrayed him. He knew exactly why she had left. He should have told Tara that he'd be waiting for her when she got back, but he'd stood there mute as he'd helped her unload their suitcases at the airport.

Again fear of rejection and hurt had prompted him to keep his feelings to himself. He'd convinced himself that letting her go was the best thing. She would come back if and when she wanted. Second-guessing his decision didn't help, so he had to live with the consequences of his actions.

As he came back around the lake toward his parents' house, the Christmas lights on the bushes and the eaves twinkled in the darkness. Light streamed from their windows, but the darkness coming from the other end of the house where Tara had lived reminded him that she was gone.

His mother had asked him to stop by, but he wasn't looking forward to conversation with his parents. He was sure they would bring up Tara. Caleb picked Sadie up and stomped the snow off his boots as he rang the doorbell. Sadie licked his face as he waited. At least somebody loved him.

"Hey, Caleb." His mother opened the door. "You didn't have to ring the bell."

"I just wanted to be sure it's okay that I bring Sadie inside."

"Sure." Sheila rubbed Sadie's head, and she wagged her tail.

Caleb set the dog on the floor, and she sniffed her way across the room. "So what did you want to talk to me about?"

"I know it's late, but I wanted to send these out to Tara and Hailey. I think we can do an overnight shipment. I was hoping you could load them up in your car and take them to the nearest shipping center." Sheila motioned toward the stack of boxes near the couch. "And I've picked up Hailey's bike from layaway because Tara had it all paid for."

"Did she tell you to get it?" Caleb couldn't help thinking that might be a sign she was coming back.

"No. I'm sure she didn't have time to think about that. Besides, the bike's still in the box, ready for shipment. It's in the garage."

"I'm sure Hailey will be very excited. I'll get right on it. The shipping place should still be open." Caleb let out a sigh he as picked up the boxes. "I'll get these small ones and drive the SUV over to get the bike."

"Thanks, dear."

"No thanks needed, Mom. You're the wise one for thinking of this." Caleb kissed his mom on the cheek. "Will you keep Sadie till I get back?"

"Sure." Sheila opened the door for him. "When you come back, plan on having dinner with your dad and me. He's still at the office."

As Caleb drove to the shipping station, he thought about what his mother had done. This was just like her and his dad. They always knew what people needed and didn't hesitate to help them. He should've thought to send these. Instead, he was immersed in his own doubts and fears—another misstep on his part.

Still berating himself, he replayed his last conversation with Tara. Had she been overwhelmed dealing with her mother? Would Tara welcome hearing from him after he had practically shoved her away? He debated the wisdom of giving her a call. The pros and cons marched through his mind like soldiers confronting each other in battle. Victory came to none of them.

When he finally returned to his parents' house, he was no closer to a decision than when he had left. He joined his mom and dad at the table, and Sadie lay on the floor near his chair. His mother placed a big bowl of vegetable soup in front of him, along with a crusty loaf of bread. The meal reminded him of the day he'd taken Tara to lunch at the Main Street Café. If he was honest with himself, everything reminded him of Tara.

After Caleb's dad gave thanks for the food, Caleb slathered butter on a piece of bread, then took a big bite. "Bread's great, Mom."

"Thanks, dear." Sheila eyed him. "You should call Tara and let her know the packages are on the way."

"Okay." His mother's suggestion was surely an answer to his quandary. She had no idea that he'd had no contact with Tara since she'd left. He would quit being a coward and make that call. "I'll do it after I get home. There's a two-hour time difference."

His mother smiled. "I understand. You want your privacy when you talk to her. Say hi for us."

"I will."

After the meal, Caleb said good night to his parents and headed home with Sadie in the lead. The snow had stopped falling. Caleb's footsteps sounded loud in the peaceful surroundings. The quiet left him alone with his thoughts—

thoughts about Tara. He could see her smiling face, hear her laughter, and feel the warmth of her caring nature. He loved her, and he needed to hear her voice.

Sadie bounded up the steps and waited for him to open the door. Once inside, he unleased her as he turned on the light. He shrugged out of his coat, letting it fall onto the couch. He fished his phone from his pocket and stood near the window. He gazed out on the snow-covered landscape, then down at the phone as he tapped her name.

The phone rang. His heart raced. He held his breath. No one answered. Just as he was about to end the call, a breathy hello sounded in his ear. "Tara?"

"No, this is her mother."

Caleb wondered why Sandra was answering Tara's phone. "Hello, Sandra. This is Caleb Fitzpatrick. Could I please speak with Tara?"

"I'm sorry, but Tara and Hailey have gone Christmas caroling with a church group."

"Oh, okay. I was calling to let her know that we sent her some packages. Please let her know that I called."

"Okay, I will."

"Thanks, and Merry Christmas." Caleb poked at the phone to end the call. He glanced down at Sadie, who was looking up at him with sad eyes. "Yeah, girl, it's lonely without Tara and Hailey."

The dog thumped her tail against the floor as if to signal her agreement. Caleb plopped onto the couch and stretched his legs out in front of him as he leaned back and laced his fingers behind his head. Now that he had made the initial contact, would Tara call back? Had she already settled back into her life in Montana and forgotten about him?

Sitting forward, he patted Sadie on the head as she

nudged her head against his leg. He pushed away the pessimistic thoughts. Tara was only enjoying the time she had with her grandparents. This was a holiday vacation, not a permanent thing. He tried to convince himself of that. Things would work out as God intended. But Caleb couldn't rid his thoughts of that one doubt that God's plans for him didn't include Tara.

CHAPTER TWENTY

The temperature hovered just below freezing, and Tara's breath created a cloud as she sang the familiar Christmas song. The wind rattled the bare tree branches, and she snuggled down inside her hooded coat to ward off the chill. Tara glanced down at Hailey, who didn't seem to be bothered by the biting cold. She probably remembered that hot chocolate was in her future.

Hailey's sweet little voice joined the chorus, and Tara's heart overflowed with love for her child. Tara wished she could generate the same feelings for her mother. Some forgiveness for her mother had gained a foothold in her heart. That gave Tara a little peace.

Tara hadn't realized the dire condition of her mother's health until they arrived in Montana and discovered that her grandparents had contacted hospice care. During the week they'd been in Montana, Sandra's health had deteriorated day by day. Tonight Tara had left her phone with her mother in case she needed immediate help and wouldn't be able to get to the landline that her grandparents had in their home.

In such a short time, Hailey had bonded with her grandmother, and Tara worried that the little girl would suffer great heartbreak when the end came for Sandra. Living in a state of uncertainty dampened Tara's Christmas spirit. Not hearing from Caleb dampened her spirits, too.

Every day she hoped for a call from him, but none came. What kept her from calling him?

As they walked back to the church building where they would have hot chocolate and cookies, she let her last conversation with Caleb float through her mind. Had there been any hint that he wanted her to come back? None that she could recall. She only remembered the way she had metaphorically poured cold water on the kindling of their budding relationship just days before their final talk. Why was she always making the wrong choices?

Maybe Caleb had used her mother's appearance as a convenient way to end their relationship without actually saying so. That would explain why she hadn't heard from him, and she didn't want to make the mistake of pushing herself on someone who wasn't interested.

Back at the church building, Tara joined Hailey as she indulged in more than her fair share of cookies and hot chocolate. Tara hoped there wasn't a stomachache in their future, but she couldn't discourage the fun that Hailey shared with Parker's twin girls, Rose and Jasmine. They were perfect playmates for Hailey.

Besides seeing her grandparents again, another plus about being in Montana was the opportunity to reconnect with Parker and Brittany Watson and their family. Parker had been a lifeline when Hailey was first diagnosed with cancer.

Tara's emotions tried to straddle two worlds—Montana and Massachusetts. Could she find happiness in either one, or would they both bring her misery? She wasn't going to answer that question tonight or even in the next week. She thought about praying, but she didn't know what to pray for, or maybe she was afraid to pray for fear of the answer she might receive.

"Are you ready to head home? Your grandpa and I are wearing out."

Tara turned at the sound of her grandmother's voice. "Okay."

Her grandmother glanced toward the end of the table where Hailey sat. "I hate to break up her good time."

Tara stood. "That's okay. It's time for her to go home, too. I don't want her to get overtired."

On the drive home, Tara's mind jumbled with her evening's thoughts. Could she ever make sense of anything that was happening? She wanted answers, but she wasn't finding any.

"Good news that your mother didn't call us."

Her grandmother's statement interrupted Tara's musings. "True."

"She probably fell asleep in the big brown chair," Hailey said. "She likes that chair."

"She does." Tara smiled, and for the first time a tender spot for her mother opened in Tara's heart. She closed her eyes and drank in the serene feeling. If she could just have serenity where Caleb was concerned, her mind would be completely at peace.

When they arrived at her grandparents' house, they found Sandra asleep in the big chair, as Hailey had predicted.

Hailey tugged on her grandmother's arm. "Grandma Sandy, wake up. We're home."

Sandra blinked. When her gaze rested on Hailey, Sandra smiled and reached out to her granddaughter. "Come sit with me."

Hailey hopped up on Sandra's lap and began telling her

grandmother about their evening. Hailey reached into her coat pocket and brought out a folded napkin. "It's a cookie I saved for you."

Sandra took the cookie and hugged Hailey, then set the napkin-wrapped cookie on the table next to the chair. "Thanks. I'll save it for tomorrow. Would you like for me to read you a story before you go to bed?"

Hailey wasted no time in getting into her pajamas and brushing her teeth before she returned with a book. She climbed back onto Sandra's lap and settled in for her story time. Tara took a seat on the couch and listened to the rise and fall of her mother's voice as she read the story to Hailey. The sound brought sadness to Tara's heart because she had never shared such a time with her mother.

While Tara listened, she picked up her phone from the table next to the chair. Several screens were open, and Tara wondered why. Had her mother been trying to make a call and not been able to? Tara scrolled through the calls but couldn't make sense of why the screens were open.

Even in the short time she'd shared with her mother, Tara had noticed that Sandra became confused about things and often repeated herself in conversations and mixed up days and times as to when things had happened. Tara feared this was part of her slow decline. Or maybe it wasn't slow at all and had been occurring for a long time already.

When the story was over, Hailey romped around the room, giving good-night kisses to everyone. Then Tara escorted Hailey to bed. As Tara tucked the covers under Hailey's chin, she leaned over and gave her another kiss. "I love you."

"I love you, too, Mommy." Hailey put her arms around Tara's neck and clung to her. "Is Grandma Sandy going to die?"

Holding back tears, Tara held her child tighter. "We're all going to die sometime."

"I know, but is she going to die soon?"

Tara released Hailey and looked into her eyes and realized this was a conversation she needed to have. "We don't know when, but it could be soon. Let's be happy for the time we have with her."

Hailey smiled. "Mommy, that's the best thing to do."

Tara squeezed Hailey tight. Her little girl had brought Tara to a defining moment. She would love her mother and care for her mother and forget the past. The only things that counted now were the days ahead in which she could erase the heartache and fill that time with everything good. She would make this a Christmas to remember—one filled with love.

***

The following evening, moonlight made the frosty windows sparkle as Tara padded into the kitchen. The frigid temperatures couldn't diminish the warmth that filled the house or the warmth that settled into Tara's soul and brightened every corner of her heart. The smell of freshly baked bread and chili on the stove wafted through the room. This Christmas Eve signaled a new beginning.

"Did you get your mother settled?" Concern knitting her brow, Grandma Pitman turned from the stove.

Tara nodded. "Yeah. She's so tired. I told her I'd bring her a tray. I can't believe how fast her health is going downhill."

"Maybe it's how early the sun sets this time of year."

Tara shrugged. "I wish I could say we're all hibernating, but she's more disoriented than ever."

Grandma Pitman grabbed a stack of bowls and plates from the cupboard and put them on the counter. "I'd better get the table set."

"You relax." Tara took the bowls. "You shouldn't have to cook and set the table, too. I'll do this."

"Okay. You don't have to twist my arm." Smiling, Grandma Pitman sat at the kitchen table as she cradled a coffee cup in her hands.

After setting the table, Tara joined her grandmother. "Do you want me to get Grandpa and Hailey? They're playing a game."

"Let them finish their game. The chili is in the slow cooker." Grandma Pitman tilted her head as she eyed Tara. "You've been in a good mood today."

Tara nodded, knowing her improved outlook came from her plan to gladly share in her mother's remaining days on this earth. "You were right about my mom. She's doing her best to make up for all those lost years, and I'm going to help however I can."

Grandma Pitman reached over and covered Tara's hand. "You won't regret that decision."

Tara nodded as she blinked back tears. "I'll take Mom her tray and tell Grandpa and Hailey to wash up for supper."

When Tara returned to the kitchen after serving her mother, everyone else was seated at the table. She sat beside Hailey, who gave her a broad smile. Laughter and congenial conversation floated through the air as Grandpa filled each person's bowl with chili. Then he gave a prayer of thanksgiving for the food. His prayers had always soothed Tara, and today was no different. When he prayed, Tara could tell he talked with God often. She needed to follow his example.

Just as they were clearing the table, the doorbell sounded through the living room. Grandpa Pitman got up to answer the door.

Grandma Pitman frowned. "Who could be ringing our bell? We aren't expecting anyone."

"Tara, Hailey, come see what has arrived for you." Grandpa's voice carried from the other room.

Hailey jumped up and raced to the living room. Tara followed close behind but stopped short when she saw one large box and several smaller packages.

Grandpa looked her way. "From Caleb Fitzpatrick."

"We can't open them until tomorrow." Tara tried to smile, but her heart was breaking. That big package was obviously Hailey's bicycle. Caleb had sent them all. That surely signaled that he didn't expect them to come back.

"Not even one?" Hailey tugged on Tara's arm.

With difficulty, Tara held her smile in place. "Maybe one tonight."

"I can hardly wait." Hailey danced around the room.

Tara watched, wishing she could borrow some of her daughter's happiness. Tara surveyed her surroundings and everyone else's smiles. This was her family. They loved her, and she loved them. That should be enough to make this a wonderful Christmas. She would think about that and not about the man who had her heart back in Massachusetts, though she apparently didn't have his.

***

No return phone call. No "thank you." No "Merry Christmas" wish. Caleb stared out his office window at the falling snow and wondered why they hadn't heard from Tara. Even if she didn't want to talk to him, he couldn't fathom her reasons for not saying thank you to his parents for sending the gifts. Had he been completely wrong about another woman?

Christmas with his parents and his brother's family had been a wonderful time, but Tara and Hailey's absence had left a big hole in his celebration. Just days later, he was still trying to make sense of Tara's inattention. He wanted to start a new year in the right way. Did that mean without Tara?

He opened up his desk drawer and pulled out the black velvet box. Opening it, he plopped onto his chair. He stared at the ring as it sparkled in the overhead light. He'd bought the ring just days before Tara's mother had appeared. Maybe she had saved him from a grave mistake, just as Amy had saved him when she left town without warning.

He snapped the box shut and threw it back into the drawer. The box landed with a dull thud, like the dull ache that circled his heart. Why did he seem doomed to the lovelorn set? He turned to the computer spreadsheet, but he couldn't concentrate. Maybe an early lunch was in order.

Getting his head on straight was imperative. Tax season and long, long workdays lay ahead. Caleb opened his office door and stopped midstep, his heart jumping into his throat. Tara? No. The blonde turned, and he stood there with his mouth hanging open.

Amy. What was she doing here? Why was she talking with his parents, and all of them smiling? Was he having a nightmare?

"Caleb, don't just stand there. Come over here." His mother motioned for him to join the group.

Like an automaton, Caleb made his way toward them, all the while wondering what he was going to say.

"Hello, Caleb." Amy gave him a tentative smile. "I know you're surprised to see me."

A myriad of emotions jumbled through Caleb's mind, and he couldn't form a coherent thought or sentence. Amy was the last person he had expected to see. She was the last person he wanted to see.

Amy stepped closer, her lips quivering as she tried to hold her smile in place. "Please let me talk to you."

Did he want to talk to this woman who had ripped his heart out and battered it with her betrayal? Forgiveness knocked on the door of his heart, but he wasn't sure he could let it in even though he'd told himself dozens of times to forgive her and move on.

"Caleb—"

"It's okay, Mom. I'll talk to her." He glanced at his mother, then back at Amy. "You can come into my office."

Without waiting to see if Amy followed, Caleb strode into his office and sat behind his neatly arranged dark-oak desk. Amy stood in the doorway. He motioned for her to sit in the faux leather chair on the other side of the desk. She slowly sank into the chair, her eyes full of uncertainty.

She took a deep breath. "Thanks. I know you must think I'm a terrible person. I've done a lot of bad, bad things, but I'm trying to make up for them now."

Caleb had no response. He wasn't sure he could speak without his words coming out in angry tones. He took a deep breath, trying to calm his emotions.

Amy sat on the edge of the chair as she twisted the strap

of her purse. "Is it okay if I tell you what's happened in my life since I left here?"

Still afraid to speak, Caleb nodded. She scooted even farther to the edge of the chair until he thought she might land on the floor. He just prayed that she didn't want something from him that he couldn't give.

Apprehension painted every inch of her face. "First, I want to say again how sorry I am about everything. I've already apologized to your parents."

"And you think an apology is enough?" Caleb sank back in his chair. Why had he opened his mouth?

"No. That's why I've given them the first payment on the money I took."

"You plan to pay them back?" This time his words tumbled out of his mouth, incredulity dripping from every one of them.

Amy nodded. "I've signed a repayment plan with your parents."

"And what brought this about?" Skepticism ambushed his thoughts. Why couldn't he be as forgiving as his parents?

"Your parents are the kindest people I have ever met. They treated me with compassion even when I hurt and betrayed them. They turned the other cheek. They practiced what they preached when they told me about the love of Jesus. They didn't stop loving me even though I deceived them."

Caleb frowned. "So if you're saying all these good things about them, why did you steal from them?"

Amy lowered her gaze. "Because I didn't believe those things at the time."

"And now you do?"

Amy looked up. "Yes."

"What brought about this change of heart?" Caleb still wasn't sure he could believe her. He didn't want his parents to be taken in again.

"My father wound up in the hospital with deep vein thrombosis. A true crisis, not a manufactured one." Amy lowered her gaze again. "I was afraid he was going to die."

"Is he okay?"

"Yes, he recovered, and one of the nurses who worked with him is a Christian, and his testimony during the crisis made me realize that I needed to turn my life over to Jesus. He reminded me of your parents and their loving-kindness, and I knew I had to make things right with them. Kind of like how Zacchaeus, after meeting Jesus, repaid the people he had cheated."

She knew a Bible story. She had made the effort to come here in person and apologize. She had plans to pay back his parents. He wished he could accept her statements without doubt crowding his mind. He had to say something. "Thanks for making plans to repay the money you took."

Crossing her arms over her midsection, Amy looked everywhere but at him. "I wish I could make restitution for the hurt I caused you. I'm sorry I hurt you, Caleb. I know there's nothing I can do to make that right."

This conversation only caused Caleb more pain. Forgiveness wouldn't come easy. He wanted to be as charitable as his parents, but saying everything was okay would make him a liar. He got up from his chair and walked to the window, where he looked out on the parking lot that was dusted with snow. He thought he'd found forgiveness for Amy, but seeing her again made him realize he'd never really forgiven her.

Amy came to stand beside him. "Your mom says you've found a new love. I believe she said her name is Tara."

Nodding, Caleb let out a halfhearted laugh. "Yeah, I guess you could say that, but I came in second with her, too."

"That's not what your mom said. She thought you two might be headed to the altar."

Caleb shook his head. "My mom's an eternal optimist, and she sees what she wants to see."

"We should all be. After all, if God is for us, who can be against us?"

Caleb turned to Amy. "I'm glad you've found a relationship with God and that your life is on the right track now. I mean that. I know I'm having a hard time with the forgiveness, but I want you to know that with God's help, I will let the past go. It's just hard to get there all at once, right now, today."

"I understand. Thank you for your honesty." Amy gave him a curious stare. "Why do you say you came in second?"

Caleb gazed at the floor as he shook his head. "It's not really fair to say that, because she went back to her hometown to take care of her dying mother. I'm afraid she isn't coming back."

"Did you tell her you wanted her to come back?"

Caleb recalled his conversations with Tara. He knew he hadn't done that—a big mistake. He should have told her he loved her and didn't want to live without her. "I'm afraid I didn't."

"If you love her, you need to correct that right away."

Her eyebrows raised, Amy looked at him. "You're a good man, Caleb, and you deserve someone to love—someone who loves you. Sounds like you have some work to do."

Caleb smiled. "Love advice from an old girlfriend—something I never expected."

"I hope you'll take it." Amy touched his arm. "Thanks for letting me explain my circumstances."

"You're welcome." As Amy withdrew her hand, Caleb realized those old feelings of love and betrayal where she was concerned didn't hold sway over him anymore. He had moved beyond the pain. "But you haven't told me what you're doing now."

"I'm working as a teacher's aide in a small town outside of Cincinnati, and in June I'm going to marry that nurse I told you about. His name is Jonathan."

Caleb grinned, his heart lighter. "I'm happy for you."

"Thanks. I appreciate that more than you know." Amy's eyes sparkled with unshed tears. "You should go after Tara and tell her that you love her. Maybe you'll have a chance to kiss her as you bring in the New Year." Amy turned toward the door. "Now I'd better get going. I have a plane to catch."

"Good-bye, Amy." Caleb nodded. "I hope you have a good life."

"And you, too."

Plopping onto his chair, Caleb could hardly believe what had just transpired. He'd actually managed to talk with Amy without letting his initial anger get the best of him. His fury concerning her previous actions had melted away like the snow on a sunny day. He would never have believed that a visit from Amy would be a gift from God.

Sitting behind his desk, Caleb knew he'd been beyond

stupid. Why had he thought Tara had to be the one to call on Christmas? Instead of feeling sorry for himself, he should've called and told her how he felt. He only hoped she would forgive him for his neglect.

Caleb turned to his computer. He had a plane ticket to buy.

CHAPTER TWENTY-ONE

The midmorning sunshine couldn't warm the bleak landscape or the ache in Tara's heart over the sudden loss of her mother. She swallowed hard as her boots crunched across the frozen brown grass in the acreage behind her grandparents' house. She stopped at the edge of the garden plot where stubble stuck up in the plowed earth. Off to one side, the bare-branched apple trees stood guard over the little piece of land.

Tara pressed her lips together as she wiped tears from her cheeks. Her mother's fond memories of picking apples off the trees had prompted her to request that her ashes be spread beneath them. Tara stared at the dark-brown soil and wondered why God had reunited her with her mother only to take her away when they were just getting to know each other.

As Tara stood there trying to make sense of everything, she thought of Caleb and his parents. They must think she was ungrateful after not receiving a thank-you for the gifts they'd sent. Now that the chaos was over, Tara needed to call the Fitzpatricks.

She trudged toward the house and hoped she wouldn't break down when she talked to them. How would Caleb receive her call? Time to find out.

Grandma Pitman stood just inside the door as Tara approached. "Come in out of the cold."

"I am." Tara hugged her grandmother and drank in the warmth of her arms. "I need to call the Fitzpatricks."

Grandma nodded. "Yes, but before you do, I need to talk with you."

"About what?"

"Tonight."

Tara shook her head. "I know the church is having a New Year's Eve get-together. I don't feel like celebrating."

"I understand. None of us do, but Parker called. He and Brittany have invited us over. Just their family and ours. He said we can all spend the night out at their place. You know they have plenty of room." Grandma sighed. "I think it'll do us good to get out of this house."

Tara wished she could argue with her grandmother's logic, but it was probably true, and Hailey would definitely like to spend time with the twins. "Okay."

Grandma patted Tara's back. "Good. You call the Fitzpatricks, and I'll let Parker know we're coming."

Tara walked past Hailey and Grandpa, who were busy playing one of the board games she had gotten for Christmas. They were so engrossed that they didn't notice her. Back in the bedroom, Tara plopped onto the bed and stared at her cell phone. She took a deep breath and poked at Caleb's name on the screen. The phone rang twice, then immediately sent her to his voice mail. Her heart raced at the sound of Caleb's recorded voice. Should she leave a message? Would he call her back if she did?

"Hi, Caleb. This is Tara. I'm so sorry I haven't called to thank you for sending the Christmas gifts. I would've called sooner, but my mom went into the hospice facility in Billings on Christmas day and passed away the following day. Things have been very hectic with the memorial arrangements and all. I just wanted to let you know and wish you a happy New Year. Thanks for everything. Bye."

Tara ended the call and again stared at her phone, her heart still pounding. What was Caleb doing that he hadn't answered his phone? Or was he trying to avoid her? Tom and Sheila would talk to her. Would they be at the office on New Year's Eve? Tara decided to try the office first. Maybe she would catch Caleb there, too.

After three rings, Sheila answered. "Fitzpatrick Accounting. May I help you?"

"Sheila, this is Tara Madsen."

"Tara, it's so good to hear from you. How are you? How are things in Montana?"

Tara sighed. "They could be better. My mom passed away the day after Christmas."

"Oh, Tara, I'm so sorry to hear this. Are you doing okay?"

"As good as can be expected." Her grandparents and everyone at their church had given her so much support.

"I had no idea that your mother was that ill."

"None of us did. I think she knew and wanted to make sure she reconnected with us before she died." Tara fought against the tears that threatened. "I learned that she'd been dealing with her kidney issue for some time, and the doctors had told her she had less than six months to live a few months ago."

"I'm so, so sorry to hear this. We miss you, but take as much time as you need in Montana."

Tara wondered if Caleb missed her, too. She wanted to ask about him, but she wasn't sure she should. "I wanted to thank you for sending the gifts. With everything that happened, I'm just getting to it now."

"I understand completely," Sheila replied.

"How was your Christmas?" Tara asked.

"We had a wonderful time with the grandchildren. Kids always make Christmas so fun." Tara heard the smile in Sheila's voice. "Is Hailey enjoying her bike?"

"Yes, she insists on riding it even when it's way too cold."

Sheila chuckled. "That's kids. They don't seem to mind the elements."

"Is Caleb around? I tried his cell phone, but he didn't answer." Tara held her breath.

"Caleb isn't here. I'll let him know you called."

"Thanks." Something in Sheila's voice made Tara think the other woman wasn't divulging the whole story about Caleb. "Tell Tom hello and happy New Year."

"I will. happy New Year to you, too. I hope your New Year is filled with happiness. Talk to you later."

Tara said her last good-bye and ended the call. She wanted to have happy thoughts about the conversation, but her life's experiences of one bad thing after another made that difficult. Sheila and Tom wanted Tara to return. Did Caleb?

He was the most important reason to go back to Massachusetts now that Hailey's cancer was gone. She should concentrate on that one bright spot in the coming year. Her little girl was cancer-free. Her relationship to Caleb would sort itself out in the coming days. If he didn't call back, she would know where she stood.

***

The voice blaring over the loudspeaker in the

Minneapolis airport gave Caleb a headache. Would he ever get to Montana? The plane for his flight between Minneapolis and Billings hadn't arrived. Bad weather across the country had flights backed up. At least his flight hadn't been cancelled yet. Maybe his plan to surprise Tara was ill conceived. He hoped not.

He decided to stretch his legs. He grabbed the handle of his roller bag and proceeded down the concourse. Hundreds of unhappy people occupied the chairs at the gates as they waited for their delayed flights. Others wandered up and down the concourse with him. Tired children cried. Travelers were hunched over computers or on their cell phones to while away the time.

As he walked back and forth, the announcement of a gate change for his flight came over the loudspeakers. Maybe that meant his flight would leave shortly. When he reached the new gate, the agent was making more announcements. Their plane was in, and they would depart in forty-five minutes.

Caleb breathed a sigh of relief. He was going to make it to Montana today. He would see Tara and Hailey. Praying that they would welcome him, he found a place to sit. His stomach churned at the thought of rejection. He shoved the negative thought away. He'd made the decision to go after Tara, and he had to believe she would be glad to see him.

During the entire flight, Caleb tried to ignore the pessimistic thoughts that buzzed through his mind like the sound of the jet engines propelling him toward the woman he loved. As he tried to make himself comfortable in the cramped seating, the elderly woman sitting next to him looked his way.

She smiled. "Are you headed home?"

Caleb shook his head. "No, I live near Boston."

"Such a lovely city."

"Yeah, it is. So you've visited there?"

"Several years ago I went to visit my granddaughter who lives there."

"You live in Billings?"

"Yes, I'm headed home after spending Christmas with my son and his family, who live in St Paul. It was a lovely time," she said. "Are you going to Montana for a ski vacation?"

"No." Did he want to tell this stranger his reason for going to Montana? Maybe if he said it out loud, it would seem more real and take away some of his worries. "I'm going to surprise my girlfriend with a visit. I plan to propose."

A wide grin spread across the elderly woman's wrinkled face. "That's wonderful. I wish you the best."

"Thanks." Giving voice to his plans lightened his heart.

"I won't bother you anymore." The woman opened a book.

"It was no bother." Caleb grabbed the magazine from the seat pocket.

After the plane landed, Caleb retrieved his bag from the overhead bin as anticipation created a roiling sensation in his stomach. He helped the older woman with her bag.

"Thanks, young man." She smiled. "Best wishes on that proposal."

Caleb returned her smile, a good feeling in his heart. "You're welcome. It's going to be a good night and a good year ahead."

After Caleb got his rental car and was on his way out of Billings toward Stockton, the nervous energy he'd been feeling earlier returned. While he listened to the mechanical-sounding voice of the GPS giving him directions, he again pushed away the negative thoughts. He wouldn't let doubts fill his mind now. He was on his way to propose to the woman he loved, and she would say yes.

As he left behind the lights of Billings, snowflakes danced in the car's headlights. He hoped this wasn't going to be a bad storm. The farther he drove, the faster the snow came down. By the time he reached Stockton, the snow was coming down so hard that he could hardly see.

He turned onto the street at the edge of town where the Pitmans lived. The falling snow made it difficult to read the addresses. He slowed the car to a crawl as he peered into the darkness. Finally, he saw the house number he was looking for. No lights shone in the windows. Was no one home? Caleb's stomach sank. Was the surprise on him?

He trudged to the door, his shoes leaving footprints in the snow. He rang the bell as he stomped on the grooved doormat. As he suspected, no one came to the door. Now what? Had he come all this way for nothing? Maybe Tara and her family were attending a New Year's Eve party somewhere. How would he find them?

With a heavy sigh, he plodded back to his car. As he slid behind the wheel, his phone rang. He glanced at the screen. His mom. He accepted the call. "Mom, hi."

"Caleb, are you with Tara?"

Caleb let out a halfhearted laugh. "I'm sitting in front of her grandparents' house. No one's home, and I have no clue where they are."

"Oh no." His mother sighed. "Did you get my message or Tara's message?"

"I don't have messages from anyone on my phone."

"That's strange. I left you a message, and when I talked with Tara, she said she'd called you."

"When did you talk to her?"

"Late this afternoon."

"What did she have to say?" Caleb held his breath as he waited for his mother's answer.

"Caleb, there's something you need to know."

Caleb's stomach did a flip-flop. "What?"

"Tara's mom passed away the day after Christmas."

"So suddenly?" An ache filled Caleb's chest.

His mom recounted everything Tara had said. "That's all I know."

"Do you have any idea how I can find them?" Caleb stared at the snow that had collected on the windshield.

"I'll give you Heather's number."

"Why?"

"Because her uncle lives near Stockton. Maybe he can help you."

"Worth a shot."

After talking with Heather, Caleb punched in Parker Watson's number. Caleb prayed that someone would be able to help him as he listened to the rings.

"Parker Watson."

"Hello, this is Caleb Fitzpatrick, and your niece Heather gave me your number."

"How are Heather and Max doing?"

"Good." As much as Caleb liked Heather and Max, he really wasn't interested in chatting about them.

"I still haven't forgiven that girl for getting married when I couldn't be there, even though we did get to see it over the Internet." Parker chuckled. "What can I do for you?"

"I'm a friend of Tara Madsen's from Massachusetts. I came to Stockton to surprise her, but the surprise seems to be on me. She isn't home. Would you happen to know where she is?"

Parker laughed. "You called the right place. She's here with Hailey and her grandparents."

"That's a relief."

"You say you're planning to surprise her?" Parker asked.

"Yeah. I'd appreciate it if you didn't tell her I'm here." Caleb hoped he could still surprise her.

"So do you want to see her tonight?"

"Yeah, that was the plan."

"Then you'll have to drive out here to the ranch because they're planning to spend the night."

"Is it a problem for me to come out there?"

"You're welcome to come, but the weather has turned nasty. This place isn't exactly easy to find when the weather's good." A warning sounded in Parker's voice.

Caleb wasn't going to let a little snow keep him from the woman he loved. "I didn't come all the way from Massachusetts not to see Tara tonight. Please give me directions."

"Okay, but you have to pay careful attention because some of the roads aren't marked very well." Adding caution after caution, Parker went through the directions.

"Thanks. I appreciate you keeping my arrival a secret."

"You're welcome. See you in about half an hour."

"I'm looking forward to it. Thanks." Caleb ended the call.

Snow coming down all around him, Caleb drove out of Stockton as he followed Parker's directions. Darkness swallowed the car's headlights and the falling snow, but the thought of seeing Tara and Hailey filled his heart with joy.

***

The high-pitched laughter of little girls filled Parker's home theater as Hailey, Rose, and Jasmine watched an animated movie filled with silly animals. Tara smiled, knowing that her grandmother had been right about spending the evening with the Watsons. Her grandparents were upstairs playing a card game with Delia, Brittany and Parker's housekeeper.

Getting out for the evening was just the medicine her grandparents needed to take their minds off of the loss of their daughter. Tara knew this time with Brittany and Parker was helping her cope. Tara wanted to start the coming year on a positive note. This impromptu party would assist with that goal.

As Tara stood in the doorway of the theater, Parker and Brittany joined her.

"The girls are really enjoying the movie," Tara said.

"Those giggles certainly tell the story." Brittany grinned. "Do you think they'll make it until midnight?"

"They'll certainly try, or at least Hailey will."

"I'm sure Rose and Jasmine will, too." Brittany nodded. "I know one kiddo who's already sleeping. So different from last year when I was up at midnight feeding a baby."

Tara chuckled. "Yes, those first few months you are so sleep deprived that you wished you never had to see midnight."

"What a difference a year makes."

Tara shook her head. "I'm not too sure those girls will

make it. I have a suspicion that even though it's only a couple of hours till midnight, we'll find them sound asleep before they see in the New Year."

"Me, too." Brittany glanced at Parker. "What do you think?"

Parker looked up from his phone. "What?"

Brittany stepped closer to Parker. "Why are you so attached to that phone tonight? You aren't usually like that. Are you expecting a call?"

"No." Shrugging, Parker shoved the phone into his pocket. "I'm going to join the girls. They sound like they're having fun."

As Parker disappeared into the theater, Brittany looked over at Tara. "I don't know what's going on with him, but ever since he got a call about an hour ago, he's been acting really weird."

"You think so?"

Brittany nodded. "He hardly ever spends much time on his phone."

"Could it have something to do with his business?"

"I hardly think so this late on New Year's Eve." Brittany shook her head. "Maybe he's worried that this snow will turn into a blizzard. Then he has cattle to think about. Before we got married, there was a terrible blizzard, and it was a real worry for everyone involved with the ranch."

"Yeah, I remember how Blake had to deal with storms when he worked on that ranch."

Brittany patted Tara's shoulder. "How you doing? I know your mother's passing came so quickly."

"It's like a bad dream. I'm not sure it's all real." Tara swallowed hard. "It's different than with Blake. I hardly got to know her before she was gone."

"I hear Hailey talking about someone named Caleb, who seems to be a big part of your lives. Does that mean you're going back to Massachusetts?"

Tara shrugged. "I'm not sure what to do. I think my grandparents might need me here."

"Tara, there are lots of people who can look out for your grandparents, if there's someone you love back there."

Tara hung her head. "That's just it. I don't know for sure how he feels about me. When all of this happened, he insisted that I bring my mom back here, but he never said anything about wanting me to come back."

"Isn't that a good thing?" Brittany raised her eyebrows. "He knew you needed to take care of your mother and probably wanted you to concentrate on that and not worry about the future."

"Well, yeah, that's what I thought until he sent all of our Christmas presents here, including Hailey's bike. His actions signaled to me that he wasn't expecting us to come back."

"Maybe he just wanted Hailey to have it. That tells me he loves your little girl."

Tara nodded. "He's a kind man. A wonderful man."

"And you love him."

"I do, but I'm not sure where our relationship is headed." Tara sighed. "You see, I thought I knew Blake when we got married, but he turned out to be someone I didn't know at all. So I'm afraid I'll make a wrong choice again."

"I know it's kind of a pat saying, but you should pray about it."

Tara sighed again. "Well, that's definitely something I didn't do with Blake."

"In fact, let's pray about it now." Brittany held out her hands.

"Okay." Tara placed her hands in Brittany's and bowed her head.

Brittany prayed for Tara's comfort concerning the loss of her mother, and for Tara's decision about going back to Massachusetts, and for her relationship with Caleb.

As Brittany finished her prayer, Parker strode out of the theater.

"Is the movie over?" Brittany asked.

"No, but I have something I need to tell you." Parker glanced from Brittany to Tara.

A sense of foreboding hit Tara as she read Parker's expression. "What?"

Parker let out a harsh breath. "Tara, I wasn't supposed to say anything to you, but I can't let this go any longer."

"What are you talking about?" Brittany placed a hand on Parker's arm.

"That phone call I got earlier was from Caleb." Parker eyed Tara. "He was calling from Stockton."

"He's in Stockton?" Her heart hammering, Tara searched Parker's face.

"He's supposed to be on his way here to surprise you, but he should've arrived at least a half hour ago."

"Do you think he's lost?" Tara asked.

Parker nodded, then ran a hand through his hair. "When I called his number, I got his voice mail. I'm afraid he's in that cell phone dead zone between here and Stockton. I'm going to look for him."

As Parker headed for the stairs, Tara ran after him. "Let

me go with you."

Parker shook his head. "You need to stay here. No sense for you to go, too."

"But—"

"No buts." Parker gave her a warning look. "I'll find him."

Tara stepped back. "I'll hold you to that."

As Parker took the steps two at a time, Brittany turned to Tara. "I think you have your answer about Caleb right there."

Tara tried not to let worry crowd the good thoughts from her mind. "I just hope nothing bad has happened to him."

"If anyone can find him, Parker will."

Nodding, Tara steepled her hands in front of her mouth. She stared at the snow coming down like a never-ending white sheet. *Lord, please keep Caleb safe, and help Parker find him.*

Brittany patted Tara on the shoulder. "You want to finish watching the movie with the kids?"

Tara shook her head. "I don't think that'll help."

"Give it a try."

"Okay." Tara sighed as she followed Brittany into the theater. As her eyes adjusted to the dim light, she sat in the big comfy chair next to Hailey, who hardly took her eyes off the screen when Tara sat down.

Tara tried to concentrate on the movie, but it only reminded her of the time Caleb had watched it with her and Hailey. Afterward he'd had Hailey in stitches of laughter as he imitated one of the characters. *Please, God, don't take away another person I love.* Tara blinked back tears. She would believe that God would give the answer that she wanted to her prayer. Parker would find Caleb. When he got here, she would tell him that she loved him. She wasn't going to be afraid of her feelings anymore.

Just as the movie ended, an upstairs door banged shut. Tara jumped up from her seat and raced up the stairs. Parker entered the kitchen, but he was alone. Tara's stomach sank. "You didn't find him?"

Parker's face broke into a smile. "I found him—"

"Then where is he?" Tara asked.

Parker laughed. "Patience. He's paying the tow truck driver."

Tara didn't wait for another word from Parker. Without bothering to get her coat, she sprinted out the door. Snow danced in the headlights of the tow truck. Caleb and another man stood silhouetted against the brightness.

The presence of the other man stopped Tara in her tracks. Her heart racing, she watched their exchange until the driver turned back to his truck. Not waiting another second, Tara launched herself toward Caleb. She threw her arms around him. "You're all right. I was so worried."

Holding her tight, he chuckled. "If getting stranded means a greeting like this, I'll get stranded more often."

Tara stepped out of his arms and looked up at him. "I'm not laughing. I imagined all kinds of terrible things that could have happened to you."

"You'll have to rein in that wild imagination of yours."

Tara tried to frown, but all she could do was smile. "What happened?"

"Some kind of animal, maybe a deer, ran across the road. I swerved to avoid hitting it and went into the ditch. I couldn't get out. Of course, it had to be in a spot where my cell phone wouldn't work. I just prayed that someone would come along and find me. God sent Parker."

Resting a hand on Caleb's arm, Tara stopped. "I'm so glad you came."

"That's good to hear. I wasn't sure how you'd feel about it." Caleb brushed snow from her hair and face. "Aren't you getting cold without a coat?"

"Just being with you makes me warm." Tara gazed up at him. "And I don't want you to have any doubts about the way I feel about you. I love you."

Caleb pulled her into his arms and held her tight. "And I love you."

Tara closed her eyes and drank in the warmth of his words. He'd come all the way to Montana to tell her. "I've missed you."

"Me, too." Caleb continued to hold her as the snow fell around them. "I'm sorry to hear about your mom. I didn't know until today."

Tara stepped out of his arms and looked at him. "You got my message?"

"Actually, no. My mom told me." Caleb pointed toward his rental car with the mashed front end. "Let me get my suitcase, then we can get out of this snow and talk about all this. I've had enough of the cold tonight."

When they entered the mud room, Brittany and Parker were there to greet Tara and Caleb. Parker clapped Caleb on the back. "Glad you guys decided to come in. I thought I might have to rescue you again."

Brittany turned to Parker. "Maybe they wanted some privacy."

"You can show them the den." A lopsided grin on his face, Parker gave Brittany a peck on the cheek. "I'll take Caleb's suitcase to the room where he'll be staying, and rescue Delia and the Pitmans from the kids, *and* check on the baby."

Caleb and Tara followed Brittany through the kitchen to a small room where a sofa sat facing a wall that sported a fireplace with a glass front. Brittany flicked a switch, and flames bobbed and weaved behind the glass. "You can have a little time alone in here."

"Thanks." Tara sat on the couch as Brittany left.

Looking nervous, Caleb stood there for a moment, then glanced toward the doorway. "Sorry. I need something from my suitcase. I'll be back in a minute."

Tara stared at the flames while she wondered what Caleb could possibly want from his suitcase. She could hardly believe he was here. She wished she hadn't doubted his love or caused him to doubt her feelings for him.

When Caleb returned, he still seemed nervous. Was he wishing he hadn't come? *Stop being negative.* This coming year would be a fabulous one. Hailey was healthy, and Caleb loved them.

"Hey." Caleb sat on the couch and took her hand. "It's been quite a night."

Tara scooted closer. "I know. I'm so glad you made it here."

Before Caleb could say another word, his cell phone dinged. He fished it from his pocket and looked at it. Shaking his head, he glanced up. "Would you believe that your voice mail and my mother's just now arrived on my phone?"

"I thought you said you talked to your mother."

"I did, but she mentioned leaving me a message earlier, and she also said that you had called." Caleb put his arm around Tara's shoulders. "Do I need to listen to this message?"

Tara shrugged. "You can if you want, but you know about my mom, and I was wishing you a happy New Year and thanking you for sending the Christmas gifts."

"So now you get to wish me a happy New Year in person. I like that better."

"Me, too."

Caleb took a deep breath. "I've got something for you."

Tara widened her eyes as she looked at him. "What?"

With his free hand, Caleb reached into his pocket and brought out a tiny package wrapped in shiny red paper and tied up with white ribbon. "I bought this for you before your mother showed up. I was going to give it to you at Christmas."

"Why didn't you send it with the other gifts?"

Caleb chuckled as he handed her the gift. "If you open it, I think you'll understand why."

Tara gently pulled the ribbon, and it fell to the couch. She looked over at Caleb, who had shifted to face her. The expectation on his face made her heart skitter. Could this be a ring? She didn't want to hope and be disappointed. She tore off the paper, revealing a black velvet box that probably contained a piece of jewelry. She was almost afraid to open it.

"It's not going to bite. At least I hope it doesn't." Caleb's anxious expression remained in place.

Tara lifted the lid. She couldn't stop the tears as she stared at the diamond ring, sparkling in the firelight. She swallowed hard as she looked up at Caleb, but she still couldn't manage to speak.

"I love you, Tara, and I love Hailey. I want us to be a family. Will you marry me and make me the happiest man alive?"

Pressing her lips together as tears threatened again, Tara nodded and threw her arms around his neck. When she finally gained control of her emotions, she released her hold. "Yes, I want to marry you."

"Let's put this on your finger." Caleb fumbled with the ring as he slid it onto her left hand.

"I love you," Tara said. "I'm sorry I can't keep from crying."

"As long as they're happy tears." Caleb pulled her into his arms and kissed her.

When the kiss ended, Tara held out her left hand. "It's beautiful."

"I'm glad you like it." Caleb took her hand. "Should we find Hailey and tell her?"

Tara jumped up from the couch. "She'll be so excited."

"Whoa. This deserves another kiss." Caleb stood and pulled her into his arms again.

Tara melted into his embrace and into the kiss. Happiness tied her heart in a bow. After the kiss ended, they stood in each other's arms for another minute.

Finally Caleb stepped away. "Let's talk to Hailey."

Hand in hand, Tara and Caleb found their way to the basement TV room, where everyone was gathered.

Hailey raced their way as soon as she saw them. "Mommy, how did Mr. Fitz get here?"

Caleb leaned down and picked Hailey up. "I got here on a plane so I could see you and your mommy."

Hailey gave Caleb a big hug. "Did you bring Sadie?"

Caleb laughed out loud as he set Hailey on the stool at the counter of the basement kitchenette. "No, my mom and dad are taking care of her. Would you like to come live at my house and have Sadie as your dog?"

Hailey's little face scrunched up in a puzzled frown as she looked at her mother. "Can I do that?"

"You can when Caleb and I get married. Is that okay with you?" Tara held out her left hand to show Hailey her ring. "Caleb asked me to marry him, and I said yes."

A smile absorbed Hailey's whole face as she looked at Caleb. "You get to be my dad?"

Caleb nodded. "If that's okay with you."

"It's better than okay. It's super, super, super fantastic." Hailey raised her arms over her head in a victory pose as she let out a loud cheer.

In the next few minutes, congratulations, hugs, and more tears filled the room as Caleb and Tara shared their news. When the commotion died down, Caleb took out his cell phone. "I'm going to call my parents and tell them the good news."

"Isn't it a little late for that? It's almost two o'clock back in Massachusetts." Tara raised her eyebrows.

"Yeah, I forgot about the time change." Caleb pocketed his phone. "I'll have to wait till morning."

Parker stepped to the middle of the room. "It's almost midnight, and we're going to have a time of prayer to end this year. Every year has good times and bad, but we're ending this year on a high note."

As Parker gathered the group into a circle, everyone joined hands. Hailey insisted on standing between Tara and Caleb. Tara smiled at Caleb over the top of Hailey's head. He was going to make a great dad. While Tara's heart overflowed with love and happiness, folks in the circle took turns giving thanks for good times in the past year and praying for God's guidance in the new one. A couple minutes before midnight, Parker ended the prayer.

"Thanks, everyone, for joining me in prayer. Now let's find a countdown somewhere." He walked across the room and turned on the big-screen TV.

After a little channel surfing, he found a station ready to do the countdown to the New Year. Brittany passed out noisemakers, which the kids grabbed with abandon. Tara held hands with Caleb, while Hailey stood in front of them, her eyes wide with excitement. The chant of the countdown filled the room.

"Happy New Year!" The chorus filled the air.

Caleb put an arm around Tara's waist. He pulled her close and kissed her while noisemakers buzzed around them. Everything faded into the background as Tara's heart and mind were consumed with this one man who was making her dream come true.

They would have a family to call their own.

Dear Readers,

Thank you for reading *A Family to Call Ours*. I hope Tara and Caleb's story touched your heart and brought you a lesson about the positive effects of helping others. Both Tara and Caleb learn how to trust in God's plans for their lives.

I would love for you to write a review and let other readers know what you think about *A Family to Call Ours*. You can do so by posting an honest review wherever you purchased this book and also on Goodreads or Book Bub.

Please consider mentioning *A Family to Call Ours* on your social media sites, especially where you talk about reading! Word of mouth is the number one reason people pick up unfamiliar books. Every review and mention helps.

I've had so much fun writing these stories. If you haven't read the other books in the series, I hope you will check out the other books in the Front Porch Promises series. You can find a list of the books below.

If you would like to get information on my upcoming books, please sign up for my newsletter on my website.

Merrillee Whren

ABOUT THE AUTHOR

Merrillee Whren is an award-winning and a *USA Today* bestselling author who writes inspirational romance. She is the winner of the 2003 Golden Heart Award for best inspirational romance manuscript presented by Romance Writers of America. She has also been the recipient of the RT Reviewers' Choice Award and the Inspirational Reader's Choice Award. She is married to her own personal hero, her husband of forty plus years, and has two grown daughters. She has lived in Atlanta, Boston, Dallas, Chicago and Florida but now makes her home in the Arizona desert. She spends her free time playing tennis or walking while she does the plotting for her novels. Please connect with her on social media or her website.

https://twitter.com/MerrilleeWhren

www.merrilleewhren.com

OTHER BOOKS by MERRILLEE WHREN

Dalton Brothers Series
Four Little Blessings
Country Blessings
Homecoming Blessings

Kellersburg Series
Hometown Promise
Hometown Proposal
Hometown Dad
Hometown Cowboy

Front Porch Promises Series
A Match to Call Ours
A Place to Call Home
A Love to Call Mine
A Family to Call Ours
A Song to Call Ours
A Baby to Call Ours
A Place to Find Love

Pinecrest
Second Chance Love
Second Chance Gift
Second Chance Forgiveness

Novellas
Puppy Love and Mistletoe
Puppy Love and Jingle Bells
Puppy Love and Christmas Cookies

Other Books
Miracle Baby
Second Chance Christmas

Village of Hope
Annie's Hope
Kirsten's Mission
Melanie's Resolve